MW01140240

changing forever

Lisa De Jong

Copyright © 2014 by Lisa De Jong

Without limiting the rights under copyright reserved above, no part of this publication may be reproduced, stored in or introduced into a retrieval system, or transmitted, in any form, or by any means (electronic, mechanical, photocopying, recording, or otherwise) without the prior written permission of the above author of this book.

This is a work of fiction. Names, characters, places, brands, media, and incidents are either the product of the author's imagination or are used fictitiously. The author acknowledges the trademarked status and trademark owners of various products referenced in this work of fiction, which have been used without permission. The publication/use of these trademarks is not authorized, associated with, or sponsored by the trademark owners.

ISBN-13: 978-1499514322
ISBN-10: 1499514328

Edited by Madison Seidler
Cover by Mae I Design
Interior Formatting by Kassi Cooper of Kassi's Kandids Formatting

Contents

"If we don't change, we don't grow. If we don't grow, we aren't really living."

– Gail Sheehy

Prologue

YOU KNOW HOW IT'S SO EASY to remember every detail of your favorite movie? You remember every word said, every little thing that happened, and in what order. That's how that day is for me, but it's not a movie. It's a real life nightmare … one I continue to wake up in every single day of my life. Every detail haunts me to this day, and at this point, I think they always will.

I remember everything about that dreary, cool autumn morning. The light rain that fell from the gray sky, keeping the newly fallen leaves from blowing in the wind. I remember the red shirt I wore, the large hole in the knee of my favorite blue jeans, the smell of maple brown sugar oatmeal that permeated the small kitchen.

I remember watching the little white car back out of the driveway, but I didn't realize then that it would be the last time. I'd seen that smiling face every day for years, rewarding all of the good things I'd done. The smooth voice inside soothed me to sleep when nothing else could. The warm hands that held mine as we crossed busy streets in our small town.

When I was young, I didn't think so much about the things I should have said, the things I should have done. That came much later when I had time to look at things in retrospect and had the knowledge to process it all. They say wisdom comes with age, but it's not because of the things you learn with time, but the events you live through.

changing forever

I wish I would have known what was coming because there's so much I would have done differently.

But it's too late now.

That smile I can only see in pictures.

That voice I can only hear in my head.

Since that day, I've hated red, and I can't stand the smell of maple. With one event, my entire life is lived differently.

But the worst part is the words last spoken between us weren't necessarily the ones I wanted to remember for the rest of my life.

I can't change it now, but learning to let go isn't easy.

If I can move on from the past, I can have everything I've ever wanted. I'll be happy for a change ... or at least that's what I think ...

Chapter 1
Emery

"WHAT ARE YOU DOING UP SO EARLY?" It sounds like I failed at my mission not to wake up my new roommate, Kate. She turns in her small twin bed and runs her finger below her tired eyes.

"It's Saturday," she adds, covering her face with her forearm.

I smile as I pull on my old tennis shoes. "I'm going to check out the rest of campus. You're welcome to come."

"It's too freaking early for that. I plan on staying in bed until my date with Beau later. You should go back to bed, too."

"Not happening. There's too much I want to see," I say, sliding my purse strap over my shoulder. "Go back to sleep. I'll be back later."

Kate lifts her arm, staring me down with her dark green eyes. "Grab some coffee while you're out. You're going to need it." With that, she rolls around and quickly drifts back to sleep, leaving me to my own devices.

I've been a small town girl since the day I was born. It never really bothered me much when I was younger, because back then, all I needed were a couple friends to play dolls with, and I was content.

Life was simple. Dreams were simple.

But as I got older, things changed, and I wanted more.

And now, I'm here, living day one of my new life. A life I've spent the last few years planning and working toward. There's no script or master plan. I just want to come out of it with my degree so I never have to go back to that small town again. It's all part of a bigger dream.

As I step outside, the hot summer sun beams down on me, forcing me to pull my sunglasses from my shirt collar. When I arrived on campus yesterday, I didn't get a chance to see everything because it was too dark, so now's my chance. I'm quickly realizing this place is almost as big as the town I grew up in. It certainly has more things to do and see. If I knew it wouldn't earn me an unwelcome audience, I'd probably be skipping through the grass because I've dreamed about this for so long. It's a moment I'd thought about for hours at night while lying in my bed … it means everything to me.

When my dad told me he couldn't afford to send me to college, I thought my world ended. I'm not one to let anything get me down, though, and the next day I woke up with a better outlook. I spent hours each night studying, getting perfect grades on everything just so I could get a full scholarship.

It worked. I'm here now, and even though no one can see it, I'm jumping up and down inside. This is my kind of adrenaline rush … my ride around the track at one hundred and fifty miles an hour. I'm trying to slow it down, to take it all in.

Besides voices and laughter, campus is quiet, and I love the serenity of it all. It's full of life, students walking about, the grass covered in blankets where some sit chatting or reading books. I like that it has the same quiet, small town feel as where I grew up—with so much more possibility.

The space between the buildings reminds me of a park—full of green summer grass and an abundance of mature trees—but my favorite part is the river that separates the east and west sides of campus. I can see myself sitting there with a book on days like this; the quiet sound of the water is the perfect backdrop to a good story.

The buildings themselves are a mix of old and new, some brick, some contemporary architecture. I don't see how someone wouldn't feel at home here; it's so diverse in everything—like Disney World for young adults, because I can spend days exploring and never get bored.

This whole experience is different for me than most. Is it about freedom? Yes. But it's also about taking a step toward who I want to be. I think most come here to figure it out, but I already know. When I'm done with this place, I'm going to be Dr. Emery White, child psychologist, and move to a big city. I'm going to make a difference in the lives of others.

It's what I am meant to do. It's what I wish someone would have done for me.

After crossing the walking bridge that goes over the river one more time, I dig through my purse and pull out an elastic band to tie my brown hair into a ponytail. If I ever move out of Iowa, one thing I'll never miss is the humidity and what it does to my long, thick hair.

As I fumble to zip my purse back up, I run into a large, solid body, sending me back a couple steps. I've been sweating since the moment I stepped out of the dorms, and now my face is burning from embarrassment, making the heat seem that much worse.

"You should probably watch where you're going," a deep, male voice comes from a few feet in front of me.

Slowly, I lift my eyes and find myself staring blankly at very toned calves and working my way up to an equally defined torso. *Holy mother of God ...* this guy doesn't have a shirt on, and his black mesh shorts hang low on his trim hips—showing off everything. There's at least a six-pack there, maybe even eight. I don't let my eyes stay there long enough to figure it out. Ogling isn't usually my thing, but this guy is impossible to ignore.

After lifting my eyes from his muscular chest, which glistens with a thin layer of sweat, I close in on his face. It's been my experience that a guy either has a killer body or good looks, but not both. Blinking, I try to keep my expression from giving away my amazement. They just don't make guys like this where I come from. That, or I don't see it because of the baggy t-shirts and jeans they wear.

"Are you done yet? I have a game to finish." The sound of his amused voice brings my head up the rest of the way without even thinking about it.

My theory is completely debunked when I finally see the rest of him. Unable to speak, I take in his damp, sandy blond hair and brazen blue eyes, highlighted by the bright sunlight. Unbelievable.

His lips quirk at the sides as he slowly scans my body. I can't decide if I should be relieved or embarrassed that I chose a pair of shorter cut-offs and a white tank this morning. I mean ... I'm in shape because I'm constantly on the go, but I have no idea how it looks to him. I'm probably less than a five on this guy's scale.

I want to turn around and run the other way, but he interrupts my plan before I get a chance. "Do you speak?" he asks, rubbing his hands along his strong jaw, which is peppered with a light shadow of facial hair. I'm not usually a fan of it, but it works on him, making him look older than he probably is.

I adjust my purse strap on my shoulder, wishing I'd at least put a little make-up on this morning. Back home I never cared much, but this is a whole other world ... one that's going to take some getting used to.

"Sorry," I finally reply, shaking myself out of my stupor. "I guess I can't do two things at once."

A cocky smile appears on his face, bringing out more of his strong, masculine features. Square jawline. Chiseled cheekbones. If my heart rate wasn't already high from all the walking I did today, it's on a 200-mph race out of my chest right now.

"If you ever want any lessons on multi-tasking, find me. I could teach you a couple things."

He just knocked himself down a couple notches on the hot meter. I know guys like him. They're all about girls and fun, or should I say, having fun with girls. So very self-important, and he doesn't know it yet, but I'm his worst nightmare. I can't stand his type, and I'll never give him what he wants so he shouldn't waste his time on me. With looks like his, there are lots of other girls who will be happy to cater to him.

"I think I'll pass. I prefer to hang out with people who aren't so full of themselves," I say, keeping my eyes up to avoid getting sucked in by his magnificent body again. His looks are the only thing still holding my interest.

"Chambers, this one looks like she'd like to be full of you," his friend, who I hadn't even realized was standing next to him, pipes in.

I step back and watch as Mr. Half-naked-and-sweaty gives the friend a look that would send an MMA fighter packing. It works. The guy walks back to the grassy area, tossing the football high in the air for another shirtless guy to catch.

"Gavin's an ass. Ignore him," he says, momentarily bringing my attention back to him.

"It's not a big deal. I know plenty of assholes so it's nothing new."

"Blunt much?"

"Every day."

Scanning our surroundings, I try to figure out an escape plan. This is awkward, and I'm ready to get back to my idea of a perfect Saturday. So far, my college life is unblemished. My day has been perfect … I'm not going to let this guy ruin that.

"What's your name?" he asks, running his fingers through his damp hair, letting it fall every which way. He's got this accidental sexiness to him, but he knows exactly what he's doing.

"Chambers, hurry up. Your new friend can wait!" his friend shouts with the football tucked under his arm.

"Calm the fuck down! I'll be right there!" His voice softens as he focuses his attention on me again. "I should probably get back over there."

"Nothing's stopping you," I say, pushing back a loose strand of hair that had blown in my face.

As I take a couple steps back, his friend, Gavin, approaches again, passing the ball back and forth between his hands. "Numbers are odd," he remarks, raking his eyes up and down my body. "Maybe your new friend wants to stick around and play a little football."

A grin spreads across Mr. Sexy's face as he looks at me. "I don't know, Gavin. She might get hurt playing with the big boys."

I shift on my feet, crossing my arms over my chest. "There's nothing hard about catching or throwing a football."

"I'm not a girl, and I don't throw like one either."

Gavin laughs, tossing the football at the guy who's become my Saturday distraction. "Show her what you got. Words don't hold the same weight, Chambers."

I open my mouth to argue, but I'm silenced by the football falling at my feet. The guy I now know as Chambers bends in front of me to pick it up, sliding his shoulder against my bare leg. I flinch, taking a small step back. I should walk away right now, but I don't. When he straightens, his body is close to mine again. The smell of musk and sweat hits me as he raises his hand, brushing a piece of hair off my cheek. "Let's make a bet. I'm going to walk over by the oak tree over there and throw you the ball. If you catch it, you're free to go. You drop it, and you're mine tonight."

My eyes widen, genuinely shocked by his bold words. College is promising to be quite an adventure. "Not happening."

6

"I didn't mean that quite like you think. Besides, there's a reason you're still standing here." He slides his tongue over his lower lip while staring down at mine. "Maybe we should find out why that is."

"You think you have me all figured out, don't you?"

"Prove me wrong," he says, his eyes searing into mine.

"I don't think you can catch a ball—not one thrown by me."

He's challenging me, and I've never been one to back away from a challenge. "One ball. I catch it, and I'm out of here."

He smiles, nodding to the grassy area. "Stand over there."

I do as he asks while he walks about twenty yards away from me. *Why am I even doing this?*

"Are you ready?" he yells, pretending to throw the ball.

Taking a deep breath, I place my hand over my eyes to block the sun. After regaining some of my composure, I drop my hands to my sides, and nod, waiting for ball to fly through the air. *Please let me catch this.*

He fakes it one more time before he lets go, sending it straight at me. I don't know much about football, but it looks like a well-thrown ball. Putting my hands up, I move a few inches to my right, and when I feel the leather against my palm, I grip it tightly.

It all happens in a matter of seconds, and when it's done, I look down, feeling the ball in my hand. I smile, tucking it under my arm as I watch Chambers walk in my direction. When he's close enough that I know I can throw it to him, I do just that. "Looks like I win. You'll have to find someone else to play with tonight."

"Tell me your name." He stares at me with his head cocked to one side, hands resting on his slim hips.

"There's really no reason to since I don't plan on talking to you again." I smile, proud of myself for being able to think quickly with a college-aged god standing feet in front of me.

7

"Good luck then. You might need it around here." He backs away, eyes roaming my body as he pulls his lower lip between his teeth. A tingle runs down my spine; even though his personality hasn't wooed me, his looks are getting to me. The guy's walking sex, but luckily, he's walking away from me.

Not even a hot guy walking around campus without a shirt can stand in my way when it comes to doing what I came here to do.

Before heading back to my dorm for the day, I stop at the coffee shop for a latte. The quaint space is much like the rest of campus, full of students, some reading, while others are chatting around packed tables. The walls are a rich yellow, and the floors are rustic stained cement. It's another place I can see myself spending a lot of my afternoons over the next four years.

I order an iced caramel latte, letting the first sip sit on my tongue for a few seconds longer than I should. This is something I can't get back home, and I'm going to spoil myself with it as often as possible. An indulgence my dad would tell me is just a waste of money. Maybe it is, but I only have one life to live.

When I finally reach my door, I take a deep breath, part of me hoping that Kate has already left for her date. I only met her yesterday, and she seems like a nice girl, but I also need time to myself. Time to process and adjust.

As I open the door, the first thing I see is her head of long, auburn hair in front of the mirror. At least she's getting ready, I think.

Her smile reflects off the mirror when she spots me. "Hey, where've you been all day? I thought you were just going to take a walk around."

"I did. I just got a little carried away and walked the whole campus. Enjoying a little freedom, you know?"

She smiles. "Hey, what are you doing tonight?"

I pull my purse strap over my head and sit on the edge of my bed, watching her perfectly place every section of her hair. "I don't know. I'll probably just read a book or something. It's been a long day."

Hot temps, long walk, arrogant college guys ... it's definitely been a very long day.

Setting the curling iron down, she spins around in her chair. "It's Saturday night. Don't you want go out and see what this college thing is all about? There's a lot to do outside of this campus, you know."

We've only known each other for twenty-four hours, but she's already getting an idea of just how fun I can be. If she expects me to be the life of the party, she might want to deal with her disappointment now. It will be easier on both of us.

"I will some other time. I'm just too tired tonight," I answer as I pull my shoes off my feet. I'm glad I opted for sneakers over flip-flops this morning because I probably walked at least five miles.

"You're welcome to come to the movie with Beau and me. We're going to the new Liam Hemsworth flick that everyone is talking about. It won't require too much energy ... I promise." She says it as if she thinks I'm easily lured by a hot guy with a killer body and smile to match. I can be, but not when she's doing the pity invite. Plus, I've seen enough of that today.

"No, I'm good. Besides, you guys just started dating yesterday, right?" She nods, watching me curiously as I continue. "I'm not tagging along on your first date."

She laughs, facing the mirror again. "It's hard to consider it a first date when we've known each other for fifteen years."

I haven't been around her long enough to understand the dynamics of her relationship with Beau, but I get the feeling that there's a story that might be worth hearing some day.

"Honestly, I'm looking forward to relaxing before classes start on Monday. I'll go some other time, though," I say, falling onto my bed.

"If you're sure."

"I'm sure."

"Does this look okay?" she asks, glancing down at her light brown wedges and strapless black maxi dress.

I laugh. "It's exactly what I would have picked for a date. Just make sure to bring a sweater if you're going to the movie. I always think it's cold in theaters."

"Good point. I always think of that too late."

"Then again, maybe you don't need to worry about it if you're with Beau."

Through the mirror, I see her roll her eyes. "Seriously? His hand will be buried so deep in a tub of buttery popcorn, he won't have time to worry about me."

"Men."

"You're telling me."

The room stays quiet as Kate continues to get ready. For me, the silence is a little slice of heaven—a delicacy I've rarely enjoyed with my dad around. It certainly didn't help when my mom left us, and he had no one else to talk to or ask to help around the house. It also didn't help that we lived in a small two-bedroom farmhouse with only one bathroom. There was never anywhere to go to get away. For many years, I thought my dad was trying to punish me by staying in small quarters, but I soon realized the way we lived wasn't a choice. We lived with what he had. I also knew it was one of the reasons she left.

A knock at the door causes both of us to jump. I should offer to answer it, but I already know it's Beau, Kate's perfect boyfriend. When he dropped her off last night, I couldn't help but listen to their goodbye. At first I thought it was disgust I felt when he was so sweet with her, but then I realized there was a tinge of jealousy that I was mistaking for something else.

No one has ever talked to me the way he talks to her. But then again, I've never really let anyone get that close to me. I dated Clay for most of high school, but before our relationship even got off the ground, I convinced myself that we had no chance of forever and always kept a certain amount of distance between us.

"Emery, are you listening to me?" Opening my eyes, I see Kate standing over my bed with Beau close behind. She's definitely one lucky girl. He's boy-next-door cute with a protective stance to match. The type of guy most girls dream about.

"Sorry, I guess I'm tired," I lie, trying to bring myself back to reality.

"Are you sure you don't want to come along? I hate leaving you alone."

I'm almost afraid to tell her no again because it's evident from the way she's asking that she's being completely genuine. "I'll be fine. You guys go have fun."

"Okay." She smiles, glancing back at Beau. The way he looks at her, with pure adoration in his eyes, brings the jealousy back that I felt the night before. Every day I tell myself I don't want that right now, but maybe it's because I haven't found anyone worth changing my rules for.

Chapter 2
DRAKE

AS I MAKE MY WAY ACROSS CAMPUS, I relax into the last few minutes of freedom before classes begin again. It's the last of sanity before the stress of school compounds on top of the football practices I've had for weeks now. There's a certain calm I feel when I'm on campus, but not on the football field or sitting in a big lecture hall listening to hours of worthless information.

Being at school also means I'm not at home, and any place is better than there. This is a different world, away from everything.

I'm always expected to be at the top of my game when I have the football in my hand. There are talents we are born with and others we learn, and for me, football is a little bit of both. My dad used to take me out in the backyard a couple times a week to throw his old pigskin around. I picked up everything he showed me quickly, and after a while, I could throw better than he could. Every time, no matter what I did, it was a perfect spiral.

Sometimes I wish I could hide from my talent. I wish I could blend in with every other college guy and not have all the weight on my shoulders. But this is what God gave me, and hopefully some day I'll make enough money to take care of my mom and younger sisters. I have to be at my best for the next couple years to have my shot in the pros.

I just need to hold on a little longer.

I need to stay focused.

It's just so fucking hard ... I always have to be the hero, but when it bleeds into an expectation of perfection, it becomes too much. Some days I just can't fucking take it anymore, and I want to disappear, to blend in. Some days, I don't want to be Drake Chambers.

As I open the door to enter the lecture hall for Speech 101, I take a deep breath. It's another semester. Another class I'll have to drag my feet through. *Three more years*, I tell myself.

I pick a chair toward the back of the room and throw my bag on the floor before relaxing into my seat. With any luck, the professor will hand us our syllabus and send us on our way.

"Please take a seat and pull out a notebook and pencil," the professor says from the podium. I keep my eyes on her just long enough to note that she's not the typical buttoned-up scholar. She's younger with long, red hair, dressed in a knee-length black dress and sandals. If nothing else, I can spend my Monday, Wednesday, and Friday mornings eye-fucking that toned body of hers. "I know it's our first class, but I have a project I'd like everyone to work on. If you thought this was going to be easy, or we'd just sit here and discuss the syllabus for an hour, you might want to reevaluate your schedule."

Okay, her fucking attitude is going to kill it for me. Shaking my head, I reach into my bag and pull out what she asked. Too bad this class is a requirement for graduation, and I can't afford not to graduate.

"My assistant is going around with a handout for everyone. When you get it, turn to page two and read about the group project. It will be twenty-five percent of your grade this semester." She pauses, checking to make sure she has everyone's attention. "One last thing. I'll let you choose your partner, but please avoid working with someone you already know. You'll get more out of it this way."

Great. I hate projects, and even more than that, I hate group projects. It's hard to find the time to get together with people when I have workouts, practices, and games. Maybe I'll find a hot chick and convince her to carry my weight. I've done it before, and I can do it again.

Noticing the guy two seats down eyeing me like his next big hunt, I stand and head in the opposite direction. He's not going to be down with the game I'm about to play. As I walk past the upperclassman, who Professor McGill calls her assistant, I grab a handout from his hand and glance around the room.

I need to find the one ... the girl who's going to help me pass this class. It's obvious from the way a couple blondes from across the room watch me that they know who I am. Those are the ones I avoid; they'll just expect something I'm not willing to give them. I learned last year that there are too many girls who want to be *the one who tames the wild quarterback*. The only problem is, I'm not the wild guy they all think I am.

I don't date because I don't have time. I can count the number of girls I've had sex with on one hand. I always make sure I end things before they go too far emotionally. There's just way too much going on in my life with football, a part-time job, and family drama to add a relationship into the mix.

When I hear some of the other guys on the team talk about their conquests, I feel like a saint. One of my wide receivers has a different girl every weekend, literally. I've seen him get in too many situations where last weekend's girl bumps into him while he's with his latest. He hasn't quite figured out how easily some of these girls get attached, and I'm waiting for it to come back and bite him in the ass.

After walking almost the whole way up the center aisle, I start to doubt my plan. The pickings are slim, and if I can't find someone, I won't have any choice other than to drop this class and try again next semester. I don't have time to deal with this shit right now.

"Hey," I hear a soft, sweet voice say from behind me. When I don't turn around right away, she continues, a little unsure this time. "Umm, excuse me."

Glancing over my shoulder, I get my first look at her. She's definitely cute ... in a sweet, innocent sort of way with her long, chocolate brown hair and large brown eyes. I bet those eyes have gotten her out of trouble a time or two. She also happens to be the same girl who ran into me while I was tossing around the ball with the guys Saturday. The one who can catch a ball and throw a perfect spiral. She didn't seem to know who I was then ... or she didn't care.

"Can I help you?" I ask, turning myself the rest of the way around.

Her eyes widen with her own realization as she tucks a piece of her hair behind her ear, allowing me to focus on the contrast between her creamy skin and dark locks. I don't stop there, lowering my gaze to her long, bare legs. I noticed them right away the other day, and I thank God she chose cutoff shorts again today.

"I was wondering if you have a partner yet. I was reading through the syllabus, and I guess everyone else got a head start."

A grin spreads across my face as I look up to her hooded eyes. "So you're the only person left in this class who doesn't have someone to work with?"

She scans the room, clearing her throat. "I think we're the only two left."

"Are you sure this isn't your way of trying to see me without my shirt again?" I tease. This is how I've gotten through the last nine years. There's nothing I take too seriously outside of family and football.

Her mouth hangs open as she looks from side to side then finds me again. "If all I wanted to do is look at a guy without a shirt, I'd stay home and browse Pinterest. At least the guys on there can't talk back." She pauses, a more serious look appearing on her face. "I just assumed you didn't have a partner since you're just standing here."

"Well, you assumed right this time, but don't make a habit of it. Most people are wrong about me."

"Do you have a name?" she asks, tucking more hair behind her ear.

She's not throwing herself at me or pretending she has a low IQ just so I take pity on her. She actually doesn't have a fucking clue who I am.

"Drake. Drake Chambers."

Her eyebrows pull in as if she's thinking really hard. It's actually kind of cute. "That name sounds familiar."

"Maybe it's because Gavin called me Chambers after you ran into me Saturday."

She winces. "No, that's not it."

"You'll figure it out eventually."

She nods, her lips pulling up at the corners. "It's nothing Google can't fix."

This girl is quick, and I kind of like sparring with her. It might be the highlight of my fucking day.

"Well, should we get started?" she asks as she wraps her arms tightly around her notebook. Her expression is hard to read. It's like we're in the middle of a poker game or business deal.

"It sounds like I don't have much of a choice." I let her lead the way, watching the way her shorts mold to her body as she walks. Her body curves in all the right places, and she's toned where it counts. Not bad. Not bad at all.

We grab two seats near the front of the room, neither of us speaking at first. She's reading her syllabus, or should I say, pretending to read it. I catch her eyes lifting from the paper a few times, watching me in the same way she watched me the other day. If she thinks she's being sneaky, she's wrong.

"You never told me your name," I say, resting my arm across the top of my chair.

"I usually don't share with strangers."

Sitting up, I lean in close to her. "I think we're moving past being strangers. What's your name?"

She shifts uncomfortably in her seat, glancing up at the clock that hangs above the door. It's good to know I can affect her in some way. "Emery."

"Emery? That's different."

Ignoring my remark, she picks up her pencil again, working hard to keep her eyes off me. "Let's get to work. We don't have that much time left."

"I'm going to be straight with you, Emery. I'm not going to be able to work on this much outside of class."

Her eyes widen. "Seriously? You had time to play around with your friends Saturday."

"Look, you picked me. I can't do much with my schedule."

She crosses her arms over her chest as her eyes narrow on me. Maybe I should feel guilty for the way I am, but I don't. Besides, she's even hotter when she's pissed. "We'll get a better grade if I just do it all myself anyway."

Her comment should offend me, but she's probably right. She has perfectionist written all over her. I bet she spends her weekends reading and studying, thinking that if she takes one day off, she'll fail out of life.

She doesn't say another word as she starts jotting things down in her notebook. I thought this was what I wanted, to sit back and watch her do all the work, but I have to bite my lip to hide my grimace. If this is what I want, why do I feel so fucking annoyed with myself?

"Emery." She stops writing but doesn't look up. Again, that unfamiliar guilty feeling hits me in the face. "Why don't we exchange numbers, and I'll try to find time to get together this weekend."

"Are you sure you can squeeze me in?" she asks as she taps her pencil against her lower lip. Her tone is sharp, and for a second, I consider sticking to my original plan, but maybe she deserves a break.

17

My high school coach always said I was too cocky. He said it would hold me back, but so far he's been wrong, and I'm not planning on changing anytime soon. This is who I am. It's what my life has molded me to be. It's how I deal with all the other shit.

"I can try to make an exception for you."

Chapter 3
Emery

WHEN I GET BACK TO my room after class, Kate is standing in front of the full-length mirror with a black dress in one hand and an emerald one in the other. It's kind of funny because it's exactly what I would have done if I had to make a decision on what to wear.

Initially, I thought it would be a little weird getting stuck in a room with a stranger and be expected to get along while living in a tight space, but it's been pretty easy so far. We've found enough similarities in our personalities to bury any differences.

She's outgoing, and I'm happy to stay locked in our room with a book.

She's always smiling, and I'm always trying to find a reason to.

But yet, we're doing okay.

"Are you going somewhere?" I ask, throwing my backpack onto my bed.

"Beau is going to take me out to dinner to celebrate my first day of college." She smiles shyly, holding the green one directly in front of her. "Which one looks better? It's so freaking hot outside, and these are the only sundresses I have."

"Where's he taking you?" I ask, surveying the dress. She's so pretty ... that dress won't do her justice.

"Hmm, he mentioned pizza or hot wings, but I'm not sure. Somewhere casual, I guess," she replies, replacing the green dress with the black. I like this one better, but something is still missing. She needs something that screams summer and reflects her bright personality.

The wheels start turning in my head as I open my own closet door and pull out a colorful, flower-printed dress I'd picked up on clearance this summer. I've never worn it, and it's just going to go to waste if Kate doesn't.

"Here," I say, handing it to her. "Try this on. I think it's fitting for the occasion."

Her eyes widen as she places it so she can see it in the mirror. "Wow. This is gorgeous, but Emery, it still has the tags on it. Don't you want to wear it first?"

I wave her off, taking a seat on the edge of my bed. "I don't have anywhere to wear it. Besides, it'll look better on you."

"No, it won't, but if you aren't going to wear it, I will."

"It's all yours." It's hard to take my eyes away from the mirror as she sways her hips back and forth to see the movement of the flared skirt. I don't often have anything to offer someone, and this feels good. "From what I've seen so far, I think you hit the boyfriend lottery."

She looks back at me, her expression not as cheerful as it had been a few seconds ago. "Coming to college was a big deal for me. I think this is his, "Congratulations, you made it through day one," celebration."

I nod, thinking of everything I went through to get here. Everything I gave up. "I get it. I just think it's really nice that you have him here with you."

Her smile returns. "Me, too."

While she's busy styling her hair and applying her make-up, I power on my laptop so I can get started on my to-do list. After checking my emails for anything new, I hesitantly type *Drake Chambers* into the search engine and tap my foot against the old hardwood floors while I wait for results to pop up.

What if he's a convicted felon, or worse yet, a member of one of those crazy boy bands that girls gush over?

Thousands of hits pop up, and I instantly know why his name sounded familiar. He's the quarterback of the freaking football team. Scrolling down the list of articles, I find stories about his high school days and recruitment to Southern Iowa. Lots of schools wanted him.

Drake Chambers is a big deal.

"Hey, what are you doing?" Kate stands behind me, peering over my shoulder. Glancing back, I notice she's in my dress, and it really does look great on her. Much better than it would've looked on me.

"I was Googling this guy I have to work with in speech."

"Why?"

"Because he's an entitled asshole."

She leans in closer, resting her elbow against my shoulder. "Wait, you're working with Drake? How the heck did that happen?"

"You know him?" Of course she knows him. He's probably left his jerk tracks all across campus by now.

She stands up straight, biting down on her lower lip. "I should probably just tell you, but—"

"Please tell me you've never had a thing with him. I swear, Kate, I will never look at you the same," I say, watching the smile form on her face.

Her laughter fills the room. "Hell no! I may be a little bit addicted to football, mainly Southern Iowa football." She pauses, trying to gain control over herself. "Besides, I think Beau hangs out with him every once in a while. How did you get paired with him?"

I remember looking around the lecture hall earlier for anyone who looked like they hadn't already picked someone to work with, and after coming up empty on my first scan of the room, I spotted him. He was standing with his back to me, and with his shirt on, I didn't recognize him as the guy I ran into the other day. His toned body and perfectly fitting jeans should have clued me in that he's a jock.

"I sort of picked him," I admit shyly. I can be very naïve, but at least I admit to it.

"Seriously. I get that you don't watch TV or follow football, but maybe you need to start."

"I'm screwed, aren't I?" At least he gave me his number at the end of class and semi-offered to help me with it. I highly doubt he'll answer, though.

"I think you're more than screwed."

Resting my head against the top of my chair, I think about all the possible scenarios. He could actually come through and help me, but from Kate's reaction and his own admission, that's unlikely. It's more likely that I'll be completing this project by myself.

Whatever happens, I'm going to do what it takes to stay on track. It's just what I do, no matter what gets in my way. Drake Chambers isn't going to change that.

"So have you decided on a topic yet?" Drake asks as he sets his stuff on the desk next to mine. We spent all of Wednesday arguing over topics, no closer to picking one than we were when we began. His stubbornness matches mine, which isn't a good sign for us.

I stare up at him, annoyed. When we left class the other day, we'd both agreed to think of something we could talk about in front of the class for fifteen minutes. The way he just said it, like it was solely my responsibility, pisses me off. I'm actually starting to think he likes to piss me off.

"Obviously I'm going to have to because I can't count on you." Looking back down, I jot the date on my notebook and wait for the professor to enter. The sooner we can get this class over with, the sooner I can get away from him.

A few seconds later, I see him inching closer out of the corner of my eye. "Don't be mad. I warned you. I may be a jerk, but at least I'm an honest one."

I wait until he sits back in his chair before I chance a look in his direction. I really don't get this guy. He seems intent on making me do this thing on my own, but he also shows signs of having morals every now and then. It's so freaking confusing sometimes.

"How are you going to make it through life if football doesn't work out for you? Because you know, nothing is guaranteed in this life. Absolutely nothing."

His nostrils flare as we stare at each other. Maybe I should be scared, but I'm not. Life's dealt me worse than Drake Chambers. "You don't know shit," he growls.

"I probably know a lot more than you think," I say, facing front again.

Very few people have gotten under my skin like Drake. He has irritated me every time we're within twenty feet of each other, but when I know I'm going to see him, there's also this level of excitement I've never felt before. I like fighting with him. He's a challenge for me. Maybe it's the way he carries himself: confident, cute in a rugged I'm-not-afraid-to-get-dirty sort of way, and witty enough to keep me on my toes. I've never known anyone quite like him before.

The constant battle is both invigorating and irritating, but I'm not going to stop until I win. I haven't quite decided what winning entails, though.

Professor McGill lectures the entire hour, leaving no more time to banter with Drake ... not that I have anything left to say to him. I can feel his eyes burning into me. He's pissed, but I don't care. He's the one who started this.

As soon as the lecture ends, I pick up my backpack, not bothering to take the time to slip my notebook inside. I just want to get out of here as soon as possible.

"Emery! Wait."

I should keep walking, but I stop, turning on my heel. It's just the type of person I am. Always trying to do what's right. One of these days I might learn how to do what I want instead.

"Look, I can get together tonight after practice, if it means that much to you." His tone is different than how he's talked to me during our few other encounters. Monotone. No teasing. No arrogance. It matches the blank expression on his face.

"Don't worry. I'll take care of the whole thing." Determination fuels me as I walk away. Stubbornness doesn't allow me to look back, even if a tiny voice in my head is begging me to take what he's offering. It's obvious that he's not a stupid guy, because he's been playing this game a little too well.

He yells my name a couple times, but I ignore it. It's what I wanted … to make him feel guilty for being such a jerk. So why do I suddenly feel like the bitch?

Having a conscience sucks sometimes.

Instead of going to the library in between classes like I planned, I decide to run back to my room and enjoy a few quiet moments before I have to head to biology. I'm too wound up about having to work on this stupid project by myself to study anyway.

When I open the door to my room, Kate is propped on her bed with a textbook on her lap.

"Hey," she says, looking up from her homework. The stress must show all over my face because her head tilts as she eyes me carefully. I've never been good at hiding my emotions.

"Hey," I answer back, attempting to fake a smile.

She stands, taking a couple hesitant steps in my direction. "Are you okay?"

"I'll be fine. Speech was just a little rough today, that's all," I answer honestly. It's probably one of many difficult days I have to come, and I need to learn to deal better. No matter how much I want it, nothing's ever going to be perfect.

"Do you want to talk about it?"

Lisa De Jong

"There's not really anything to talk about." It's a lie, but talking about Drake isn't going to make things with him better. Right now, I just need a few minutes alone to get a grip on my emotions. I hate when I feel like I don't have control. "I'll be right back."

She nods, sitting back down in the center of her bed. Her eyes never leave me, though, and I can tell she's reading right through me as I step out of the room.

Since I was little, I've had this way of dealing with life when it gets overwhelming. Call it my form of meditation— my way of dealing with all the loud noise in my head. I shut myself in the bathroom and lock the door behind me, because at home, it was the only place I could escape to that had a lock. Leaning back against the counter, I take a few deep breaths and let everything go—all the irritations, all the things that are holding me back from being the person I want to be.

Maybe I wouldn't have such a hard time dealing with my emotions if Mom hadn't left us the way she did. I was too young to understand, but too old to forget. She hurt me. She ruined my dad. He was a man who spent hours outside taking care of the farm, but he'd make time for me every night when he came inside. We' built forts, made animals out of Play-Doh, and read books. He was Daddy, my safety blanket when it thundered or the rickety floorboards of our old house creaked.

Then, after she left, he was always busy. If it wasn't the fields, it was cooking or paying the bills. My imagination became my nightly playmate, which was good sometimes and scary at others. I used to think about what it would be like to be a real princess and wear big, sparkly pink dresses. I used to pretend I was older and wear the heels and purses she left behind. That always led to other thoughts … like what all my friends were doing with their moms. I imagined what it would be like to shop with her, get our nails painted, and cuddle on the couch with a movie. Things I never got to do.

One day, not long after she left, I heard my dad telling my grandma that my mom always had dreams that would never come true if she stayed with us. That was when I first realized I had big dreams, too. I just don't want to let anyone down the way she did to make them come true. I'm determined to do it the right way ... before I make a mistake that I can't go back from.

I have to remember that now, even when little roadblocks like Drake pop up. *That's all he is*, I think as I straighten up and look in the mirror. The front of my long hair sticks up from the way my fingers gripped it, and my mascara is smeared from pressing my eyes in the palms of my hands. It's nothing a brush and washcloth can't fix.

I just wish it were that easy to fix the damage inside of me. It's been years, and I need to find some way to let it all go.

Taking a deep breath, I walk back into the room, noticing Kate hasn't left for class yet. "Do you want to walk to class with me?" I ask, hoping to ease her worry. We have the same major, and have biology class together on Mondays, Wednesdays, and Fridays.

"Yeah, give me just a second," she says, throwing her books into her bag.

It's obvious from the number of times I catch her looking at me while tucking her books away that she's still not convinced I'm okay. The last thing I want to do is take someone down with my bad mood.

"We're having a study group tonight for biology. Do you want to come?" I ask, sitting on the corner of my bed. This is normal Emery.

"Maybe. I'll have to check with Beau first to see if he has any plans." She slips her bag over her shoulder and steps into her flip-flops.

"You two seem to spend a lot of time together. Don't you ever just want to do your own thing? When do you have time to study?" I ask as I chip away the polish from my nails. When she doesn't answer right away, I look up. With the strange tension I'd already caused, this probably wasn't the best time to mention Beau. It's not my business anyway.

She shrugs. "We're making up for lost time. It's hard to explain, but right now, I need all the time with him that I can get. And don't worry about my study time. I get plenty of that done when I'm with Beau."

I smile. "Whatever. I guess if Beau was my boyfriend, I would want to spend every minute I could with him, too."

"Have you ever had a serious boyfriend, Emery?"

The weight on my chest becomes a little heavier again as the smile falls from my face. I hate what I did to Clay, but that doesn't mean it wasn't the right decision. "This might not be the best day to talk about that."

"I'm sorry. I didn't mean to pry," she says softly in an attempt to back track.

"It's okay. Maybe someday we can talk about it, but not today." I wonder if Kate would understand me. Would she see how my past plays a part in everything I do, every decision I make? She'd probably tell me it's time to move on ... and maybe it is.

"Are you ready to go?" Kate asks, glancing around the room again.

"Yeah, let's get out of here." I stand from the bed and toss my hair over my shoulders. It's a good thing I came home between classes, because I'm already feeling a lot better after getting a couple minutes to myself and talking to Kate. Maybe she'll become a new part to my ritual.

As we make our way across campus, I run a few ideas for my assignment by Kate. Drake's not helping, and I need to make sure my concepts make sense to someone.

She nods often as I take her through my plan. "It's actually perfect. I've never thought too much about why I am the way I am, and I never knew my dad so I have no idea if I'm anything like him. From what my mom says, probably not. I can tell you've thought about it a lot, though."

After shrugging my shoulders, I tuck my fingers into my front pockets. "Thanks. I guess I'm just very passionate about it."

When we get to our classroom, we take our seats right next to each other in the front of the room. Our professor is an older gentleman on the verge of retirement, and he isn't always the easiest person to hear or understand.

"Are you ladies going to the game tomorrow?" I swear to God. I thought I was done with him for the day, but as it turns out, there's nowhere to hide from Drake Chambers. Until right now, I had no idea he was even in this class. Maybe this is the first time he's been to biology this semester.

"We have better things to do. Like memorizing all the past presidents in order of their presidency," I reply, not even bothering to turn around. The cockiness that was missing earlier in the hallway is back, and I have my shield up.

"What about you? Are you memorizing the presidents with the brown-eyed devil over here?" he asks Kate. He probably sees her as his next conquest, and I'm going to put that idea to bed right now.

"She's hanging out with her super nice and very sexy boyfriend," I interject, catching Kate's eye.

"I think she can answer for herself." By the sound of Drake's voice, I know he's closer, and as I feel his warm breath against my neck, I know he's too damn close.

Kate interrupts, "I don't know why you two even bother talking to each other."

"If Professor McGill hadn't assigned us to work on a group project, we wouldn't have to," I answer, glaring at Kate. She knows why I'm stuck with the jerk.

Even though I can't see Drake, I can still feel him right behind me. "Speaking of that stupid fucking project, are we still getting together tonight?"

"I can't. I have study group."

"When don't you have study group?" Closing my eyes, I try to pretend that his proximity isn't affecting me.

"Tomorrow," I reply, opening my eyes again. Not able to hide from him any longer, I turn to face him, hoping he'll back away. That he'll see anger written all over my face and leave me alone.

He doesn't.

I notice his once blank eyes are now lit by fire. Whatever mask he had on earlier has come off, and this is what's left. I don't necessarily like it, but I want to make it burn hotter.

"I have a game," he finally replies.

"Well, then it's going to have to be Sunday." I try to keep my eyes on his, but his perfect pink lips are hard to ignore. Impossible actually.

"Have it your way, but I won't be up until at least noon, since there's a party tomorrow night," he says, sounding matter of fact. Like it's something I should already know. Those lips don't seem quite as perfect anymore … in fact, the more he opens his mouth, the less I like them.

"Yeah, I'd hate for you to miss the party. Nothing like wasting a night getting drunk."

Kate groans. "Seriously, you guys. Lecture is about to start."

"I can't stand him," I whisper to her, turning around in my chair.

"I see that. Can you finish this later?"

Drake sits back in his seat, giving me the space I've been craving. "I'll call you on Sunday when I get up."

"You gave him your phone number?" Kate asks, her eyes going wide.

"Of course she did." Drake smirks, twirling his pencil between his fingers.

"God, I hate him," I say as we wait for the professor.

"Sometimes people mistake hate for like," Kate says, her smile growing bigger.

Without missing a beat, I ask, "Did you ever hate Beau?"

"No," she says without even a second of hesitation.

"Exactly."

Chapter 4

DRAKE

TODAY ENDED WITH ANOTHER GAME in the win column, which means tonight's party is going to be crazy. Some Saturday nights I'm pumped to go, and others I'd rather stay home. Tonight, I'm leaning more toward the latter.

My shoulders are killing me, and I fell hard on my side, leaving a decent bruise on my hip. My body is screaming at me to lay low, but I always feel like it's my duty to go because I'm the quarterback ... the leader of the team.

Tonight I'm riding with Gavin, and if I'm lucky, I'll be able to sneak out after a couple drinks and get a good night's sleep.

"Got a girl lined up for tonight?" he asks as we come to a slow at a stoplight. We managed to ride quietly up to this point, listening to rap songs on the radio.

"No, dude, you know it's not like that for me. I leave that shit to you guys." Since the day I stepped foot on this campus last year, I felt like there was a difference between the way I am and the way my teammates expected me to be. It made me uneasy at first because I was the new guy ... the fucking freshman, but I think they're used to it now.

"Don't act like you're so fucking perfect, Drake. College isn't supposed to be your ticket to sainthood." He pulls in front of tonight's party house and turns off the ignition. "Have a little fun."

30

Ignoring him, I open my door and step out into the stale summer air. I'm going to need another shower when I get back to my room tonight because this hot, humid weather is ridiculous. I walk up the sidewalk that leads to the oversized brick house, taking the front steps two at a time. From the outside, I can tell this place is packed, which means it's probably hot as fuck in there.

Before going inside, I turn back around, causing Gavin to practically run into my chest. "I never said I was perfect. Besides, you don't have to fuck a different girl every weekend just because you play football."

I watch his eyes double in size under the porch light. I let Gavin give me shit about a lot of things, but I'm sick of hearing about this.

"Now, let's go inside and get drunk."

Without waiting for a response, I push open the door and step inside the foyer and into the view of everyone in the large, packed living room. The crowd erupts just like they do when I make a play during the football game. This is the part I hate. The attention. The invisible pedestal. This isn't what I'm about.

Gavin pats my back, pushing me forward. "Showtime, Chambers."

I put on the customary grin and work my way through the crowd, giving high-fives along the way. It's so fucking hot in here, and bodies are pressed so close that I have to shoulder my way through. A few girls grind up next to me as I pass them, but I don't play along. I'm not in the mood for that tonight.

If I can find the booze and down a couple quick drinks, it'll loosen me up. I can make face, and then get the hell out of here.

After spotting the keg near the door to the kitchen, I push harder through the crowd, needing my space and something cold to drink. It's difficult to get through when everyone wants a piece of me.

"If it's not Drake Chambers. Good game, man." I don't know the guy in the fraternity shirt, but he's manning the keg, which makes him cool in my book.

"Thanks," I say, taking a glass of the cold amber-colored liquid from his hand. I down it quickly, passing the cup back for more.

"You missed a couple big passes down the field when your receivers were wide open. How could you not see them, man?"

Fucking great ... this again. Every week, no matter how good I play, I always hear about what I can do better. Whenever someone tries to give me football lessons, I think back to when I was younger, and that's the last place I want to go right now. My dad pointed out every missed throw, every time my footwork wasn't good enough, and when I took too many unnecessary sacks. My team could win by thirty points, and it still wasn't good enough.

There's already way too much pressure sitting on my shoulders without hearing Dad's voice in my head. I don't need to hear that I can be better. I don't need to hear that I'm not perfect. I used to get so tired of that shit. Now I have everyone on my case. I guess that's what happens when you're in the public eye.

"That's easy to say when you're not the one on the field. Things look a little different when you have three hundred pound guys coming after you."

"There's no way those guys were more than two-fifty," he scoffs. He hands me my refilled cup, and I quickly move away in an attempt to avoid any more shit from him. As the school's football star, I'm also supposed to stay out of trouble, and listening to this guy much longer is going to get me in all kinds of it.

With a quick scan of the room, I spot some of my teammates huddled in the corner and make my way to them. They know better than to question my skills.

I don't get far before a small, bony hand wraps around my bicep. "Drake."

Without looking back, I know it's Olivia. Last year, after a night of way too much drinking, I ended up in bed with her. I regretted it as soon as I woke up the next morning, and she's been unable to take no for an answer ever since.

Glancing over my shoulder, I see her in one of the shortest skirts I've ever seen and a tiny top to match. Not that it surprises me. "What do you want, Olivia?"

She moves her manicured hand to my shoulder, bringing her lips close to my ear. "Do you want to go upstairs? I haven't seen you in a while."

"I'm hanging with the guys tonight," I say, trying to free myself from her grasp.

Her long nails dig into my arm, holding me back. "Please, I miss you." Her generous pink lips pucker while she twirls her finger through her shoulder-length blonde hair. She's hot, I'll give her that, but she's not what I'm after. Not that I'm after anyone right now.

"We're not happening. Ever."

She licks her lower lip as she stares at mine. "We already did."

"It was a mistake," I say quietly, shaking my arm loose. The last thing I want to do is cause a scene.

"Over here, Chambers!" one of the guys shouts. I push past Olivia, and if I'm lucky, she'll stay away from me the rest of the night.

"Drake!" I hear her yell after me. I don't look back. I wish there was a way to erase the night we spent together because this isn't worth it. It wasn't worth it then.

When I finally reach the guys, I'm greeted by high fives and a full cup of beer. If I could stay locked in this corner of the room, the rest of the night wouldn't be so bad.

"A week off, and then Michigan State is rolling in. Are you ready?" It's Cooper, one of the defensive ends.

"I'm always ready, but with an extra week to prepare, they better watch it. Have you guys been studying film?" I ask, taking another sip of my cold beer.

"Nah, we'll start on Monday. One game at a time," Cooper answers, looking past me into the packed crowd. "What's up with you and Olivia?"

I grimace, rubbing the back of my neck. "Nothing. Absolutely nothing."

"She's looking over here, and if I were you, I'd go after that. It might loosen you up before the big game."

Looking behind me, I see her huddled with a couple of her friends, all six eyes on me. I don't even want to think about what they're talking about. "I'll be loose enough. Don't worry about me."

When I spin back around, all my teammates are giving their full attention to the girls. "Fuck it," I say, downing the last of my beer and pushing my way back to the keg. My original plan to leave after a couple drinks fails, and the rest of the night becomes a blur.

If you asked me how old I was when I got my pro jerk card out of the cereal box, I wouldn't have an answer. It came piece by piece … like a puzzle. Every day, it was another chip added to my shoulder. Another problem I had to find a resolution for.

It's all a weight that's been building up for years. I don't have time to step back and think about it too often, but when I do, I'm not happy with the person it's made me.

One day, I was a kid, who did nothing but ride his bike and play on the small town football team, then suddenly I was left to watch over my mom and two younger sisters. It wasn't fair, but I had to deal with the hand I was dealt.

I did the best I could, but it never felt like enough. My mom fell apart, and I don't mean in a slow, predictable kind of way. She used to pack each of us the perfect lunch every morning, even cutting the crust off our sandwiches, but that all changed suddenly. She became someone who barely came out of her room, and it was hard to understand the reason for that at such a young age.

I still don't understand why she "left" us, but I try to hold my shit together. I try to set a good example for my younger sisters. It's not always easy, though.

I certainly don't like how I've been acting around Emery. I'm an ass, a jerk, a dickhead, whatever you want to call me. She doesn't deserve my shit, and she didn't ask to enter the world I created. Not that I really asked for the circumstances of my life to make me this way.

Grabbing my phone from my nightstand, I dial her number, part of me praying she doesn't answer and the other part hoping she does. I drank a little more than I intended to last night, and I'm paying for it this morning. My mouth's dry. My head pounds. I'm not in the mood to study, but I feel like I owe it to her.

"Hello," she answers in a soft, hesitant voice.

"Hey, Emery, it's Drake." I squeeze my eyes shut and run my fingers through my hair. I probably sound like an idiot.

"I know who it is ... I just never expected you to actually call."

I wince. She always says what's on her mind; I'll give her that. "I said I would. I'm the honest jerk, remember?"

"Okay, honest jerk. I'll try to remember that."

After taking a deep breath, I continue, "Look, I'm sorry about the other day. I was having a bad morning, and I took it out on you."

Her voice is quiet when she replies. "I understand. It's just that school and my grades ... they're really important to me."

"I know," I say, stopping her. School is her football. I get it.

"I either need to know you're in this or you're not. If you're not, I need to move forward with it on my own." Her voice is low, sad almost. Like I'll break something inside her if I don't help her with this.

changing forever

As I lay in bed earlier this morning, I decided that I was going to treat this like football. I'm Emery's teammate, and I'd be a coward to let her down. It's not about what I want to do or what I don't want to do. It's about what's best for the team.

"I'm in."

I hear her let out a deep breath. I've really been doing a number on this girl's patience. "Can you get together this afternoon? We really need to pick a topic so we can start researching," she says, sounding hopeful.

"Yeah, that's why I called actually. Can you meet me in one hour?" I rub the palm of my hand over my tired eyes, trying my best to get myself in good enough shape to study.

"Yeah, I'll meet you in the coffee shop, but don't stand me up, Drake. I don't often hand out second chances."

Grimacing, I rub my fingers along my forehead. I hate coffee. Actually, hate might not be a strong enough word.

"I'll be there," I say hesitantly, hanging up before she has time to change her mind.

I stretch out on my bed again feeling a little bit better about myself. Spending part of my Sunday working on this project won't kill me ... it's the right thing to do. Unfortunately, the overwhelming smell of stale beer is the only thing hitting my senses at the moment, and a shower is definitely in order before I go anywhere today. I grab a clean pair of jeans from my dresser and a plain gray t-shirt from the shelf in my closet. I'm so fucking glad these things are somewhat in style because they're all I own. All I can afford actually.

As I walk out of the room and into the hall, I notice the quiet. It's a nice change from the usual rowdiness that fills the narrow space. If my conscience would allow it, I'd crawl back in my bed and sleep the rest of the day away right along with everyone else.

I shower as fast as my aching head will let me. The hot water feels good on my sore muscles and reminds me that it might not be a bad idea to sit in the sauna later.

After pulling my clothes on and brushing my teeth a couple times to banish any remaining smell of alcohol, I head out to meet Emery. The last thing I want to do is be late for my second chance, because something tells me she was serious about this being my last one.

Fall is starting to move in, and the temps are a little cooler today than they were yesterday. It only takes me a few minutes to find the coffee shop, and surprisingly, I'm ten minutes early. I guess that's better than the alternative, given my current standing with Emery. The place is packed, leaving only one chair at the bar open, which won't work at all. I stand against the wall just inside the door, waiting for Emery before making any decisions on what to do next.

Luckily, she's not far behind me, appearing in the doorway a couple minutes later with an oversized bag over her shoulder. She looks so fucking hot in tight jeans and a fitted black t-shirt. I think her simplicity separates her from other girls, and I guess simple is sexy.

"Hey," she says, tucking a strand of hair behind her ear. I've noticed she does that a lot.

"Hey," I answer back, shoving my hands deep in my pockets. "I couldn't find a table. Do you want to go somewhere else?"

She smiles, glancing over her shoulder and out the window. "Why don't we grab our drinks and go sit out by the river?"

I pull my hand from my pocket and rub it along my jaw. What she's proposing sounds nice, but it also sounds a little too cozy for me. I don't do cozy well.

"Lots of people study outside," she adds, adjusting the strap of her bag. Her eyes brighten as she shifts her gaze between me and the window. How am I supposed to say no to her and those big brown eyes?

"I guess we're going out by the river then," I say, placing my hand on her lower back to guide her to the counter. I don't realize I'm doing it until we're halfway to the register, but then I can't let go. It feels better than I'd ever admit.

My hand drops away when we stop at the end of the line. "What are you going to get?" she says, glancing back at me.

"I don't know. I can't stand the taste of coffee."

She points her painted purple nail up to the menu board. "I bet the smoothies are good. I haven't had one, but I notice lots of people ordering them."

"Yeah, I'll give that a try. What do you want? I'm buying."

She looks back at me, her eyes wide. My offer is obviously a surprise to her, but have I really been that much of an ass? "You don't have to do that."

I lean in close, my chest hitting her back. "It's just a drink, Emery. Don't argue with me about this. Besides, I think I owe you."

"You don't, but because I'm not in the mood to argue, I'll take a medium iced mocha with no whip," she says, crossing her arms over her chest. She's stubborn, but I like the challenge.

I step back to give her some space, but I'm still close enough to smell her perfume. I usually can't stand the stuff, but hers reminds me of strawberries with a hint of vanilla. It's sexy with a side of sass but not too overpowering. From what I know about her so far, it suits her perfectly.

"Next," the barista calls, waving me forward.

Stepping up to the counter, I order and pay for our drinks. They don't ask for my name, but it must not have been a secret because a couple minutes later it's called, and our drinks are placed on the end of the counter. After handing Emery her coffee, we walk outside and start toward the water.

This is my second year here, and I've never once taken the time to just sit outside. It's hard to think about that kind of stuff when I rarely have free time. Every extra minute I have is devoted to football ... my dad taught me how to live and sleep it.

"You're kind of quiet over there," Emery says, interrupting my thoughts.

"So you Googled me?"

"What?" she asks, nervous laughter escaping her.

"The other day in class ... you knew I played football."

"Oh yeah," she says, shaking her head. "You didn't think I could work with you if I didn't know who you were, did you?"

"I didn't expect anything less from you."

She stops about fifteen feet from the river and pulls a flannel blanket out of her bag. No wonder that thing was so full. "Does this spot look okay?"

I scan the area, making sure there's no one I recognize. It's not that I'm embarrassed to be seen with her ... I just don't want anyone to draw conclusions. A guy and a girl alone on a blanket just screams couple, especially around here. Because of who I am, it would cause a breaking news flash across campus. "This'll work."

When I look in her direction again, her lips are pursed around her straw, one arm crossed over her chest. "Is there a problem, Chambers?"

My lips quirk; I can't help it. "Just making sure no one sees me with you. I don't want to ruin your reputation."

She rolls her eyes, letting her bag fall down her arm. "I don't think I have one to ruin."

"No, you have one ... you just don't know it because it's not that exciting."

"What makes you say that?" I watch as she lowers herself to the blanket, crossing her extended legs in front of her.

I join her, sitting down a couple feet away. "Because I've never heard of you."

She runs her fingers through the grass, pulling a few pieces from the ground. I wonder what she's hiding in her eyes because she won't look at me. "It's still better than a bad reputation," she finally replies.

"Yeah, I guess you're right."

The air between us is quiet as we both focus on the murky water. The berry smoothie I picked up in the coffee shop isn't too bad ... if anything, it's keeping me busy while Emery's thinking about something else. Usually, I could care less what others have going on inside their head, but this girl is so fucking hard to read. It makes me that much more curious.

"What are you thinking about over there?"

She pulls the straw from between her lips, and glances up into the sky. "It's really nice out here."

"That's all?" I ask, raising my brow. Her large, almond-shaped eyes squint against the sun. I focus on them ... they're hard to ignore.

She clears her throat. "Speech topics. Do you have any ideas?"

"Honestly, the only thing I know is football. The only thing that interests me is football," I say, running my fingers through my hair.

She tilts her head in my direction, narrowing her eyes. "Seriously, Drake?"

"Seriously. I don't have time to learn anything else."

"Yeah. What did you do last night?"

"Went to the post-game party."

She nods, sucking the last of her drink through her straw. "We could do it on teenage drinking."

She has got to be fucking with me. That's one of the most overdone subjects ever ... I don't want to take part in beating something that is already dead. "First of all, I'm twenty. Second, I'd rather give a speech than preach," I say as I set my empty cup on the ground and wrap my arms around my folded knees.

"What if we do nature versus nurture? I've read about it before, and it's really interesting."

"How about cars?"

Her lips press into a thin, tight line. If looks could kill, I'd be flat on the floor without a heartbeat right now. "Really?"

"No, I was just playing, but the look on your face was totally worth it." I pause long enough to watch her roll her eyes. "Tell me a little bit more about this nature versus nurture. Why do you want to do it?"

She glances around uneasily, wetting her pink lips. "Because I'm proof that nature is just as strong as nurture." I'm so fucking lost. "What?"

She surveys the grassy area behind us before continuing. "I grew up with my dad, but I'm a lot like my mom. Most of my characteristics and behaviors mirror hers."

I nod, waiting for her to go on. There's sadness in her eyes. One I don't often see in others. It makes me want to know more.

"She was a dreamer. I'm a dreamer. She was a fighter, and I always have my boxing gloves on." A faint smile highlights her face. I think I've already seen her with her gloves on, and she knows how to use them.

"Did you see your mom at all growing up?"

She nods, staring down at her hands. "Until I was four, and then one other time after that."

This little glimpse into who she is has me seeing a whole new side of her. She's not perfect. She hasn't lived a perfect life. She's got her shit, just like I have mine.

I'd like to argue that we both show more nurture than nature. Stubborn. Difficult. It's a product of what our parents did to us, not what they gave us.

"I'm sorry."

"It's okay. What doesn't kill us makes us stronger, right?" she says, her eyes glossed over.

I nod, combing my fingers through my hair again. Things are getting a little too personal; it's time to get back to what we came here to do. "Are we going to split this up, or how do you want to do this?"

"Am I making all the decisions again?"

"Every once in a while I give up control," I tease.

"Fine, how about if I do the nature side, and you can do nurture? I mean, I feel strongly about nature so it should be easy."

"It just so happens that I think it's the other way around. We'll see who can convince the class." I wink, adding some competitive fire to our conversation.

"Bets on."

"So, since we're not doing this on football, can I give you a few lessons? A trade-off of sorts."

"What makes you think I don't already know all about it?"

I laugh. "For one, you didn't know who I was."

Rolling her eyes, she says, "It's just college football. It's not the damn pros."

Yep, she's pretty darn clueless. "In this part of the United States, it's more important than the pros."

"Well, I think that concludes lesson number one. Can we move onto some real work now?" she asks, chipping away at her purple nail polish.

I lean in, little by little, until I feel her reacting to me. It would be so easy to brush my lips against hers, to feel her reaction. Something tells me she wouldn't push back. "Next time, we might work on tackling since I know you've already mastered catching and throwing."

She scoffs, moving in the opposite direction from me. "In your dreams, Chambers."

We spend the next hour sparring back and forth, about our project, and life in general. When it's all said and done, I don't regret going. In fact, I kind of wish we could have stayed there longer. She's easy to talk to, and truth be told, I do like to talk about things that aren't related to football.

Chapter 5

Emery

THIS WEEK SEEMED TO DRAG ON forever between grueling study sessions and classes. For once, I'm happy it's Friday because even I need a break every now and then.

College has definitely been an adjustment for me.

There's more homework and more complex information to memorize before tests. On a positive note, Drake's been doing his share of the research since we got together last weekend, which is taking some of the pressure off me. At this point, I'm still not sure what the end product will sound like, but at least I know I don't have to do the whole project on my own.

But I'm not thinking about all that tonight. I'm going to step outside my comfort zone and leave academics behind. There was no way Kate was going to take no for an answer when she asked me to go out tonight … that's all I've done since we got there. And besides that, I feel like I have my feet under me. I know it's bound to get tougher as this year goes on, and I'm going to enjoy my little bit of free time while I have it.

"Are you about ready to go?" Kate asks, combing through her hair for the hundredth time.

"I can't decide what to wear. Where did you say we're going again?" This whole thing is making me nervous for some reason, and even though she told me twice already, I keep forgetting.

"It's a billiards bar."

I groan. Again. This does not sound like my idea of a good time. "What do people wear to a billiards bar?"

She taps her index finger on her chin, puckering her lips. "I've never been to one, honestly, but I assume jeans. How about jeans and a cute tank?"

When I turn my attention back to my closet, the first thing I spot is my brown western boots. I've never considered myself a fashionable person, but I try to stay somewhat current. "What about cutoff shorts with boots? That's not too slutty, is it?"

The laughter that erupts almost has her rolling on the floor. It's one of the things I like most about us … we've been able to find little things to laugh about. When she can catch her breath, she says, "No, that sounds cute. Not slutty, or trampy, or hookerish … just cute."

"Okay, but what shirt should I wear with it?"

"Hmm," she says, stepping next to me. "What about this?" She pulls out a black tank with beading at the top, but I shake my head. The nights have gotten cooler, and that may be a little too much skin for me.

It doesn't faze her as she dives right back in, picking out a white short-sleeve t-shirt. I recognize it; it's cut deep in the front and hugs my curves perfectly.

"That I can do," I say, grabbing the shirt from her. I quickly dress, even letting Kate twist her curling iron in my hair a couple times. When she's done, and I've had a chance to throw some make-up on, I stand back and survey my reflection in the mirror. My eyes widen as I turn from side to side. I look really good … maybe college will end up being more than just a stepping stone for me.

"Ready?" Kate asks, picking up her small black clutch from her bed.

"Yeah." I grab a yellow sweater out of my closet for later and follow her out the door. "Who did you say was going to be there?"

She shrugs. "Beau and some of his friends. My friend Rachel is going to try to make it so you can finally meet her. It's no big deal."

"I've never played pool before so I might just watch."

"Emery, you're playing. I've only played once, so we should be pretty even. In fact, you'll probably be better than me because you're good at everything," she says, unlocking her car doors.

"Whatever."

"Just relax. We're going to have fun tonight … I promise."

I'd be lying if I said I wasn't nervous. I never even went to these types of places back home because I'd told myself over and over that it wasn't my thing. I convinced myself that I couldn't have good grades and a good time. I have to admit, though, it feels like the weight of the future has been taken off my shoulders, because right now, I'm only thinking about tonight.

My hands are clammy as we pull into a gravel parking lot. The shy side of me is begging to have Kate drive me back home, while the more adventurous side that I keep locked up tight can't wait to get out of this car.

"Ready?" Kate asks.

I take a deep breath and undo my seatbelt. I need to stop thinking so much and just do this. "Let's go shoot some pool."

Without waiting for her reply, I step outside, stretching my arms above my head. Most of the spots in the parking lot are full, which means this place is probably packed.

"Is this place always so busy?"

Kate comes up beside me, hitting the button to lock her car. "I'm not sure. Beau said it's two dollar draw night, whatever that means."

I nod and begin walking to the entrance with Kate beside me. The gravel crunches under my boots, a melodic interruption of the voices in my head begging for me to get back in that car, get as far away as possible.

The building isn't much on the outside. It looks like a red rectangle with a black door. The roof barely peaks, and the Jake's Billiards sign above looks as if it hasn't been painted in several years. It's definitely not the type of place that draws you in when you drive by.

As we step inside, the smell of beer and popcorn fill my nose. I immediately notice the old, frayed, hunter green carpet, and the standard black leather bar chairs that surround the wooden tables. Besides a few lit up beer signs, the walls are pretty bare. The backroom is filled with pool tables and about one hundred people, mostly guys.

"Are the guys here yet?" I ask, gripping Kate's forearm so I don't lose her.

I watch as she scans the room. When a smile forms on her face, I follow the path of her eyes and see Beau standing in the back corner with a pool stick in his hand.

I start walking in that direction, anxious to get out of the crowded doorway, but Kate pulls me back. "Emery, I need to tell you something before we go over there."

"Yeah?"

She shifts uncomfortably, rubbing her fingers together. "Well, it might just be me, you, Beau, and one other guy playing tonight."

"Umm, what do you mean?" I ask, rubbing the base of my neck.

She grimaces, taking a small step back. "Well, it's kind of a blind date. Like extra blind because I didn't even tell you about it."

I glance over her shoulder to get a glimpse of who it is. This is so sudden ... I don't even know what I should be feeling right now.

"I'll understand if you're mad, but I hope you'll stay. It's just that I don't see you having a lot of fun, and I

Lisa De Jong

thought this would be fun. Beau says he's a nice guy." She takes another step back; it's probably a good idea at this point.

"Why didn't you just tell me?"

"Would you have come?"

I don't answer. We both know what it would be anyway.

"Give it one hour. If you're not having fun, I'll take you home," she begs, clasping her hands in front of her.

Surveying the bar, I realize most of the people in here are laughing and having a good time. Hopefully, I can handle this for sixty minutes. "Fine, what's his name."

She jumps up like she just won the lotto. "Eric," she squeals.

I shake my head as we make our way to the guys. I feel a good hour of awkwardness coming my way. The guy standing by Beau is a little shorter than him with dark hair that's just long enough to show off a little wave. And his eyelashes … they're amazingly dark and long.

"How are you ladies this evening?" Beau asks as we approach. He's greeting both of us, but his attention is focused on Kate.

"Good," I answer, clasping my hands behind my back.

Beau points to the guy I assume is Eric. "Oh, Emery, this is Eric. Eric, this is Emery."

I wave shyly, not exactly sure what to do on a blind, blind date. "Nice to meet you."

"You, too."

A long, awkward silence follows. I'd do anything to get some magic disappearing potion right now and never come back. "Umm, Beau, do you want to come with me to get some popcorn?" Kate asks.

Shit. She's already plotting to get me alone with this guy. I didn't sign up for this.

"Yeah, do you guys want anything to drink?" Beau asks, resting his hand at the back of Kate's neck.

47

I narrow my eyes at Kate, but also manage a tight smile. "I'll take a Coke or Pepsi ... whatever they have."

"Me, too," Eric answers, tucking his hands in his pockets.

As I watch Beau and Kate walk away, I fold my arms over my chest. I kind of hate both of them right now. I'd rather give a speech to the entire Senate or sing on national television than go on a blind date.

"Have you been here before?" Eric asks, breaking the quiet spell.

"No," I answer, watching the pool game at the table next to ours.

"Me either."

Standing on my tippy toes, I try to see over the crowd. Beau and Kate need to hurry up because I can't take this much longer. "So, how do you know Beau?"

"He's in a couple of my engineering classes."

"That's cool."

He shrugs. "It's all right."

This is ranking right up there with the best conversation ever. "So—"

"I never thought I'd see you here." I recognize that voice by now. Looking over my shoulder, I see a familiar smirk.

"And I never thought I'd come here," I say as I turn to him. He looks good tonight in faded blue jeans that hug his thighs and a navy t-shirt that does the same to his chest and biceps.

His eyes travel down my legs, his smile widening as he reaches my feet. "Nice boots."

I cross my feet at the ankles, suddenly feeling self-conscious about my choice in outfits. "I like them."

"I never said I didn't."

Eric clears his throat, reminding me he's still here. It feels like I'm buried in double hell. "Umm, I don't think we've met. I'm Eric."

Eric reaches his hand out, but Drake looks back and forth between us before accepting. "Drake."

Eric nods. "Yeah, I know who you are."

Silence takes over again as all three of us stand with our arms crossed over our chests. I glance back every few seconds for a glimpse of Beau and Kate, but I find nothing.

I am so going to kill her for this one.

Drake finally speaks up, ending the silent stand-off. "Well, it was nice seeing you, Emery, but I'll let you get back to your boyfriend."

"Oh, he's not my boyfriend," I reply quickly.

Two guys. Two sets of eyes … on me. I wish a hole would open up in the floor and suck me down into it.

"So, you won't mind if I steal her away for a minute?" Drake asks. "I'm playing pool back here, and we're short a player. Our fourth guy should be here shortly."

Eric rubs his hand along the back of his neck, peering at me through the corner of his eye. "Yeah, sure. I'm going to go up to the bar and see what's taking so long."

I feel kind of shitty as I watch him walk away … but I also feel relief. Our date, or whatever Kate intended it to be, was going nowhere.

"You looked a little uncomfortable," Drake says, just loud enough that only I can hear it.

I nod. "Blind date."

He laughs, cupping my elbow in his hand to guide me to his table. "I didn't peg you as the type that would agree to that."

"I'm not. They tricked me."

He wiggles his eyebrows, a grin spreading across his face. "Well, anytime you need me to save you, I'll be your Superman."

Shaking myself free from his grasp, I say, "Trust me. I won't be doing this again."

"Yeah, I suppose if things get serious with Eric there, you won't need to."

"Shut up and teach me how to play."

"Wow, Chambers, you got your hands full there." I recognize the guy as the one who was playing football with Drake the first day I ran into him.

Drake's eyes stay on me as he responds. "No, it looks like you have yours full, Gavin, because she's on my team."

Before I know it, I have a pool stick in my hand, and the front of Drake's chest is pressed against my back as he tries to show me how to hit the white ball. The warmth of his body makes mine tingle in a way I'm not used to, and a part of me wants him to stay there. I hate even admitting it.

"See how we're going to do this? We're going to place the tip between your left fingers and hold the end of the stick with your right." He stands behind me, his hands right behind mine. "We're going to pull it back, and then hit the ball. Not too hard. Not too soft."

We do just that, him guiding me the whole way through. The first shot he helps me with, I make with no problem, but as soon as he leaves me on my own, I miss the next couple shots.

"You can do it," he says. "Just take your time, and do exactly what I showed you." Not long after, I get the hang of it, knocking a few balls into the pockets. I'm even able to hit one in by holding the stick behind my back; I'd seen Gavin do it and was determined to show him up because he's been teasing me incessantly tonight.

"You play before?" Gavin asks after Drake and I win our second game in a row.

"This is my first time."

"Wow," he mouths, setting up the balls again. "Do you have any plans for tomorrow night?"

"Leave her alone, man!"

"*All* right, I get it," he says, laughing.

"Oh, no way—no, no, no, we aren't together," I stutter in an attempt to clear up the confusion. "There's absolutely nothing going on between us."

"Not yet," Gavin says as he walks away with a smirk on his face.

Drake and I are about as likely as world peace. He's starting to show me he's a good guy, don't get me wrong, but he's not my type. Even if he was, I'm not interested in dating right now.

When I turn my attention back to Drake, he seems to be running Gavin's comments in his head, too, because his eyebrows are pinched together as he looks back at me.

"Ignore him," he mumbles, running his fingers through his hair. His head tilts to the side as he considers me carefully.

"I think you've told me that twice now when Gavin's involved," I say, biting on my lower lip. The way he looks at me has me shifting on my feet. Things didn't feel so uncomfortable when Gavin was with us.

"Just making sure you understand."

"Loud and clear," I say, scanning the packed bar for any sign of Kate and Beau. I spot them playing two tables away with Eric. "I should probably go back over there."

He nods, his lips turning up at one side. "Signal me if you need me to fly over and save you again."

"I can handle it," I say, walking back a couple steps.

"We'll see."

After a few more steps, I turn back around. "Does this take the place of a football lesson?"

One corner of his mouth quirks. "Not even close. We didn't even touch on tackling."

Smiling, I go back to join the others, dreading having to hang out with Eric. As I assumed it would, the awkwardness returns. Eric and I are definitely not going anywhere. I mean, just holding a conversation with him is harder than any calculus test I've ever taken.

At one point I consider going back over to help Drake, but change my mind when I notice the hands of a skinny blonde on his chest. An odd sensation fills my chest, but I don't know why; she's exactly the type of girl I pictured him with. I'm not that girl. He probably wouldn't even give me the time of day if it weren't for our project.

"Emery, are you awake?"

I rub my eyes, but when I try to open them, the room is too bright with morning sun peeking through the curtains. Why is she waking me up on a Saturday? "Kinda."

"Well, hurry up. I'm dying to talk about last night."

Rolling on my back, I throw my arm over my eyes to keep the harsh light out. Last night, after one brutally awkward game of pool with Eric, he offered to take me home. My initial reaction was to tell him no, but Kate and Beau weren't ready to leave, and I couldn't stomach another round of pool, or should I say, another hour with Eric. So I accepted, and endured exactly thirteen minutes in the car with him. I know because I watched every freaking minute tick by. It was painful, but still better than the alternative.

I even thwarted his attempt to kiss me by telling him I wasn't feeling well. Now that I think about it, I owe Kate big time ... and not in a good way.

"You know, I should have gotten up earlier and thrown a bucket of cold water on your head," I say, peeking over at her from under my arm.

She laughs. "So, I didn't make a love connection?"

"No! Not even close. What the heck were you thinking?" I prop myself up on my elbows, shooting daggers with my eyes. It doesn't bother her at all, though. She's having a good time with this.

"I'd never met him before, and Beau said he was really smart. It sounded like you guys would be a good match. I'm sorry it didn't work out."

"Are you?" I ask, rolling my eyes.

"Umm, no, I'm never going to feel bad about trying. It looked like you were having fun with Drake, though. How were those pool lessons?"

When I think back to what it felt like to have Drake's body molded to my back and his hands curled around mine, it's hard to keep from blushing. He gets under my skin a lot, but I can't deny how good he looks and the way he can make me feel. He's different than anyone I've ever met, in good ways and bad.

"Drake's a good teacher. I mean, Eric and I beat you and Beau, didn't we?"

Kate's head falls back onto her bed. "Don't remind me. I suck."

I laugh. "You're not that bad."

"Emery, I hit a ball off the table. Who does that?" she asks, losing herself in her own fit of giggles. It was funny when she did it, but for whatever reason, it's even funnier now as we relive it.

"You just need a lesson or two. You better talk to Beau."

"Don't worry. He mentioned it on the way home last night." She sits back up on her elbow. "So, what's up with you and Drake? And don't tell me nothing because I can see it."

"I don't know. We've been spending a lot of time together working on the speech, and he's starting to grow on me." I honestly don't know what to say. I couldn't stand him the first couple times we talked, but that's not necessarily true now. Sometimes I even look forward to it. "Besides, he was with a girl last night."

Kate scoffs. "He always has girls hanging on him. It doesn't mean anything."

I shrug, folding my pillow under my head. "Maybe. Hey, I'm going to run to the mall today. Do you want come with?"

"I can't. I already promised Beau I would watch football with him."

"It's okay. I'm sure you'll approve of whatever I get anyway since our closets are almost identical," I say, throwing the covers off and stretching my arms above my head. I'm looking forward to a relaxing day. Throw in a little bit of shopping, a good book, and it's my idea of perfect.

Chapter 6

DRAKE

THE FIRST THING I NOTICE when I step outside is the wet sidewalks and the smell of fresh rain. The condensed moisture used to be one of my favorite things, but that's not the case anymore. It's the nine-year anniversary of one the worst days of my life, and without a football game today, running is my only release.

I plan to stay out here until my body aches so much that my heart no longer hurts—not that it's even fucking possible. I always thought it would get easier over time, but it doesn't. Maybe it would if I dealt with it the way I should, but that's hard to do with all the responsibility I carry. I'm supposed to be the strong one, taking care of everyone else in my family, but it hasn't left any time for me. I barely know who I am anymore, because I'm too busy making sure that everyone else is doing okay and following a football dream that may not even be mine.

Campus is quiet, but I wouldn't expect anything less on a Saturday morning like this. My old tennis shoes hit the wet pavement, crunching against rain-soaked leaves. It brings me back to that morning because it was just like this … exactly like this in so many ways.

Making it even more eerie, I pass a car that looks exactly like his. Usually, I keep my eyes forward when I run, but the similarities have me doing a double take, and that's when I see her. Familiar dark hair, exotic brown eyes. As I approach the old white Ford, I watch her pound her forehead against the steering wheel over and over again.

"Damnit!" I hear her yell. I lower my head, watching as she beats her palms against the dash. I lightly tap my knuckles against the glass, trying to get her attention without scaring her.

The rain starts falling fast again, soaking through my white t-shirt. When I look through the window, she's just staring at me, mouth hanging open slightly. Anxious to get out of the rain, I knock against the window again, and this time her fingers find the lock and let me in.

She squints her eyes as she watches me climb into the passenger seat. The way her eyes roam my soaked clothes says everything … she thinks I'm an idiot, or I'm stalking her. It feels like I'm everywhere she is, or maybe she's everywhere I am.

"Couldn't multi-task again?" I ask, running my fingers through my wet hair.

"What makes you say that?"

"You can't stare at me and unlock the door at the same time," I remark, focusing in on her white knuckles. "And you know, you probably don't have to hold on to that so tightly when the car isn't even moving."

She rolls her eyes, obviously not in the mood to play any games today. "Why are you here, Drake?"

I shrug, looking straight ahead at the deserted, grassy area. "Because you let me in."

"Don't you have a game today?"

"No, it's a bye week, which means we have today off. I thought I'd go for a run to keep myself loose, but then this happened," I say, waving toward outside. The rain is falling harder now, making it more difficult to see out the windows. It also makes the weight on my chest heavier. I hate this weather. Absolutely fucking hate it, and everything it reminds me of.

We both remain quiet for what feels like forever. I can't stand it, honestly. Without anything else to talk about, my mind always goes to him, and it's exhausting. There's a chill in the air today, but the inside of her car is overwhelmingly warm. When my eyes finally wander back in her direction, she stares outside.

"Are you always up this early when you don't have a game?" she asks, breaking through the silence, but keeping her eyes fixed on the rain-soaked window.

"I couldn't sleep," I say, rubbing my palm across my chest. Her eyes search for mine, and when they find them, they stay locked there. She looks lost. Sad. I wonder if this is the real her, who she hides under the stubborn, focused girl I usually see.

Looking at her is like facing myself in a mirror. I want to know what's going on inside that head of hers, but I'm not in the sharing mood today, and I'm not one to ask for something I can't give.

"So how was your date?"

When I saw her come in with Kate last night in her short shorts and boots, I was excited. All sorts of ideas were running through my mind, but then I saw him. I couldn't stand to watch her with him, so I kicked someone off our table and invited Emery over. Never in my life have I gotten jealous over a girl, but when I saw her with that guy … I wanted to take her away from him; so I did. I told myself it had more to do with saving her from a situation that was obviously making her uncomfortable, but deep down, I knew the true motivator.

I'm not that fucking noble.

It turned out to be one of the best nights I've had in a long time because there isn't any pressure with her. We don't always get along, but she's honest and doesn't want me for my name. Things are just comfortable.

Rolling her eyes, she says, "I hardly consider that a date."

I laugh. "What would you consider it then?"

"An unfortunate circumstance. Life is full of those."
The vision of Olivia walking up to me in the bar last night
flashes through my mind. I feel like I can never escape her,
and that's unfortunate. What was even more unfortunate was
the look on Emery's face when I caught her staring at Olivia
and me. I wanted to tell her she had it all wrong, but I have
no reason to explain anything to her.

"Did an unfortunate circumstance lead to you beating
up your car? It must have done something pretty fucking
bad," I say, running my fingers along the dashboard.

"My car wouldn't start. I haven't moved it since I got to
school, and I think it forgot how to work."

I can't suppress the half-smile that forms on my lips,
but I know it doesn't quite reach my eyes. I definitely feel
off balance today. I need to get back out there and run.

"Are you okay?" she asks.

The smile quickly crumbles as I look away from her.
"I'm just tired of all this rain. It seems like there are very
few sunny days." The words are metaphoric ... so much
meaning behind them.

"It's still better than snow."

"Maybe," I say, looking over at her again. "Do you
want me to take a look at your car?"

"You fix cars?"

"Yes, I can throw the football and fix cars. Well, not
everything, but if it's something simple I can."

"If you wouldn't mind. I really didn't want to have to
call my dad," she answers as the drops fall harder against the
windshield.

"It's no problem." I smile, more genuine this time.

"Thank you." She stops, smiling back at me. "However,
there's not much you can do about my car right now ... I mean
with this rain. Do you want to look at it later?"

"Do you have to be somewhere?"

"No, I was just going to run a few errands."

I nod, leaning over to look up at the gray sky. "I think
it's supposed to clear up this afternoon. Do you want to

work on our project, and then maybe later, I can come out and take a look at this bad boy again? I could use a distraction."

Taking my mind off things might help. I can't just sit and sulk all day long.

"Do you want to meet me in the library?" she stops, surveying my drenched clothes. "Maybe in one hour?"

"This will be the first time I've been there since I've gone to this school."

"Doesn't surprise me."

"One hour then," I say, opening my door.

Jogging back to my dorm, I think about her. I find myself doing that more and more lately. It's not necessarily a good thing because I should be thinking about football and family. I owe it to him.

An hour later, I'm walking into the place unknown: the library. It looks exactly how I thought it would, which doesn't do anything to raise my excitement level. There are several tables full of students, all working quietly, and then a few other students sitting in front of their computers in a row of cubicles. Standing in here for more than five seconds feels like a punishment for me, like I've been placed in a world where I shouldn't exist.

Before anyone can question my presence, I walk around looking for Emery, but it's not easy to find her in the sea of bookshelves. The voice in my head that is always leading me to the dark side is telling me that if I don't find her in the first few minutes, I should leave. Cut my losses because it's not like I didn't try.

I feel marginally better than I did when I saw her earlier this morning. I ran for another thirty minutes after I left her at her car, but I have a feeling another run might be needed before the day is over.

I spot her hidden in the corner, surrounded by windows. Leave it to her to find the quietest, most desolate place in the library for us to meet. She looks casual with her hair pulled up in a ponytail, dressed in a worn Southern Iowa sweatshirt. She's definitely low maintenance, but it fits her. That day when she ran into me, her big brown eyes were the first things I noticed. They're always the first things I want to see.

"I made it," I say, throwing my bag onto the floor. Those eyes that always pull me in are on me now.

"Are you expecting a band to come in and play a celebratory song?" she teases, tapping her eraser against the wooden table.

"A smile would be nice."

Just like that, the corners of her lips turn up. She comes off as so tough, but yet I seem to find ways to loosen her up.

"Happy now?"

"As much as I can be in this place." Some of the familiar heaviness weighs on my chest again. I try not to think of happiness ... it's a pipe dream for me.

"What's your story, Drake Chambers?" she asks, twirling her pencil between her fingers. I swear she's seeing right into me; I just hope I'm not that fucking transparent.

I shrug. "Maybe I don't have one."

"Everyone has one."

"Not everyone has one they want to share," I say, looking down at the wood table. Really, no one knows my story, and Emery isn't going to get her name on an exclusive list.

She nods, staring off into the rows of bookshelves.

"Do you still need me to fix your car?" I ask in an attempt to change the subject.

"Do you still want to fix my car?"

"Of course. I'll take a look at it after we leave here."

"So are you ready to get started on this? I kind of know what I want to do, but I need to do some research."

I rest my elbows on the table, leaning in as close as I can. "You got to go first last time. I think we should start with your football lesson."

"Funny, Chambers. Don't forget we're in the library."

"Doesn't matter. I'll flip your lessons around. We'll work on tackling another day," I say, watching her eyes go wide. I fucking love how simple words affect her. She reminds me a lot of the good girls from my high school. They were always the most fun to tease.

"Okay, I'll play. What do you want to teach me?"

"The difference between offense and defense." I pause, watching her expression shift to that of someone who's in the second hour of a long presidential address. I'm going to get a rise out of her no matter how hard I have to try. "I'm the quarterback, so I'm in charge of leading the offense down the field. Our job is to get down to the end zone as often as possible. The defense's job is to make sure the other team doesn't score. The offense has to score more than their defense lets the opposing team."

"Sounds easy enough."

I shrug, leaning in closer. "It's not nearly as easy as it sounds. If someone isn't where they're supposed to be, or if one guy isn't playing like he should, we lose. Consider it a bigger scale team project."

She tilts her head, seemingly hanging on my every word. As a smirk forms on her face, her eyes seem to brighten. "So am I on offense or defense?"

"I always have the ball, Emery. Always."

She shifts her eyes to the window, doing her best to avoid me. It's the truth. I always have to be in control. If I'm not, all I feel is chaos inside, and I can't even think. I get the feeling that Emery is the same way so it will be a miracle if we get out of this able to stand each other.

"Well, let's see if we can work on your passing skills. How is your portion of the project coming along?" she asks, focusing her eyes back to me.

Lisa De Jong

"I just need to pull some facts from the web, and I'll be all set," I say, eyeing her carefully.

"I don't want you to take this the wrong way, but do you really think that's enough?"

"I guess we'll just have to see who can be more convincing," I say, twirling my pen between my fingers.

"You're on. I'm going to get a book so I can get started," she announces, rising from the table.

After I watch her disappear into the rows of books, I pull my laptop from my bag and make a few notes. This assignment isn't going to be easy, but I have a feeling we're going to pull it off just fine.

That's what teams do.

To an extent, Emery has a point about nature, but for me, I think that's only good as long as someone is nurturing it. If my dad were still around guiding me, I'd probably be a whole lot like him. Maybe I'm a little bit like him now, but it's hard to say because some days, it's hard to remember what he was like. I remember football, and the last day we spent together, but no matter how hard I try, anything beyond that is difficult. It would have been helpful if my mom could have at least talked to me about him, but she rarely says his name at all.

When Emery isn't back a few minutes later, I go looking for her, weaving in and out of bookshelves. I'm not a fan of libraries, and she's the only thing that makes it halfway tolerable to be here. I actually look forward to seeing her in class these days; last night and today was just an added bonus. I'll never tell her this, but she's making today the best worst day of the year just by spending some of her time with me. It's kept my mind off things at least temporarily.

I finally spot her when I round the corner to the history section, literally running into her. She startles, covering her chest with her hand.

"Hey," I say, gripping her upper arms to hold her steady. "I didn't mean to scare you."

61

Her dark brown eyes look up, and something shifts inside of me. Maybe it's the way the front of our bodies touch, or the way her sweet smell invades my senses. Something has been pulling me toward her the last couple times I've seen her, and being like this makes it hard to ignore.

"It's okay. I should probably stop running into you like this." Her heart is beating against my chest, heightening all the feelings I've been trying to bury.

The longer we stay locked in a staring contest, the more I realize this moment was inevitable. I haven't been honest with myself because it's always been easier for me to live in my make-believe world. Drake's world.

I hate these emotions, but yet there's something that feels so damn good about having her this close to me. My heart is begging me to take a chance with the one person who hasn't asked me for anything. The one person who's taken my shit and thrown it right back at me.

Before I even realize what's happening, my lips inch closer to hers. I don't have any control. Or maybe I don't want to have it anymore, because I'm passing the ball to her. My hands slide up her arms, cupping her cheeks, but my eyes never leave hers. I'm waiting for her to stop me. We've gone ten rounds since I've met her, and I never thought it would lead to this.

This isn't supposed to happen, I think to myself as I feel her warm breath against my skin. So close. "Emery," I whisper, my voice desperate.

"Drake," she says quietly, pulling some of the fabric from my t-shirt between her fingers. She has no idea what her touch is doing to me. No fucking idea.

"Can I help you two find anything?" *Shit.*

I pinch my eyes closed to regain some of my composure. "No, I was just getting ready to leave."

Dropping my hands, I glare at the librarian, silently begging her to walk away.

Lisa De Jong

"That sounds like a good idea," she says, glancing back and forth between Emery and me before disappearing around the corner again.

This suddenly doesn't feel right. I shouldn't be doing this with Emery ... she deserves so much better. I know I'm not the guy for her, and I never will be.

The fate of interruption proved it.

Neither of us should be here doing this.

Finally, I step back and give Emery her space, the awkwardness leaving it almost impossible to even look in her eyes. "I need to go. Let me know if you need anything else from me to finish the presentation."

I take two steps back, watching confusion cloud her features. "What? We haven't even started."

"I'm sorry. I have to go," I say, turning to walk away. I can't look back because I'm not a strong enough man to face the consequences of my actions. She's not the first girl I've let down, but she's the first girl who's made me feel guilty about it.

Chapter 7
Emery

IT'S BEEN A WEEK SINCE DRAKE CHAMBERS almost kissed me. I felt like things were changing between us, but I never expected that. I surprised myself by actually wanting it to happen, which only made it that much worse when it didn't. I've almost convinced myself that I made the whole thing up. That there's no way he was about to kiss me. Why would he?

I'd watched him walk out of the library, only stopping to quickly throw his bag over his shoulder. I was unable to form the words to stop him. We're too different; I know that. He's worried about memorizing all the offensive plays in the playbook while I'm obsessed with having everything my family never did.

Two different people.

Two different worlds.

Two different dreams.

Now it looks like he's skipping class. Maybe he's trying to avoid doing any of the work on our speech, but I know him better. If he didn't feel like helping out, he'd still come just to give me a hard time.

He's avoiding me.

"Are you and Drake ready for the presentation next week?" Professor McGill stands at the side of my chair with her perfectly manicured hands clasped in front of her.

"We will be," I say honestly. Whether he shows or not, I'll be ready.

"If you see him, let him know he'll receive a zero if he doesn't show."

I nod before she walks away, pretty sure I won't be seeing him anytime soon.

When the hour is up, I quickly head for the door and disappear outside. I completed everything for the speech last night, thinking Drake wouldn't be of any help to me today or any time before the project is due.

As soon as I step outside, rain hits my cheek. It feels like all it does is rain these days, and while some people can't stand when it rains, I find it relaxing. Today, though, it just kind of reminds me of the time I spent with Drake in my car last weekend, and I wish the sun would come out and make it all go away.

"Em, wait up!" *Kate.*

Slowing my pace, I wait until I see her feet next to mine on the pavement. "Hey, are you done with class?"

"Yes, actually I was just coming from the library. You?"

"I just got out of speech. I think I'm going to head home and relax."

She groans. "You're not sitting alone in that room tonight. Come out with me and Rachel." Here comes the customary *you-should-be-doing-something-other-than-sitting -in-our-room-on-a-Friday-night* speech. After what she put me through last week, you'd think I'd be off the hook for a while.

"I really just need to be alone tonight," I say, glancing over at her. The way her lips press tightly together before she looks at me tells me she's not settling for my answer this time, and I'm not in the mood to argue. "Hey, what if we do something tomorrow night?"

Instantly, a smile spreads across her face. "Beau's having a little get together at his apartment. Come with me."

My first thought is I hate parties. I mean absolutely despise them and would rather go anywhere but. It must be written all over my face because she speaks before I get a chance. "I haven't been to a party in over three years. I hate them—like really hate them. Will you please come with me?"

I take a long, deep breath, weighing all my options in a matter of seconds. "Fine, I'll go," I say with about as much emotion as a mime at the circus. I really don't want to, but I'll do it for her.

"Seriously? You just made my day," she says, wrapping her arm around my shoulder.

Kate's the first person in a long time who I've actually wanted to please. She has a kindness to her that makes it almost impossible to let her down.

"Yes, I'll go with you."

She pulls me into a full hug. "Thank you. Thank you." Pulling back, she adds, "I have to go. I'm supposed to get ready at Rachel's tonight."

"Well, if you need anything, you know where to find me," I joke. A chill runs through my body as rain continues to soak my hair and clothes. It doesn't feel as good in October as it did in September.

"You should probably start carrying an umbrella, Emery," Kate says as she walks backward, starting to put distance between us.

I laugh. "And what about you? It's going to take you all night to fix that hair."

She looks up to the gray sky and says, "I love when it rains."

She walks off without another word, leaving me to start my usual Friday night. Alone. More miserable than I'd ever admit.

And wondering where Drake is right now.

The minute I woke up this morning, I wished I hadn't told Kate I'd go to this party. I'd only ever been to a couple with Clay, and even though they weren't horrible, they weren't that fun either. What's the point of getting drunk until you puke or disappearing into a bedroom with some guy you barely know?

"What are you wearing tonight?" Kate asks as she pulls on a pair of jeans. Our styles are very similar—too similar, really.

"I think I'm going to wear the faded skinny jeans with my white dolman sweater and brown booties."

Pulling a royal blue sweater over her head, she says, "That sounds hot. We both have good taste in clothing. Now, we just have to find you a man."

I scoff, laying my outfit on my bed. "The last thing I need right now is a man. Besides, your match making skills suck."

"How long has it been since you had a boyfriend?" She eyes the outfit I have laid out and grabs a turquoise beaded necklace from her jewelry box, tossing it onto the bed.

"Three months," I answer, pulling the towel from my wet hair.

Understanding washes over her features as she sits down at her desk to begin her make-up. "How long did you date?"

"Almost four years."

She spins around so quickly I'm surprised she doesn't leave a black mark under her eye with the mascara wand. "Seriously? That's a long time. Why did you break up?"

Four weeks ago, I would have never told her, but I trust her now. She's done nothing but earn it. "I guess I knew a long time ago there wasn't a future for us. He's a nice guy, though, and I guess I was afraid to hurt his feelings so I waited until right before I left for school."

"Wow. It must have been hard after all that time."

As I think back to it, the pit I felt in my stomach that day reappears. To him, I was everything. His past, present, and future, and I thought about what I would say for so long, I was numb to him. The way I did it, waiting so long, was a mistake. "It was."

Kate stares down at the floor, fingering the raindrop necklace I see her wearing every day. "I was with someone before Beau, too. He died of cancer earlier this year."

With no idea of how I should respond, I stare at her, waiting for her to continue. I know there is a lot about Kate I don't know, but I'm not expecting this. When she speaks again, her voice breaks. "You need to find a way to be happy, Emery. You can't close yourself off for the rest of your life, because you're going to miss out on all the little things that make life great."

"What do you mean?"

"Do you know how I know you weren't in love with your high school boyfriend?" I shake my head, wondering how she could know much of anything without ever seeing us together. "When you love someone, like that deep down, absorbent kind of love, you want to spend every minute you can with them. Being in love is the best feeling in the world, and once you have it, you'll never want to lose it."

We stare at each other for several seconds before I grab my sweater and pull it over my head. This is much deeper than I usually let myself go, and I'm ready to come back up to the surface. After slipping my jeans on, I whisper, "Sorry about your boyfriend. What was his name?"

She closes her eyes and swallows. "Asher."

"I like that name," I say honestly.

"It fit him," she says, smiling sadly.

We finish getting ready without saying another word. I don't know what we were thinking settling on the topic of old boyfriends before a night out, but the damage is already done.

"Are you ready?" she asks, pulling on her brown leather jacket.

I take one last look in the mirror, applying one more layer of lip-gloss. "As ready as I'll ever be."

"Oh, come on, it's going to be fun."

Rolling my eyes, I grab my purse and follow her to the door. It's one night. I can do this.

Since Beau lives off campus, we take Emery's car. I'm sure she knows the way like the back of her hand.

"Who's all going to be there?" I ask.

"Oh, it's actually going to be small. Beau, his roommate, Rachel, and a few other couples from what I understand. Low key."

"No football players?" I ask, only half joking.

She glances over at me for a split second, wiggling her eyebrows. "None that I'm aware of. Is there a certain someone you wanted to be there?"

"No," I answer quickly, turning my attention out the window.

I never said a word to Kate about what happened with Drake in the library the other day. I've already analyzed it enough on my own, and I don't need anyone else helping me out.

It's not long before we pull in front of Beau's apartment complex. Kate jumps out of the car and waits for me on the curb as I take a few deep breaths. *God, I hope this night goes by quickly.*

Chapter 8

DRAKE

THERE ARE A MILLION REASONS why I shouldn't be at this party tonight. One, there's a full keg waiting for me at the frat house where some of my teammates belong. Two, I only kind of know a couple of people who will be here tonight. Three, my whole body aches like a motherfucker and belongs in a goddamn ice bath after the game I had this afternoon.

"Hey, dude, do you want another beer?" It's Beau. He invited me here, and I'm waiting to see how long it will take before he regrets it.

"No, I can grab something. I need to walk around anyway. My body is so fucking stiff."

"Don't go too far. My girl should be here soon, and she's bringing a friend," he says, taking another swig of his beer.

"I'm not in the mood for a set-up tonight, Beau."

He grins, a hint of mischief in his eyes. "Oh, you might like this one."

"Doubt it," I say, walking away from him.

I met Beau last year. He lived across the hall from me in the dorms and was the guy I'd hang out with when I needed to lie low. There were several times we got drunk and played stupid video games until one of us passed out from exhaustion or alcohol. With the demands of football and family, sometimes it's just what I need.

Lisa De Jong

After grabbing a couple cold ones from the fridge, I hear the door click open and look over.

It's Beau's girl. He hasn't officially introduced me to her yet, but I recognize her as Kate, the girl who sits next to Emery in bio. I take a few steps forward to formally introduce myself, but the bottles almost slip from my hand when I see who's with her. I should have guessed that Emery would be the friend she would bring tonight.

I'm obviously not someone who has good luck, and I'm a little pissed that Beau wasn't straight with me about this "friend."

I haven't seen her since I left her standing in the library. Not because of chance but because I've been avoiding her. There's too much there. Too much I'm starting to feel whenever I'm around her, and I can't deal with it right now.

Those couple times I almost opened up to her—in her car and the library—I wanted to, and that scares me. I don't know what life outside of my hiding is like.

Emery's not the typical girl, but there's so much about her that I'm attracted to. Her smile. Her drive. Her ability to take me out of a shitty mood, even though sometimes she can frustrate me and put me right back in it. I never imagined being affected by anyone like her, but it doesn't matter.

She's better off without someone like me.

As I watch them walk toward Beau, I contemplate my next move. I can walk out that door and pretend I was never here. I can stand back and watch her, hoping she doesn't spot me. I can man up and apologize for leaving her alone the other day. But right now, I feel like half a man, half a man who's falling for the one girl who doesn't treat me like I'm just the king of the football team.

Before I have a chance to decide what I'm going to do, her eyes find mine. I'm not okay with how I feel whenever I stare into those eyes.

There's something about this girl that gets to me.

I start toward her, and when I'm only a few feet away, Emery pulls Kate by the arm to the corner of the room. I should be offended, but just like everything else, I let it roll off me. I'm good at it.

I have been for a long time.

It's another sign of things that just weren't meant to be.

Walking up to where Beau stands with a couple other guys, I ask, "Why didn't you tell me Emery was coming?"

"Would you have come?" He pauses, taking a swig of his beer. "I saw you with her last weekend, and unless my eyes were playing tricks on me, I'd say you like her."

"I'm probably the last person she wanted to see tonight." It's true. I almost kissed her, and then left her without any explanation. To make matters worse, I left her to finish our project on her own. At this point, she probably considers me the king of all assholes.

"What's going on between you two? And don't tell me it's nothing."

"Emery is my speech partner. That's it," I say, running my fingers through my hair.

"Whatever. The only girl I've ever looked at like that is Kate." He smiles, but it quickly falls from his face when he sees the expression on mine. I hate how he reads me, but he is the expert. The guy's been a lovesick puppy from the day I first met him.

"Look, I should probably be going. She doesn't want me here."

"Stay," Beau says quietly. "Emery's cool."

When I look up again, she's gone. I scan the room and spot her standing with Kate, talking to a couple of guys I don't recognize. It really shouldn't be that big of a deal for me, but she seems like she's having a good time, and maybe she hasn't been as affected by this crazy back and forth as I've let myself be.

"I appreciate what you're trying to do, Beau, but I don't want to ruin the night. Maybe we can catch up next weekend after the game."

He nods, giving me the green light to go. I walk out the door, careful not to let anyone stop me. I want to get out of here. It's better that way ... for both of us.

It's like I'm on the football field—the score is tied—and there's fifteen seconds left in the game. I have a choice of either letting my running back take the ball to run the clock out and go into overtime, or throw a Hail Mary from the fifty-yard line into the end zone. On the field, I'd always pick the Hail Mary.

This time, though, I picked the safe run.

I'm a coward, afraid of the risk. I should've walked up to Emery and apologized for being such a selfish ass, but instead I'm standing alone with my back against the fucking wall outside Beau's apartment door. All that stands before me is worn brown carpet and marked up white walls ... not at all how I pictured this night.

One of these days I'm going to have to man up and face her. Until I know what version of the truth I'm willing to give her, avoidance is my game.

As I start walking down the hall again, the door clicks behind me.

"Are you going to stop or just ignore me?" I immediately recognize the voice, but it's the pissed off version.

If I were to hand the ball to my running back on this play, I'd simply walk out without even looking back at her. Now that she's called me out, it's not that easy.

Running my fingers through my hair, I ask, "What do you want me to do?"

"For one, you can stop ignoring me." By the sound of her voice, I can tell she's closer.

For the first time in a long time, I'm going to throw the long pass on the football field. As soon as I turn around, I get a glimpse of her angry brown eyes. I hate that I'm doing this to her. "Look, I'm sorry I didn't help more with the speech. This is who I am, Emery. I fuck things up."

She steps closer, eyes of fury burning into me. "What the hell happened in the library the other day? Why did you just leave? Why haven't you been to class all week? You can't just check out without an explanation."

All I can do is stare at her. She's so fucking beautiful, but it's not necessarily the kind that immediately captivates me. It's the kind that grows more and more as I get to know her. It might be fucked up, but I think she's even sexier when she's pissed.

"Is that all you got, Drake? You're just going to stare at me like an idiot? Well, fuck you, too." I immediately miss the nearness of her body as she backs away from me.

"If you're worried about Monday, don't be. I'll tell Professor McGill you did most of the project," I say quietly as she moves farther away.

"This isn't about the stupid project, and you know it."

She begins to walk away again, but before she can get too far, I grab her arm and pull her back to my chest. "What is it about then, Emery?"

"You, Drake. I don't let many people in, but I gave you a chance, and this is where it got me. I guess it just proves that I really shouldn't trust anyone." There's a hint of tears to come in her voice, and I can't hate myself any more than I do right now.

"What do you mean you gave me a chance?"

She shakes her head and looks up to the ceiling. "Honestly, I wanted to drop you as my partner that first day in class, but I thought I saw something. Every once in a while, you show me the human side of you. The one that seems to care." She stops suddenly, covering her face with her hands. "Jesus, I even told you stuff about my mom."

The raw emotion in her voice causes a painful tightness in my throat. "Please don't ... not over me," I say soothingly. My lips betray the part of me that wants to keep my distance, pressing a kiss to the top of her head.

"I'm not," she answers, rubbing the back of her hand across her eyes. "Let me go, and we'll just pretend that this, or the other day in the library, never happened."

This is my chance to make it all go away, just like I wanted. I can let her go right now, and we can go our separate ways. But I can't. For once, my heart is speaking so much fucking louder than my head. "Come with me."

Her body tenses in my grip. "What?"

"I'm going to be honest. I don't know what I'm doing or what I want. Just come with me."

"I don't think that's a good idea," she says, shaking her head.

"We might regret it tomorrow or a week from now, but right now, it's all I want. Come with me."

"I'm with Kate. I can't just leave her." Her eyes are trained on Beau's door. I know what she's thinking, but I'm not ready to let her go.

"She's with Beau ... she'll be okay. Besides, were you having fun?" I know this isn't her idea of a good time.

"I haven't been here long enough to form an opinion. Maybe I should stay and find out." She smiles.

"We're just leaving a party together. I'm not asking for sex."

Her smile falters slightly. "That's great because the last thing I want to do is have sex with you ... or take those tackling lessons you've been promising." She stops for a few seconds, glancing down at her feet. "So what did you have in mind?"

Grabbing her hand, I lead her the rest of the way down the hall. "It's a surprise. I'm going to show you how to live a little."

Chapter 9
Emery

I DON'T KNOW WHAT I WAS THINKING getting into Drake's car with him. Now, I'm at his mercy, going almost fifty miles an hour down a busy street. I had the best of intentions to stay away from him, but the minute I saw him, I lost my will. It was partially anger that pushed me to confront him, but it was also the part of me that wasn't ready to let him walk out of my life so easily.

The last few days have honestly kind of sucked. He's the one person besides Kate who I talk to on a regular basis. He's the one person who's gotten a glimpse of who I am when my nose isn't stuck in a book.

"Where are we going?"

"You're not nervous, are you?" he asks, drumming his fingers against the steering wheel.

"I think someone's nervous, but it's not me," I reply as I cross my arms over my chest.

He laughs. "Are you saying you trust me?"

"Are you avoiding my question?"

He dares a glance in my direction, immediately locking eyes with me before turning his attention back to the road. "No, I'm not nervous. I'm just anxious to get where we're going."

A welcome silence occupies the rest of our trip across town. I mentally go through all the places he could be taking me. Pizza? Coffee? Movie? By the time he pulls onto campus, I've given up, resigned to go with the flow for once.

He parks in one of the lots next to Kinnick Stadium and turns off the engine. I stay still, waiting for him to give me further instruction as I look out at the dark night sky. When I can't take it anymore, I glance over at him only to see someone who suddenly looks lost. I've seen that look before … every time I look in the mirror I see it.

"Drake?"

Closing his eyes, he lowers his chin to his chest. I'd give anything to know what's going on in his head right now. "Let's get out of this car," he says without even looking my way.

"Okay," I mumble, opening my door to follow him. This has been one strange night.

I stand back and watch as he opens the trunk and pulls out a worn fleece blanket and a flashlight. I have no idea what he has planned, but I hope he realizes how chilly it's getting outside.

He holds the items under his left arm and entwines his fingers on his free hand with mine. I'm hesitant, but it feels too good to let go. "Have you ever been out here before?"

"I've never been a big fan of football. No offense."

"What's not to like about football?" He unlocks a door on the side of the stadium and leads us down a dark hall with the flashlight lighting our path.

I follow close behind, afraid of tripping over something on the narrow pathway. "It's more like, what is there to like?"

He laughs. I've heard it a few times now, and it's a sound I'm really starting to like. "My goal is to get to you to a football game this season. Once you go, you'll be hooked."

"That sounds like a challenge."

He stops, looking straight at me. "I like a challenge. Plus, I have confidence in the quarterback's skills to draw you in, and it's considered part of your lesson."

"The quarterback seems to have a lot riding on his shoulders," I say honestly.

We continue down the dark hall until we reach another door. As soon as he opens it, the vast football field greets us, lit by a few lights above.

"Are we supposed to be out here?"

He shrugs, looking up to the blank scoreboard. "No one specifically said not to be."

"If we get in trouble for this, I swear I'm going to—"

Placing a finger over my lips, he says, "Live a little. Besides, we're just going to set this blanket in the middle of the field and enjoy the night sky. The lights go out in eight minutes."

I open my mouth to tell him we should leave. It's not worth the risk … neither of us can afford to get in any trouble. But I want to be here with him. I just have to decide if he's worth the risk.

"What's holding you back?" he asks, noticing my reluctance. His index finger rests under my chin, making it impossible to look away from him.

"I can't afford to lose my scholarship."

He removes his finger and breaks eye contact, grabbing my hand in his again. "You're not going to get in any trouble. Let's find a spot before it gets too dark."

When we reach mid-field, he drops my hand and lays the blanket flat on the ground without uttering a word. I'd started to relax while walking across the field, but those doubts and worries are creeping back up again. Even when I was on my first date with Clay, I didn't feel this way. And this isn't even a date … I don't know what this is.

He sits on one side of the blanket and pats the spot next to him. "I don't bite."

I smile in an attempt to ease the tension between us and take the spot beside him, careful not to get too close. "Do you come out here often?"

I feel him staring at me, but I continue to look at the empty bleachers behind the end zone. There's nothing to see really, but it's keeping my nerves in check.

"I do some of the maintenance work out here for some extra cash so between football and that, I guess you could say yes."

And just like that, the lights flash off, leaving us alone with a better picture of the stars in the otherwise dark sky. I'm thankful the rain ended earlier because it's giving us a perfect view.

"You know, when you asked me to leave with you, this is the last place I thought you would take me," I admit, propping myself on my elbows.

He chuckles, and out of the corner of my eye, I notice him mimicking my position. "Where did you think I was going to take you? I'm just trying to score some originality points."

Biting my lower lip, I turn to get a better look at him. "Mission accomplished."

Sometimes quietness between two people can be awkward, but I'm finally getting to the point with Drake where it's not as uncomfortable. Being with him actually relaxes me. Like when I'm with him, I'm free to think about other things besides my grades and how I'm going to write my research paper that's not due for two more months. Even when we're bickering, I'd rather be with him than most other places. It's weird, and I know I've only known him for a short time, but there's definitely something different about me when I'm with him.

"What are you thinking about over there?" he asks, resting his warm hand on top of mine. It sends those crazy butterflies loose again. The ones I've been feeling whenever I'm around him.

"How nice it is to do something besides study. Sometimes I overwhelm myself, you know?"

"I feel the same way. I stress out when I have a game but being out here now, like this, is one of the most relaxing things ever. I'm always working toward making the pros, and if I'm not throwing the football, I'm not any closer. School, work ... it's all necessary, but it's not going to get me to where I'm going."

I turn my head until I feel the worn flannel blanket against my cheek. He's staring straight up at the dark sky, but I know he sees me from the corner of his eye. "I get what you're saying. I wish I could skip undergrad and go straight to grad school."

"What do you want to be when you grow up, Emery?" he asks, finally turning his eyes to me.

I swallow, feeling the empty pit in my stomach. Usually when I tell someone what I want to do with my life, they ask why. I have my manufactured answer, but I know that won't work with Drake. And maybe, just maybe, if I extend a small branch to him, he'll give one right back to me. "I want to be a child psychologist."

The corners of his lips turn up. "So I'm lying with the future Dr. White? What makes you want to do that?"

His smile slips as he watches me struggle to form an answer. It shouldn't be this hard after all this time but it is. "I want to help children who are hurting, especially the ones who no one else can reach. The ones who bury everything inside so deep that it takes a special person to help them find who they are again."

"But why do you want to do it?" His voice is low and soothing, like he knows he's about to get more from me than just an answer to a simple question.

Closing my eyes, I see that. The day things changed.

My mom has had the old wooden jewelry box sitting on her dresser for as long as I can remember. If I tried to explain it to anyone, it wouldn't do the box's beauty justice, but the hand painted pink roses on the top are what draw me in. Pink's my favorite color, and nothing beats the smell of my grandma's rose garden. The old box makes me think of so many good things, but I don't understand why she's giving it to me today. I know how much she loves it.

It's not my birthday, and Christmas is months away. The last couple days I haven't listened to her as well as I should have, picking ripe tomatoes from the garden and sneaking away to eat them. I also snuck into her closet and made a huge mess as I tried on all her high heels. Maybe she's giving it to me because she wants me to be better.

"Emery, baby, open it up," she says softly.

I follow her instructions, afraid she'll change her mind and ask for the box back. As I open it, the welcome smell of cedar hits my nose. Inside is a silver locket with roses etched into it. I recognize it as the one she said grandma gave her when she graduated from high school. She's only told me the story ten times, and I've always hoped she would give it to me when I graduate high school. But I'm only four and that's a long time away.

"Can I wear it?" I ask, running the cold metal between my fingers.

"Yes, I want you to have it." A tear slips from her eye, but I didn't think much of it, not then.

"Why?" I ask curiously.

She shakes her head, using her sleeve to wipe her eyes. "I don't need it anymore, and I want you to have it."

"Can I put it on?"

"Why don't you leave it in there for now so you don't lose it. Take it on up to your room. I'm going to go run some errands, but Beth is downstairs, and she's going to watch you." Beth's in high school, but she stays with me a lot in the summer when my mom needs a break.

"Okay," I say, wrapping my arms tightly around her neck. "Thank you, Mommy. I love it."

"I love you, baby." Her voice breaks, but at the age of four, things like that don't send up many warning flags. As I disappeared up the stairs, I didn't think it would be the last time I'd see my mom in a long time.

I tell Drake everything. Maybe it's because we're tucked away in the dark, and I feel less exposed because he can't see me. He's quiet, and I'm grateful he lets me get everything out uninterrupted.

"I'm sorry you didn't have your mom growing up," he says when I'm done. His hand still rests on mine, squeezing it every now and then.

"You know, after a while, you learn to adapt. Sometimes I just wonder if I overcompensated."

"In the end, I think things always work themselves out."

A breeze blows through, sending a chill down my spine. "Did I tell you what was in the locket?"

He shakes his head, staring at me intently.

I reach my hand under my sweater and pull out the tiny silver heart. I've worn it around my neck every day since my mom left me. Opening it, I wait for him to find it with his flashlight. "It's her. She put her picture inside."

He studies it for a minute before looking back up to me. "You look a lot like her."

"I've been told that a time or two," I say, feeling the tears building in my eyes.

We sit silent for a while, me trying to recover from giving away so much of why I am who I am … and him … I think he's coming to grips with the fact that I'm not perfect. Or my life hasn't been anyway.

"Have you seen her since?" he asks, cutting through the silence.

I nod, not willing to go into any more detail. I've given him enough for one night. "What about you? Any secrets you're hiding?"

He wets his lower lip before his eyes find me again. "Nothing I want to share."

Looking away, I try hard to squash the regret I suddenly feel. I gave him more, so much more than I've given anyone, and he doesn't want to share anything about himself. I passed the ball to him, and he doesn't want to run with it. I guess I thought if he told me something, we'd be forever bound by our secrets.

He runs the back of his fingers against my cheek, bringing my attention back to him. "Emery, I don't want you to think I don't trust you, but there are things I don't talk about. With anyone."

"It's okay. You don't have to."

Besides the loud truck going by on the street, it's quiet again. I'm about to ask if he'll take me home when he speaks again. "Do you remember how big it seemed when we walked in today and the lights were on? Do you remember stepping out onto the field?"

"Yes, this place is huge."

He nods, agreeing with me. "I get sick before every game. Everyone thinks I'm this cool, calm, collected guy who can just step onto the field and make magic happen, but inside, I'm scared to death. You step out here and there's voices, the roar of the crowd, reporters wanting to ask a few questions … it's too much sometimes."

"Why do you do it then?"

"Because I'm good at it. Because it's going to get me somewhere."

"There are a lot of things out there that will get you somewhere."

He lets go of my hand and sits up. "It was his dream, and I need to see it through."

Sitting up next to him, I ask, "Whose dream?"

"My dad's," he replies, running his fingers through his hair. My hand reaches up to rub his back, but before I actually touch him, I pull away, not sure if it's my place.

"Why did you say it was his dream?" I ask, remembering his exact words.

Glancing at me with pained eyes, he says, "Let's leave that one alone."

I'm disappointed, but in a way, I understand him. It's not easy to open up, and it takes a lot of trust. Maybe he just hasn't gotten to that point with me yet.

The wind has picked up, and I wrap my arms around my legs to chase away the chill. "Are you cold?" Drake asks as he runs the back of his hand up and down my arm.

"A little."

"Let's get out of here," he says, standing up. "I'll give you a ride back to your dorm."

Part of me wants to stay here so I can pretend for a little longer. Pretend that this is all I have to do, sitting on this worn blanket staring up at the stars, but it's not reality.

Standing up, I stretch my arms over my head to loosen my stiff back. It's been a long day. It'll be nice to throw on some sweats and crawl into my warm bed.

Drake rolls up the blanket and tucks it under his arm, taking my fingers between his again. "You don't mind this, do you?" he asks, raising our joined hands up slightly.

"It's okay," I reply shyly.

He smiles, leading us back across the dark field and down the dark hall. He doesn't say a word until we're back to his car. "This night didn't turn out exactly how I'd planned, but I'm still glad we came."

"Me too."

He lets go of my hand, brushing his fingers across my cheek. His eyes have the intensity they held that day in the library. This time I lean in, attempting to meet him half way, but he tucks a strand of hair behind my ear and backs away. I don't know what it is about him, about us, but I've never been more pissed about a non-kiss. Maybe it's because I've never wanted someone to kiss me as much as I want Drake to kiss me.

As he walks away, I climb through the door he opened for me, and collapse into the passenger's seat. There's a familiar tightness in my chest because of what just happened.

I hate how he can brush this stuff under the rug like it's nothing, because it's starting to mean something to me.

I stare at him as he climbs in but he won't look at me. I hate this feeling. Ignoring someone is rejection in its worst form. He starts the car, quickly throwing it in drive. "Listen, can we get together tomorrow to go over the speech? I really feel bad about last week."

"Don't worry about it."

"I want to," he replies in a way that doesn't give me much leeway.

"Call me when you get up then. I don't have anything planned," I whisper, pressing my forehead against the cool window.

I wonder if he knows how much he irritates me when he comes close to taking whatever is going on between us to another level then pulls away. I wonder if he realizes how badly I want him to press his lips to mine ... so badly that I'm thinking about it right now.

Inhaling a deep breath, I close my eyes. Tonight on the football field was perfect. There wasn't anything fancy or glitzy about it. It was just us, and I opened up to him in a way I rarely do with anyone. I never feel like he's judging me, and that freedom feels nice.

"Hey, are you okay?" he asks, drawing me back in a couple minutes later.

"I'm fine. It's just been a long day." I'm trying hard not to tarnish the nice night we had.

As he pulls into an empty space in front of my building, I unbuckle my seatbelt and open the door. I'm ready for these awkward moments with Drake Chambers to end. I just want to climb in my bed and wake up tomorrow with a clean slate.

"Emery!" he yells as I make my way up the walkway.

For a minute, I think about ignoring him, but in the end, I face him, trying to bury away the stubborn part of me.

"Thank you ... for tonight," he says, tucking his hands in his front pockets.

"Yeah, it was nice. Thank you." And just like that, he turns and climbs back into his car.

I'm left wondering if he feels anything like what I feel, or if I'm just wasting my time on something that will never be.

Chapter 10

DRAKE

I FUCK THINGS UP, that's what I do. I've proven it over and over again. The other night with Emery … she gave me another chance after I acted like an asshole in the library, and I pretty much did the same thing to her all over again. I wanted to kiss her so badly, and I felt like she wanted it, too. In the end, I was too afraid of what that next step would mean.

I'm always in control, but I feel it slipping whenever I'm with her. So far, I've been lucky enough to catch myself before I fall completely. I just don't know how much longer I can hold on. Emery's not the type of girl I'm going to be able to kiss once and then walk away from, and I don't have time after football and personal issues to take on a relationship.

When I called her this morning about getting together to run through our presentation, I didn't expect her to suggest we meet in her room. I've been in girls' rooms—that's not the problem—but this is Emery. She pulls me in. She tests me. She makes me want something I shouldn't even be thinking about, but yet I can't let her go.

Gripping an iced latte in one hand, I use my other to knock. I stare at the old hollow wood door while I wait for her to answer, rocking back and forth on my heels. We ended things on a strange note last night, or should I say I did.

As the door swings open, I can't take my eyes off the girl in front of me. Gray sweats and a white t-shirt never looked so good.

"Hey." She smiles nervously, motioning for me to come in.

"I brought you a little pick me up." After handing her the latte, I walk to the center of the room, glancing around for a place to sit.

She lets out of soft moan that makes it hard to just stand here. The more I'm around her, the more I want her ... all of her. "God, this is so good. How did you know what I liked?"

Fuck. This girl has no idea what those words are doing to me. "Maybe I know everything about you."

She comes closer, her eyes roaming the length of my body. I wonder if she thinks I don't notice. "If you know everything, tell me what I'm thinking right now?"

"The way you're looking at my lips ... I'd say you're thinking about what it would be like to kiss me." I can't help the cocky grin that spreads across my face. I probably shouldn't be doing this. I've almost kissed her more than once. Joking about it now is a dick move, but I can't stop.

Her eyes snap to mine as she takes a step back. "Can we just be serious for once? Besides, not every girl wants to kiss you."

I shrug. "I'm not talking about every girl." I pull my backpack off my shoulder and throw it on one of the small twin beds. "Anyway, I listened that day in the coffee shop. I know what you like."

She practically spits out a mouth full of latte, brushing the back of her hand along her chin. "I bet you think you do."

Sitting down on the edge of the bed, I stretch my arms above my head. "Are you ready to get some work done?"

"Yeah, I, uh, put together an outline of our whole presentation." She shuffles some papers on her desk and hands me something that looks like it took more time than any research paper I've ever written. "Let's go through it a couple times until we get to the point where we don't need this."

"I'm ready."

As we go through line by line, I have a new respect for Emery. She's spent a lot of time on this, and I owe every bit of the "A" we're sure to get on this to her. The emotion she feels bleeds through her words. This is personal to her ... it's personal to me.

"I can't thank you enough for doing all this, Emery."

"You haven't been that bad to work with," she teases, sitting a couple feet away from me on the bed.

"I mean it," I say quietly, shifting toward her. Her eyes widen as I lean in to brush my lips against her forehead. I've wanted to kiss this girl for so long, but if this is all I'm going to get, I'm going to take it. "I need to go, but I'll see you tomorrow."

She nods, closing her eyes for a brief moment before finding mine again. Those beautiful brown eyes are going to undo me, and I don't know if I have anything left in me to fight it.

When I walk into class, my eyes roam the room, looking for her. Today is the day we make our big presentation, and I'm not sure where we go from there. I should leave her alone, but I'm not sure I can.

"Hey, I'm over here." I'd recognize that voice anywhere.

Looking to my right, I spot her sitting front and center. That should have been the first place I looked. I hope she doesn't read too much into the big fucking smile that forms on my face. It's automatic.

"Are you ready?" she asks as I take the seat next to her.

"Are you kidding me? This is nothing compared to leading the team down the field for the game winning score."

"Do you compare everything to football?" She gives me a sideways glance, and she looks really fucking cute doing it.

"It's all I know," I say honestly.

"I think you know a lot more than that," she whispers, pulling our speech notes from her backpack.

Class starts, and I pretend to listen to each pair as I glance down at the package I brought for Emery. I picked it up and put it back down a handful of times before even leaving my room this morning. I still haven't decided if I'm going to give it to her or not because I don't want her to think it's more than it is.

Hell, I don't even know for sure why I'm giving it to her. Maybe I'm scared that after we give our presentation, there won't be any reason for us to spend any more time together. Usually, I'd be happy to walk away, but this time I don't want to.

When our names are called, I take a deep breath and walk to the front of the room in the same way I walk onto the football field every Saturday. Even if I'm not ready for this, I'm going to fake it like I am.

Emery goes first, like we'd planned, talking about nature and how she's come to believe it affects the way we handle our nurture. I'm lost in every word she says until she starts to stumble. She's talking about studies done on children who weren't raised by their biological parents, and how even when they've never spent a day with them, they can have similar behaviors and characteristics.

I take over for her, trying to make the transition as seamless as possible. I'm relieved when I look out the corner of my eye and see the appreciation on her face. I wasn't trying to tell her in any way that she couldn't do it. I only wanted to help and show her that I understand everything she's going through. I continue on with my part. How what we're taught from a young age determines how we react to things until the day we die. Those first few years are important ... so fucking important.

When we're done, we take our seats and listen to the remaining two presenters. It's actually hard to concentrate because all I can think about is whether or not I'm going to go through with my plan. It's a step ... no, it's a *huge* leap for me.

Professor McGill speaks, bringing my attention back to the front of the room. "I'd like to thank you all for the time you put into these presentations. I'll have your grades to you by the end of the week."

As she walks away from the podium, the back and forth debate continues in my head. In the end, after a quick glance toward Emery, I decide I have nothing to lose. She might say no, but then we wouldn't be any different than we are now. But there's a chance she might say yes, and I haven't decided what that means for me yet ... or us.

She stands, putting her things into her backpack. It's now or never. When I see the sad look that still covers her face, the words just come out. "Can we talk outside?"

She surveys the room before her eyes find me again. "Why can't you talk to me here?"

"Just give me two minutes," I whisper, careful that no one overhears.

Sighing, she throws her bag over her shoulders and starts toward the door. "You're scaring me, Drake."

I follow her out the door like I'm some sort of lost puppy. I've never cared this much about what a girl thought, nor have I gone out of my way to try to get to know one.

As the door closes behind us, I take a deep breath. I started this and now I have to finish it. "Are you okay?" I ask, tempted to reach up and stroke my fingers across her cheek.

She startles, looking up and down the long hallway. "I started to think about my mom, and I lost it. I guess it doesn't matter how much time has passed ... it still hurts."

I cup her face in my hand, rubbing my thumb along her cheekbone. "I just want to know that you're all right."

"I'm sorry I blew it. Thank you for taking over for me."

"There's nothing to be sorry about."

She nods, her sad eyes locking with mine. I think a person can tell the minute they care about another person by how much they absorb the other person's emotions – taking them as their own. I'd be lying if I said there wasn't a twinge of pain in my chest right now. This girl, so sweet, so beautiful, is hurting, and I want to make it all go away.

Breaking eye contact, I reach into my bag and pull out the gift I packed inside. As I hand it to her, my fingers tremble. Whether she opens it here or later isn't really up to me, but I'd rather not look rejection in the face.

"What is this for?" she asks, looking between me and the handle of the bag wrapped around her fingers.

"Consider it a thank you for not giving up on me," I reply, rubbing my hand along the back of my neck.

"Can I open it?" she asks, fingering the layer of tissue paper that peaks over the top.

Shit. I don't know if I'm ready for this. "It's up to you."

A smile lights her face as she pulls the first piece of tissue paper out and then the next. My heart races when she gets to what's underneath and removes it from the bag. "It's your jersey."

"This Saturday is homecoming, and I'd like you to come to the game. Everyone should experience at least one football game in their life, and you just happen to be the first person I've let wear one of my jerseys."

She pulls her bottom lip between her teeth, looking at me with unasked questions in her eyes. I want her to say yes, because for whatever reason, knowing she is there will give me an added boost. I want her to see me doing what I do best. I want her to know that I'm not the fucking failure I've made myself out to be. We're more alike than she thinks; we simply focus our energy on different things.

"Do you have to know now?"

"No, you can hold onto it. For what it's worth, I really want you to come." I sound more nonchalant than I feel, but I'm trying the best I can to mask my disappointment.

She folds the shirt back into the bag. "I want to ... it's just ..."

"Just what?" I ask, taking a step closer to her.

"I don't know what my plans are yet. I might be doing something with Kate."

Maybe I know her a little too well already because I suspected she might play this card. "There are three tickets in the bottom of the bag. Bring whoever you want."

Her eyes widen as she watches me. She's used to being the smartest girl in the room, but not this time. I close the remaining space between us, leaving only inches between our bodies. She watches me intently as I lean in, my lips brushing against her ear. "I want you there. Don't let me down."

I hear her sharp intake of breath and back away, keeping my eyes on her as I walk backward down the hall. "See you Saturday, Emery."

Chapter 11

Emery

WHY CAN'T THIS DECISION BE EASY? Like choosing whether I want butter on my popcorn or pepperoni on my pizza. But no, I'm trying to decide if I should go to the football game. Not just any football game, but the one where the starting quarterback just happens to be the one guy who I've let get under my skin. The one guy who makes me want to break my own rules.

I struggle with it because it's like opening a door with no idea what's behind it. I'm not the kind of girl who does that. I live in this safe, pre-planned world I've created, and while it always feels like something is missing, I'm content. Right now, it's enough. Drake's intentions are unknown to me, and that scares me … it brings me out of the safe shell I've been hiding under.

I manage to avoid him Wednesday and Friday by coming to class right before it starts and grabbing a seat in the back. I feel like I'm back in middle school again because I'm working so hard at avoiding a potentially uncomfortable situation. I have no idea what to say to him, and I don't want him to ask me if I'd made a decision yet.

I'm starting to feel something for Drake Chambers, and I'm scared he may never feel the same way. I have this tough as nails exterior, but inside I'm a tangled mess. When one of the only people you love and trust leaves you at such a young age, it's hard to get over. I didn't understand it. I didn't know how to deal with it. It broke me. And because of that, I close myself off to avoid getting hurt again.

I glance toward the door when I hear a key in the lock and wait for Kate to barrel in. She does a few seconds later wearing her gray Southern Iowa Hawks sweatpants and sweatshirt. Her long hair is tangled in a knot at the top of her head, and it's one of the few times I've seen her with her glasses on.

"Good morning," she says, throwing her bag onto the bed.

"Hey, how was your night?" I ask, wiggling my eyebrows at her.

"It was good." She plops herself down next to me on my bed. She never asks first, but it doesn't bother me. Kate's different than most girls I know, wiser and more mature. She's very easy to be open with.

"And?" I ask, nudging her with my elbow.

"And nothing. I told you, we're not in any hurry." She rolls to her side, facing me. "Besides, you have no room to talk. When's the last time you had sex?"

"Three months."

Her mouth opens then closes again. Kate's speechless.

"What? Did you think I was a virgin? Why does everyone think that?"

"It's just … when you were talking about your high school boyfriend, it didn't sound like you had that type of relationship." Her green eyes are as big as I've ever seen them.

"I'm smart, but that doesn't make me an angel."

"I'm sorry. You just didn't seem like the type to risk it."

"Risk what?"

"Getting your heart broken."

I laugh, a serious, gut-shaking laugh. "In order for a guy to break your heart, you have to feel a certain way about him. Clay had a special place in my heart, but it was different than what you have with Beau."

"What do you mean by that?"

"Your relationship seems so effortless, and you guys enjoy being with each other. I've never seen you fight once. What I had with Clay was so much work, mostly because I never truly invested in it."

"Beau and I were friends forever, though. We understand each other."

"So why did you wait so long to get in a relationship?"

An uneasy feeling washes over her face. "I liked him for a long time, but things happened that kept us apart, or should I say *I* kept us apart."

"Yeah, I guess I kind of did the same thing with Clay. I never really gave us a chance to be anything more than high school sweethearts. I was too afraid he'd hold me back."

"Do you think you could have had something more permanent?"

"I'll never know. I mean, I think I did too much damage in the beginning by keeping him at arm's length to ever give us a happy ending." I stop, wondering how the heck we always end up having these types of conversations. I guess, in a way, it's good that I feel like I can open up to Kate, and it allows me to see that I created some of my misery myself. Not everything can be blamed on my mom.

"So are you and Beau doing anything today?" I ask, ready for a subject change.

"Beau's going to the homecoming game."

"You're not going?" I'm surprised. They seem to do everything together.

"No, I told him I wanted to hang out with you. Besides, he is going with Cory and a couple other guys."

The mention of the game brings the bag I have hidden inside my backpack to the forefront of my mind again. I'd all but decided not to go, but I wonder what Kate would think of it.

"Drake gave me something the other day after our presentation."

"Really? What was it?"

Scooting down to the end of the bed, I lift my backpack from the floor and pull out the black gift bag with yellow tissue paper. I haven't looked at it since he gave it to me. "Here," I say, handing it off to Kate.

She pulls out the paper first, coming up with the number twelve black and gold jersey with Chambers across the back. I wonder if the players are even supposed to hand them out. "Oh my God. Why did Drake Chambers give you his jersey?"

"He wants me to go to the game today. He even put three tickets at the bottom of the bag," I say, nervously playing with the edge of the comforter.

She reaches her hand to the bottom and comes up with a white envelope with my name scrolled on the top. She tears it open and pulls out the contents, laying them on top of my bed. Three tickets are fanned out, but there's also a folded piece of notebook paper. One I would have never known was there if it hadn't been for her.

"I didn't know there was a letter," I say, pulling it from her fingers. I don't hesitate to open it.

EMERY,

THIS IS THE FIRST TIME I'VE EVER LOANED ANYONE MY JERSEY. PLEASE COME TO THE GAME. I WANT TO SHOW YOU SOMETHING I'M GOOD AT, BECAUSE I'VE ALREADY SEEN HOW AMAZING YOU ARE.

DRAKE

P.S. NO-STRINGS INVITE.

In my haste to read what Drake wrote, I didn't notice Kate leaning over to read right along with me. "You need to go, Emery. I'll call Rachel, and we'll go with you."

"I can't." I don't want to be judgmental, but I know Drake's just going to break my heart. He's already scratched it a couple times, and we're not even in any sort of relationship. We've never even kissed ... I have no idea what he wants from me.

"Why not? This is one of the sweetest things I've ever seen, and the fact that it came from Drake Chambers says something."

"Why is he doing this?" I ask. It's a question I've asked myself over and over the last few days. Why does he care so much whether or not I go to this?

"I think he likes you but just doesn't want to admit it. Sometimes guys need a little push. I mean, do you know how long Beau liked me before he actually said something?" She stops, picking the jersey up off the bed and throwing it over my shoulder. "Put this on. The game starts in a little over an hour. We can still make it."

I open my mouth to argue, but the look she's giving me warns me not to waste my time. I stand up and pull on a pair of jeans and a long-sleeve white shirt from my dresser, ready to see what this football stuff is all about.

"I can't believe you've never been to a game before," Rachel says as we walk into the packed stadium. This is the first time I've met her, but it doesn't feel that way. The three of us quickly fell into a rhythm and haven't stopped talking since.

"Hey, give her a break. I've never been to one either— not in college anyway," Kate replies, saving me from having to come up with an explanation.

"Cory drags me along to almost every home game. The only reason I didn't have to go this time was because Beau invited him. Tell him thank you."

Kate laughs. "I will."

Rachel nudges my shoulder, pointing to three empty seats in the front row of the student section. "Drake scored us some good seats. We should have painted our stomachs or something. Maybe we could have gotten ourselves on TV."

"I'd never do that," Kate chimes in as we take our seats.

The teams are just taking the field and, oddly enough, I'm nervous. Not because I'm here, but for Drake. I remember what he told me that night on the field, and I wonder how he's doing right now, especially since it's homecoming. Maybe I should have texted him to wish him good luck, to let him know I'm rooting for him.

As the teams settle on their respective sidelines, I notice number twelve jumping up and down on the green turf. He's rubbing his hands together like he's cold, and breathing into them as his eyes scan the stands.

I feel a knee in my back and spin around, slightly annoyed. "Hey." It's the girl with shoulder-length blonde hair who I've seen around Drake before. "Is that Drake's jersey?"

"Yes it is," Rachel answers for me, not bothering to even turn around.

Before I turn back to the field, I notice the girl mouth "wow" as her eyes continue to take me in. "Don't get to used to it. It's not like you're the first girl to show up here with that on. In fact, I will almost bet you that it's back on me by next weekend."

Rachel turns around, her hands closed in fists. "You know what, Olivia, I'm here every weekend, and I've never seen you or anyone else wearing his number."

Olivia makes a clucking sound with her tongue as she looks away from us. I spin around, intent on enjoying the game.

"Don't listen to her. But for the record, I still can't believe he wanted you to wear that," Rachel says, loud enough that only I can hear it.

"What do you mean?"

"It's not so much that he gave it to you, but that he gave it to anyone at all. He doesn't give many people the time of day." I kind of know this. I've known him long enough to see how he is.

"I think he has a lot going on," I say, watching Drake lead the offense out to the field for the first time.

Kate leans in next to my other ear. "Maybe I shouldn't tell you this, but Olivia had a fling with him last year. And when I say fling, I mean, they had sex at a party, and he didn't even ask her name the next morning when he woke up. He told Beau about it because she won't leave him alone."

Bile rises from my stomach when I think about him doing that to anyone. Why is it that I can't see it? Why is he different around me? "We're not like that. I mean, we're not dating so you don't have to worry about me."

Kate stares down at the football field and points her finger for me to look, a huge grin on her face. "We'll see. Besides, something tells me he wouldn't do that to you."

I follow the direction of her gaze and see Drake with his hand over his eyes, looking up to where I sit with my friends. When he sees me, he smirks and then walks off to join his teammates in the huddle.

Rachel bumps her shoulder against mine. "Looks like someone is happy you made it."

I smile, wrapping my arms around my body to shield myself from the cool breeze that's whirling around the stadium.

I don't know a thing about how football works besides the little things that Drake's told me, but Kate and Rachel give me a play-by-play, allowing me to catch on quickly. The teams are pretty evenly matched in the first half, tying each other over and over again, until the very end when Southern Iowa captures the lead. Watching Drake take his team down the field is an adrenaline rush. If I'm feeling like this from the bleachers, I can't imagine what it feels like for him.

At halftime, his team heads toward the locker room, but Drake stays behind, talking to one of the brunette cheerleaders who's been cheering on our end of the field the entire half. A burning sensation fills my chest, surprising me yet again. Why do I feel this way about a guy I can never have? The breeze blows some hair into my eyes, but I quickly shove it away as I turn my back to the field, unable to see him anymore.

I hate feeling jealous, and of all people to get jealous over, why does it have to be Drake? I know better than to let myself get hung up on a guy like him. Especially after hearing about Olivia and the way he treated her. Little Miss Short Skirt down there is probably his plan for the evening.

"Do you want to grab a drink or something?" Kate asks, holding her hair back from her face.

"I think I'm going to use the restroom." At this point, I don't even know if I want to stay for the second half because being here doesn't feel right anymore.

As I start toward the cement stairs, I feel a hand on my shoulder and spin back around. It's the cheerleader Drake was talking to on the field. "I'm supposed to give this to you." She slips a small piece of paper in my hand and quickly disappears.

"What's that?" Kate asks over my shoulder.

"I don't know."

I unfold the note, immediately recognizing Drake's handwriting.

IT LOOKS LIKE YOU'RE HAVING FUN. WAIT FOR ME OUTSIDE THE LOCKER ROOM ON THE EAST SIDE AFTER THE GAME.
DRAKE

Folding it back up, I hold it against my chest. Every time I'm about to give up on him, he reins me back in. And if he thinks that little gestures like this are going to earn him points, he's probably right.

Chapter 12

DRAKE

AS THE WARM WATER FALLS on my back, I relive the final plays of the game in my head. Wisconsin stormed back after halftime, taking the lead, and I struggled with almost every pass I threw in the third quarter. I came back strong in the fourth, though, and in the final minute of the game, down by one point, I got my chance to lead my team down the field.

It's when I excel … when I have the most pressure on me. I threw four perfect passes, the last one in the end zone to give my team the win. It was closer than I would have liked, but in the end, all that matters is getting the win. How we got there isn't as important.

"Chambers, are you going to the party tonight?" It's Trip, my center. The guy likes to have a good time just like most of my other teammates, but he's cool.

"Maybe." I shut the shower off, grabbing my towel from the hook.

"There's no maybes today, man. Donovan invited two sororities, and I hate to tell you this, but you need to get laid."

"Shut up," I say, walking toward the locker with my last name spelled across the top.

"And that's why," he shouts, laughing behind me.

In football, your teammates are like your brothers. You do anything for each other to keep the team unified, even if that means going to a party you'd rather skip.

When I wrote the note earlier inviting Emery to meet me tonight, I wasn't sure whether she would show up or not. I've messed with her a lot, and she's probably thinking this is just one of those times.

I pull on my faded blue jeans and a green polo, topping it all off with a brown blazer that Coach insists we wear to and from the field on game day to keep up a professional appearance.

As I slide on my brown dress shoes, I glance around the locker room, watching most of my teammates leave. Deep down in the pit of my stomach, I'm worried she's not going to show. It's easier to sit inside and tell myself she might be out there waiting for me, than to actually see she's not.

After waiting a couple more minutes, I gather up my gym bag and head out the door.

Holding my breath, I glance up and down the hall, looking for any sign of her. She's not here. The game ended almost forty-five minutes ago, and she's had more than enough time to make it down here.

I guess this is what I get for sticking my neck out, for taking a chance, and most importantly, for being an asshole. Only one girl in nineteen years has truly interested me, and I fucking blew it before anything ever started.

"Drake."

As I spin around, I let out the breath I've been holding. She's standing a few feet in front of me, and I have to admit my jersey has never looked so good.

"Hi," I say, quieter than I intended. She takes a few steps in my direction, causing one side of my mouth to turn up. She looks so damn hot, and for a second, I let myself picture her in nothing but my jersey. It's never going to happen, but a guy can dream.

"You take a little longer in the shower than the other guys," she teases, nervously brushing some of hair behind her ear.

This time, I'm the one to close some of the space between us. I use my fingertips to move a few strands of hair she missed, causing her to briefly close her eyes. "I was giving you time to get down here."

She smiles, tilting her head to the side. "You thought I wasn't going to show?"

I laugh, avoiding her eyes the way I'm about to avoid the truth. "Nah, I knew you'd show. It's a once in a lifetime opportunity."

"Really?"

I shrug. "Of course, who wouldn't want to spend the night with me?"

"You're probably right but, if I spend the night with you, I'll probably never want to do it again," she teases, stepping back far enough that I can't touch her, which is probably a good idea on her part.

"Okay, smartass, let's get out of here. We have plans." I start down the hall, not grabbing her hand like I have in the past when we were alone. I invited her to go with me tonight because I know she'd never go to a party like the one we're about to experience on her own. I also know that I'll have a much better time if she's with me ... I want to get to know her better.

There's a connection I feel toward her, but I also know we can't be more than friends. There have been times I've wished I'd met her at a different point in my life—a time when I had less pressure, and things were stable. I think if given the opportunity, we could have something really fucking good between us.

But, I've got my drawbacks, and she deserves someone better than me.

When we step out onto the parking lot, there are a few players still lingering about. I'm not ashamed of Emery, but I don't want them to get the wrong idea about why we're together so I place my hand on her lower back, hurrying us along. This is the first time I've ever been near them with a girl who I'm serious about ... one I actually want to have a real friendship with. The last thing I want is for Emery to be a part of their stupid fucking locker room chatter. She doesn't deserve that, and she's certainly not going to become the team's latest ping-pong ball.

Quickly opening the passenger door, I use my hand to guide her into the seat and shut the door before hurrying to the driver's side. I make sure no one is watching us before climbing inside.

I pull my car out of the lot before looking over at Emery. Her elbow is propped up against the door, her forehead resting against her closed fist. I'd say she's not very happy right now.

"Are you okay?"

"Why wouldn't I be?" She won't even look at me.

My temper starts to creep up as I grip my steering wheel tighter in my hands. I always have the best intentions, but my execution sucks. "Look, I'm sorry about what just happened. I don't want the guys to get the wrong idea about you."

Her head snaps in my direction, a confused look on her face. "Wrong idea about what?"

"About what we're doing. I haven't been in a single relationship since I got here, so anytime I'm with a girl, it's—"

"For sex?" she cuts me off.

I scrub my hand over my chin while I formulate my response. Technically, the answer is yes, but I don't want her to think it happens all the time. "If you want me to be honest ... yes, but it's probably not like you think."

She looks down at her fingers before moving her eyes back to me, her mouth opening and closing a couple times before she finds her words. "Are you embarrassed to be seen with me?"

My mouth falls open before I regain my composure. She's wrong. She's so fucking wrong ... she should be embarrassed to be seen with me. "No, I'm not embarrassed to be seen with you. I didn't want the guys to think we're together like that. You're not the type of girl they're used to seeing me with, and you don't deserve the things they'd say if they thought we were."

"I'm a big girl. I can take care of myself."

I pull up to a stoplight, taking the opportunity to sneak another look at her. "I know, but I'm not going to put you in that position if I can help it."

She shakes her head, keeping her sights on the passing streetlights.

"Have you ever been to a college party?" I ask, trying to do what I do best and change the subject.

She studies me for a few seconds before she answers. "I went to Beau's."

"Emery, that was a get-together, not a party."

"What's the difference?"

Normally, I would laugh at this conversation, but Emery's not dumb. She's just naïve, and I want to help her open her eyes to the world outside of her studies. "I could count the number of people at Beau's on my fingers and toes. What I'm talking about is a packed house, kegs of beer, and loud music."

"Then no, I've never been to a college party before."

I pull my car onto the street that will host tonight's post game party, looking for a space to park. "We're going to change that then."

After squeezing my car into a small space, I turn it off and pull my blazer off my shoulders. "Ready?" I ask, reaching for my door handle.

She opens the door without replying, and I'm left to try and catch up.

"Emery!"

She keeps walking, following the crowd to the front door of a two-story brick house. She needs her space. I get it, but if she thinks she's going to run away from me and disappear into that house by herself, she's wrong. So fucking wrong.

The crowd inside slows her progress, allowing me to catch up. "What do you think you're doing?" I ask, lightly wrapping my hand around her wrist.

She tries to pull away, but I don't let her go. "Let go of me."

"Answer my question."

"You have a lot of nerve, you know? You can't walk through a freaking parking lot with me, but you want to go to a party together. You don't make any sense."

Letting go of her wrist, I step back. I'm a fucking walking contradiction. All the things I was worried about back in that parking lot are nothing compared to what people are going to think if we're here together. I get so caught up in the little things sometimes that I miss the bigger picture. I guess I thought when we got to the party, we'd blend in, but I forgot who I am. There's no chance I'm going in there unnoticed.

"That's what I thought," she says, pulling my jersey over her head. "Why don't you give this to someone who has time for your mind games. I've got better things to do."

And just like that, she turns, walking deeper into the packed crowd. I should follow her, but I know I deserve it, and she needs her space.

I wanted to protect her. Fuck, maybe I wanted to protect myself. Every minute I spend with her is beginning to mean something to me. I want to be around her, and watch her do things that might make her smile. She's so closed up all the time, and I know she'll regret it at some point. There are things in life everyone should experience. I had every intention of doing this with her, but I never imagined she would read so much into the distance I was putting between us.

After circling the living room, I walk into the kitchen and find her grabbing a soda from one of the coolers. At least she's not drinking, I think, as I lean my shoulder against the wall to watch her. The cheerleader who brought the note to her at halftime, Missy I think her name is, appears at her side, and they start talking. When Emery rolls her eyes, I can only assume they're talking about me, and I take it as my cue to disappear again. That's my plan for the night—give her some space while keeping her in my sights.

I'm not more than three steps into the crowd when a small hand wraps around my bicep. As I turn, I realize it's not who I'd hoped.

"Hey, Drake, good game today." Fuck. It's Olivia. I swear she has a GPS chip embedded under my skin or something.

"Thanks," I mutter, scanning the people around me. It's about time I find Emery again.

"Do you want some company tonight?"

"Do I look like I want company tonight?" I haven't looked her in the eyes once. That should be a hint.

"You're obviously looking for something. Let me help you," she says, snaking her finger between two of the buttons on my shirt.

I pull her hand away from my chest. "That's not going to happen tonight or any other night. How much longer is it going to take before that sinks in?"

She purses her bright red lips as she looks over my shoulder. "It's your loss," she says, leaning in to kiss my cheek before I have a chance to react.

I watch as she walks away with a grin on her face. Girls like her make me want to lock my sisters up for the rest of their lives. I guess I want them to be more like Emery. I don't want them to chase after guys, especially ones like me.

After straightening my shirt, I walk to the corner of the room where a makeshift bar is setup and throw back two beers. I need something to loosen all the damn tension in my body. Two probably won't cut it, but I need to keep an eye on Emery.

Scanning the room again, I see her standing with Cole Dillon, laughing at whatever he's talking about. Cole's one of the few guys on the team who I don't consider to be a complete dickhead, at least when it comes to the way he treats girls. He's one of the only guys who doesn't disappear into a bedroom every Saturday night at these parties. He's also the type of guy Emery deserves, which makes watching this that much more difficult.

I stay put, trying to convince myself she's a big girl and can do what she wants, but I'm not good at this, and it all goes out the fucking window when he puts his hand on her arm. My jaw clenches as I walk to where they stand, ignoring the crowds of people I pass. Just as I reach them, Emery throws her head back in laughter again, and Cole looks at her with a loving glint in his eye. At this point, he'll be lucky if I throw the ball to him at all next Saturday.

When Emery finally sees me, she stops, putting her hand on Cole's forearm. "Hey, Drake, why didn't you tell me Cole was so funny?"

My cheeks are probably bright red, because my face is fucking burning. "I guess I didn't realize Cole was a comedian off the field." There's a venomous bite to my voice. The way his expression changes tells me he heard it.

"He was telling me stories about the team's road trips. I'm surprised any of these guys have girlfriends." She smiles, bumping her shoulder against his. If she's trying to irritate me, she's doing a great job.

I clench my fists at my sides, trying hard to hold myself back. "I think it's time for us to go," I say, staring straight at her.

"But I'm just starting to have fun. Besides, you didn't really want to come here together anyway. I'm sure Cole will give me a ride home." She looks up to Cole again, and I swear to God she winks.

I can't do this anymore. I know she's mad about what happened earlier, and if she's trying to get back at me, she's succeeding. I can't remember the last time I wanted to punch somebody, especially someone I like.

Grabbing her free hand in mine, I walk to the door, giving her no choice but to follow. At first she drags her feet, but I'm almost double her weight. She's not going to win this battle.

"Drake!" She tries to pull her fingers from mine, but I win again.

"We're leaving," I say, not bothering to look back.

Before I can take another step, Cole's in front of me, eyes blazing. "I don't think she wants to leave with you."

"She came with me. Now get out of my way, Dillon. She's fine," I seethe. I just want to get the fuck out of here.

He glances back at Emery, and then steps out of my path, allowing me to walk past.

"Are you sure you don't want to leave with Olivia?" I hear her faint voice behind me.

I stop, looking back. "What?"

She looks hurt. Genuinely hurt. "I saw you with her earlier. She must be good enough to be seen with here."

Something snaps inside me. We continue to fight our way through the crowd, but before we reach the door, I change the plans. She tries to pull away from me, but I don't let her. Maybe it's the two drinks I've had or the emotion I'm drowning in, but I find myself pulling her into the half bath off the living room. The look on her face when my eyes catch hers again is one of shocked surprise.

When we're both inside, I push the door shut, reaching behind her to lock it. She doesn't take her eyes off me, and I can't take mine off her. This girl … I don't know what she's doing to me.

"You're good enough, Emery. In fact, you're too fucking good for me. Don't you get it? I want you so bad right now, but I'm fighting it because you *should* be with someone like Cole. He can be what you need … I can't."

Her eyes widen as she stares at me. "He's not the one I want."

Grabbing her hips, I pull her body so it's flush against mine. She trembles in my hold, but the hungry look in her eyes begs me to continue.

I run my fingertips up her sides, feeling the smooth texture of her t-shirt against my skin. Her chest heaves as my lips move toward hers. She's hesitant. I feel it. I see it. This isn't the first time I've done this to her, or the second.

I stop when my lips are so close to hers, one might think we're actually touching. Her warm breath tickles my skin, making it impossible to think. "I'm going to kiss you."

She nods, resting her palms against my chest. And I do. First brushing my lips across hers, then holding them there, getting used to the feel of her skin. As my tongue traces the seam of her lips, my fingers find the hem of her shirt, moving up inside to caress her smooth stomach.

It's the first time, in over a year, I've kissed a girl when I wasn't completely drunk. And even though it's been a while, I don't remember it ever being like this. My whole fucking body trembles with need ... one I've been fighting for far too long.

"Emery," I groan as I pull my shirt over my head, "I want this so fucking much."

She responds by wrapping her arms around my neck, pulling me closer. Even with her shirt between us, I feel her breasts pressed against my chest. It heightens my need, making me lose control of the rational part of my brain.

I run my hands down her back, stopping when they reach her perfect ass. Lifting her in my arms, I seat her on the edge of the sink and step in between her parted legs. My cock twitches when I press my body into hers. I want all of her.

My tongue moves with hers before traveling down her throat, tracing a line along her collarbone. "You taste so fucking good. So good," I say, my lips moving along the center of her throat.

She moans as I roll my hips against hers, creating the friction I've been craving. "Drake."

I need more. I want to taste more of her warm skin, to feel it against mine. Grabbing the bottom of her shirt on both sides, I begin pulling it up.

"Stop!" she yells, pushing against my chest. I freeze in place, wondering what the fuck just happened. This moment was more real than anything I'd experienced in a long time. For once, I'd let myself follow my heart, and it led me to her.

"Not tonight," she adds, her palms still resting against my skin.

I lift my head, allowing me to see into her big brown eyes. There's so much confusion in them, so much pain. I just want to make it all go away. "I can't," she whispers.

I cradle her cheek in my hand, caressing her soft skin with my fingertips. "I didn't mean to push you."

She tightly closes her eyes then opens them again. "I want to. I just … I can't."

Before I realize what I'm doing, my mouth is closing in on hers again. Just hearing her say that she wanted me fuels the fire that I'm finding impossible to put out. My lips brush against hers, but then stay frozen, waiting to see if she pulls back.

When she doesn't, I brace my hands against the wall on either side of the mirror, effectively caging her in. It's the only way I can keep my fingers from touching her soft skin. As my tongue presses between her lips, she scoots to the front of the sink, pressing our bodies close again.

After a few minutes of tugging and teasing, my lips move to the sensitive skin below her ear. "Do you want to stop?" I ask, nipping her earlobe between my teeth.

"Just kissing, Drake. Nothing more." I pull on her earlobe again, enjoying the moan that escapes her lips.

"I'll take whatever you're willing to give me right now," I whisper, pressing my lips back to her skin.

She's so controlled, but I'm crumbling a little more every time I'm with her.

Chapter 13

Emery

HIS LIPS ONLY TOUCH MY NECK, but the tingle runs down the entire length of my body. Ten minutes ago, I was pissed off, and now I'm struggling to keep it from going any further. I've never felt this way before. No control. No worries.

It feels so damn good.

I've written him off a few times, but he keeps coming back, and there's a reason I let him. I see through him … there's a raging fight going on inside of him. He's struggling. I'm struggling. We're both addicted to the fight.

His thumb brushes across my breast, and that action, coupled with the friction of him pressed between my legs, gently rolling his hips against me, pushes my body over the edge. He covers my lips with his, swallowing my moans. It's euphoric … the first time I've ever had an orgasm without the help of my own fingers. With passion, it is so much better, so much more intense.

As my body winds back down, he covers my face in light kisses, rubbing his hands in circles on my back. I should be relaxed, but the tension is returning … this is where the awkwardness starts to seep in. Should I return the favor? Does he expect me to? Do I even want to?

"What's going through that pretty little head of yours?" he whispers so close to my ear, I feel his breath.

"Who said I was thinking?" I reply, trying to keep my voice even.

Brushing my hair behind my shoulder, he exposes my neck. "Your body is tense. Let me fix that for you." His lips press to my exposed skin while he uses his fingers to lift my chin, giving him access to my throat.

He continues, tracing where his lips were with the tip of his tongue. Slowly, all my worries begin to fade away. This isn't a test. It doesn't require a study guide or a plan. It's about us, locked in a moment.

When I'm relaxed again, he pulls back. I miss his kisses almost instantly. After helping me straighten my clothes and pulling his own shirt back over his head, he grips my hips and slides me down off the sink. "We should probably get out of here before someone needs to use the bathroom the way it was intended," he says, a sexy grin showing on his face.

I nod, returning his smile. "Did you have something in mind?" Right about now, I'd go just about anywhere with him.

As he watches me, watching him, something changes in his eyes. He's leaving me again, pulling back. "I should probably get you home," he says, scrubbing his hand over his face.

For the first time since he pulled me into this bathroom, he's not touching me. He's not looking at me. He's checking out again; we've gotten to the point where I feel it coming. My chest instantly tightens, making it almost impossible to keep the uneasiness out of my voice as I grip the doorknob and pull it open. I'm going to be the one doing the running this time. "It looks like we're done here anyway."

Maybe I'm expecting him to grab me and tell me I misunderstood. Maybe I want him to ask me what's wrong so I can release weeks of pent up anger. But he doesn't. Why would he when he knows exactly what's bothering me? The apologetic look on his face when I glance back over my shoulder tells me that much, but I still feel used. Like sometimes I'm good enough for him to take the next step with, but not good enough to take the one after.

I push past the crowd of students who have gathered in front of the door and make my way down the front steps without looking back again. I should be able to walk home; it's not that cold outside and from my recollection, we can't be more than a mile from campus.

"Where the fuck are you going?" he asks as I continue down the sidewalk. I ignore him, not wanting to get into this any deeper than what we already are. Ten minutes ago, we were treading with ease. Now, we've gone under ... seconds away from drowning.

They say the ones worth fighting with are the ones worth fighting for.

I'm not so sure about that.

"Emery!" I hear his heavy brown shoes hitting the pavement, and I quicken my pace. Soon after, a large hand wraps around my arm, stopping me in my tracks. "You're not walking home. Now get in the fucking car."

I wiggle, trying to free myself from his hand. "You know what, Drake? I'm done. Just let me go, and we can pretend this night never happened."

"It shouldn't have happened. I think we both know that." Guilt echoes in his voice.

"I didn't regret it until you pulled this again. Why do you do it? Why do you pull me close and let me in only to drop me on my ass again? I'm done."

Under the illumination of the streetlight, his nostrils flare as his eyes scan mine. He looks like he wants to say something, but he doesn't. He loosens his grip, and I shake myself away from him. He doesn't say another word as I start back down the sidewalk again, but I hear his footsteps behind me.

I'm so done with him, done with this. Out of all people, why did my heart have to make an exception for him? Why is the one person who gets under my skin, the one person whose fingers I want on my skin? It must be a version of self-rebellion ... my body's a freaking traitor, especially my heart. I replay the moment I saw him with Olivia ... right before she leaned in to kiss his cheek. When she walked away, she passed me, brushing against my shoulder with a huge grin plastered on her face. It was right after that when Cole Dillon found me.

With every block, my anger rises. One side of me wants to turn around and scream in his face, but deep down, I know he won't give me what I want—an explanation. I'm better off to just keep going. Go back to the place I was before I met him.

When I reach the door to my building, he's still behind me. I guess he gets one point for not being a complete asshole and leaving me to walk home alone in the dark.

After shutting myself inside, I lean against the wall away from his view. I wait, taking several deep breaths to calm my nerves before chancing a look out the window. I spot his retreating figure in the distance, his shoulders slumped, hands obviously buried in his pockets. It's better this way, I think, as I watch him disappear into the night.

"Hey, Emery, how was your night?" Kate spent the night at Beau's again, and I miss her. It's nice to have a girl to talk to.

"You know me. I did some studying and read a book. Oh, and to keep things really interesting, I ate almost a whole pizza by myself," I announce with artificial pride.

She laughs. "Control yourself, Emery."

"I'm trying," I say, pulling my covers up. It's mid-morning on a Saturday, and I haven't even gotten out of bed yet. The weather is gradually turning colder, making it more difficult to motivate myself to do anything unless I have class or study group.

Kate sits on the edge of my bed, pulling her legs up and wrapping her arms tightly around them. "Have you heard from him yet? It's been almost a week."

She wasn't here when I got home from the party last Saturday night, but she picked up on my mood the minute she walked in the door on Sunday. I told her everything. How he seemed jealous that I was talking to Cole, and then all the sudden couldn't keep his hands off me. I told her how quickly he changed again, going from hot to cold. Surprisingly, she seemed to understand. She said he's obviously conflicted with himself, and it has nothing to do with me.

I don't necessarily believe her, but there might be some semblance of truth to it.

"No," I answer, playing with the frayed edge of my old pink and black comforter.

"Maybe you should call him. Men are stubborn, especially guys like Drake. They don't like to admit they're wrong, Emery."

I sigh, remembering how he acted every time I saw him this week. "He wouldn't even look at me during class. If he wanted to talk, don't you think he would have tried to get my attention?" I close my eyes, picturing the disconnected look in his eyes every time I looked at him during class. "It's over, not that it ever started."

"You know what you need?"

Lifting my brows, I stare at her. "To disappear to an island with nothing but libraries and coffee shops?"

"No," she says, smacking my leg. "Let's have lunch. I'll call Rachel and see if she can meet us."

My first instinct is to say no, but the longer I look at her, the harder it is. Plus, I've been sitting alone in this room way too much. "Okay."

"Yay!" she screams, jumping up from the bed. "Okay, you need to get dressed ... and maybe shower."

Rolling my eyes, I throw off the covers, revealing my worn pink sweats. "Yes, boss."

She ignores me, digging her cell phone from her purse. I grab a pair of jeans and my old Southern Iowa Hawks hoodie from the drawer before disappearing into the bathroom. If this makes her happy, I'm going to do it. Maybe Kate's happiness with rub off on me.

The smell of smoked barbeque makes my mouth water as we walk into one of those bar and grills that specializes in buffalo wings. Not my first choice, but Kate and Rachel claim it's the place to be during the football game.

We find one empty table near the bar and order sodas right away. "What have you been up to, Emery? I haven't seen you since the football game."

"I had a couple big tests this week," I answer honestly. I purposefully leave out the part about being a recluse to avoid Drake.

Rachel catches Kate's eye then looks back to me. "How did things turn out with Drake last weekend?" If I didn't know better, I'd say they've been talking about me.

"Shitty," I answer as the waitress sets our drinks down. Her eyes fall on me, and I smile. "We're just talking about a guy."

The waitress laughs, pulling her small notepad from her pocket. "Well then, that's the only word needed to describe them. What can I get you ladies today?"

We take turns ordering, each choosing a different flavor of wings so we can share. As soon as our waitress is out of earshot, Rachel starts her line of questioning again. "What happened?"

"Nothing and everything ... all at the same time. Things were going okay at first, but then he got pissed off and pulled me into a bathroom where we shared a kiss that was better than any sex I've ever had. Oh, and the best part, after he was done with me, he went back to being an asshole. That pretty much sums up the night."

Her eyes grow wider as she listens. "Why did he get pissed off?"

I scoff. "I was talking to Cole Dillon."

"He was jealous," Kate chimes in.

"Then why is he being such an asshole?" I ask, swirling my straw in my cup.

"Because he's fighting it." Kate covers my forearm with her hand. "If you really want to pursue this thing with Drake, you have to fight for him. He's not going to do it himself."

I know she's right, and while part of me is drawn to Drake, I'm ready to cut my losses and concentrate on the goals I laid out when I came to school. All of this is just taking time away from the things I should be focusing on.

"I think it's a lost cause. Besides, I have other things I should be concentrating on. It's not worth the risk," I say. My eyes catch a play from the Southern Iowa game on the big screen behind the bar. The camera is on Drake. He's under center, scanning the defense. As soon as the ball is snapped, he steps back, pumping his arm a couple times before letting it go to his tight end. It's the perfect pass.

Rachel's eyes catch mine. "Are you sure he's not worth it?"

I'm about to tell her he's not when he's sacked on the next play. My eyes are glued to the screen as I watch him, silently begging him to get up. When he reaches up with one hand and pulls his helmet off, I watch him grimace. Covering my face with my hands, I make it easy to hide my eyes if I need to. I just want him to get up. Instead he covers his shoulder with his hand and pinches his eyes shut. All I can do is watch as the training staff runs out to the field.

After a couple minutes, he's able to stand with help and makes his way over to the bench. I watch, waiting to get a glimpse of his face. His brows are drawn together as one of his trainers work on his shoulder. When he's done, Drake gets up and starts pacing up and down the sideline, trying to do circles with his injured arm.

The camera stays on him as he watches the rest of the drive from the sideline, and when it ends in a punt, he heads into the locker room, a look of anguish on his face.

When the wings arrive at our table, I nibble on one, leaving the rest of the basket untouched. "See, Emery, you care," Rachel says, looking between me and the television.

"I never said I didn't. I just don't know if it's worth it."

"Maybe you should go check on him after the game. Make sure he's okay," Kate adds.

As soon as she suggests it, I know I want to. But will he want me there?

Chapter 14

DRAKE

JUST OPENING THE DOOR to my dorm hurts like a bitch. The medical staff confirmed my shoulder isn't badly injured, and my collarbone isn't broken, but they said it would be sore for a few days. I wasn't able to return to the game, but the team was able to pull out a win, keeping us alive for the conference championships.

I fumble with the buttons on my jeans, trying to unfasten them so I can replace them with lounge pants and fall into bed. Just as I finally have success with the last button, there's a knock at the door. "Shit," I mutter under my breath as I tug my shirt down to hide my open fly. I don't want to answer it, but it could be Coach, and if I leave him hanging, out will come the search party.

As soon as the door swings open, I lose all knowledge of the English language. I haven't let myself look at her since the night we kissed.

"Hi," she says quietly, her eyes falling on my right shoulder.

"What are you doing here?" It doesn't come out quite as I intend, but the pain in my shoulder is overriding any common sense right now.

Her eyes pierce into mine, sympathy mixed with anger. "I came to check on you. To see if you need help with your shoulder."

"It's fine. I can take care of myself. I always do." As I reach up to rest my arms against the doorjamb, I wince, grabbing my shoulder in pain.

"You're not fine. You're stubborn, and there's a difference," she says, walking right on past me. This is my room, and I should tell her to leave, but I can't ... I kind of want her to stay.

"Make yourself at home then," I say, slamming the door shut with my good arm.

"Sit down," she says, pointing to my desk chair.

I hesitate, not used to having anyone but Coach tell me what to do. That's why I play quarterback after all.

"Drake, please."

Without speaking, I do as she asks. For the first time, I notice the bag she brought with her and wonder what's inside. She pulls out two small ice packs and a small white tube, setting them on top of my desk.

"I have trainers, you know," I mumble as she kneels down in front of me.

"Yeah," she says. "Did they work on it?"

I nod, trying not to move too much.

"Does it feel better?"

It doesn't. Not at all.

"That's what I thought. Can you pull your shirt off, or do you need help?"

Admitting weakness is almost as bad as death for a football player. But what am I going to do? Lie to her, and then let her watch me struggle. "I need help."

"Lift your left arm up." I do as she asks, and she slowly slides my shirt up my arm until it's free. "Now, I'm going to try to pull it over your head so I can just slip it down your right arm, okay?"

I nod. I just don't get why she's doing this for me. I haven't done a fucking thing for her.

Her plan is successful, leaving me shirtless in front of her. The annoyance I felt when I first opened the door is starting to subside. She's right. If she hadn't come here, no one would have. Coach might have checked on me, but not like this.

"We're going to ice it for fifteen minutes first," she says, lightly pressing one of the ice packs to the front of my shoulder. "Can you hold this with your hand for a second?"

I do as she asks, feeling the release of tension from my body with every word she says. I watch as she picks up the other pack and presses it to the back of my shoulder. She uses her free hand to pick up a medical wrap, and before I know it, my whole shoulder is wrapped up, holding the ice packs in place. It doesn't feel perfect, but it's taking away some of the sting I felt a couple minutes ago.

I want her here. I want her taking care of me, but it's a horrible idea. I've spent the last week chasing her out of my head, and now that she's here, I realize I haven't made any progress.

"Thank you."

She looks down at the floor, and I'm disgusted with myself. The last thing I ever wanted to do was beat her down so much she couldn't look me in the eye. If I ever saw one of my sisters like this, I'd want to kick the ass of the guy who made them that way.

I need to fix this.

Standing, I grip her chin between my thumb and index finger, leaving her no choice but to look at me. "Thank you, Emery. You didn't have to do this."

She swallows, her eyes glossing over. "I wanted to."

It's these moments of truth and honesty that attract me to her. It's in these moments that I want to be with her. I want her to be the girl I kiss after each win. I want her to be the one who takes care of me when I'm injured. I want her to be the one who I tell everything.

God knows I need someone.

"Emery," I whisper, running my thumb along the cleft of her chin. It would be so damn easy to kiss her right now. Her eyes are practically begging me to. Hell, my body is begging me to stop fighting it.

It's an exhausting tug of war, but I don't see any other way around it.

I let her go, turning to escape her tortured eyes while tangling my fingers in my hair. *Not you, Drake. She's worth so much more than you can give her.*

I don't know why I'm so fucking scared. I've been miserable for years, but things are different when I'm around her. Maybe I should give us a shot and take my chances on the potential fucking heartache ... but I can't.

"You need to go," I say, unable to look at her.

"Damnit!" she screams, throwing the white tube against the wall. "Why do you keep doing this? Why do you look at me like I'm the answer to all your problems, and then push me away?"

I turn so fast my shoulder throbs. "I didn't ask for this!" I yell, unable to control myself any longer. "I didn't ask for you, Emery."

Her head shakes slowly as her chin begins to tremble. I'm not just messing with my life ... it's affecting hers, too.

My heart is screaming for me to wrap her in my arms.

My head is telling me to let her go before I hurt her even more than I already have.

They're fighting each other. I'm fighting myself.

"You know what, Drake. I didn't ask for you either. I've never needed anyone, and I don't need you." She picks up her bag and walks to the door before turning back to me one last time. "By the way, after the ice melts, rub some of that cream on your shoulder."

Her hand is on the knob. It's now or never. Take a risk or continue to live the way I have been. Either way, I think we're both going to get hurt; it's just a matter of when.

"I'll fuck everything up. I always do, Emery, because the one thing I can't escape is myself," I admit, waiting to see how she reacts.

Her body freezes, hand still resting on the metal knob. Maybe I screwed this up so much that it's not fixable, but maybe there's a chance she'll give me one more shot ... but at what?

I need her to put a few more seconds on the clock.

"I already told you ... I can't do this anymore. The first time it happened in the library, I thought you were just confused. Then it happened again at the party last weekend. And today ... I'm not going to let you keep doing this to me," she says, resting her forehead against the door. She hasn't looked at me yet, and it's killing me.

It may not be right, but I know how to weaken her resolve. Closing all the space between us, I press my chest to her back. She shakes her head like she knows what's going to come of this. She knows the power I hold over her body, and the way it can change how she thinks.

I grip her hip with the hand on my good arm as I move my lips close to her ear. "Please, let me show you what I can give you. No one has ever affected me the way you do. Maybe there's a reason for that."

Brushing her hair away from her neck, I let my fingertips skim along her skin. She whimpers, relaxing into my body. I almost have her ... my Emery. "Things won't be easy, and I can guarantee I'm going to try to push you away again, but don't let me."

She braces her palms against the door. "I don't know." Her voice shakes as she tilts her head back.

Sliding my hand across her stomach, I kiss the side of her neck. Softly, lips barely touching her warm skin. "What do you have to lose?"

"Everything."

I press my lips to her neck again. "And what do you have to gain?"

"Everything," she cries, shaking her head.

"Then the question is, am I worth it? Am I worth risking everything?"

She wiggles, quietly begging me to give her some space. I give her just enough to turn around, afraid that if I give her too much, she'll run away. There are tears running down her face, leaving harsh black lines. I cup her face in my hands and brush my thumbs across her cheeks, wiping some of the warm tears away. "Emery," I say quietly, trying to draw her back in.

Her eyes burn into mine. "You tell me. How do I know that this time is different?"

I wince. "I know you probably feel like you've already given me a chance, but this time *is* different. I want this."

She's reading me. Hopefully what I feel on the inside is written on my face. I need her.

"Tell me something about yourself that I don't know, Drake. What makes you, you? Why are you constantly fighting against us?"

It's like a cold bucket of water was just dumped over my head. "What?"

She removes her hands from my chest, but I catch her wrists, keeping our joined hands between us. "If you're serious about this, you'll let me in. You've never let me in the way I've let you in."

I inhale, looking up at the old popcorn ceiling. There's a lot that people don't know about me. Things that might show just how imperfect things are for me. This is probably the main reason I've stayed out of relationships. Sex is one thing, but bleeding out your life story is something entirely different. I'm not ready for that, but I want something in between ... I'm just not sure if Emery is willing to find middle ground with me.

"Let me kiss you," I whisper, moving my face close to hers.

She turns her head away from me. "I can't, Drake."

"Fuck, Emery. Didn't you listen to a word I said? Don't let me push you away."

She flinches. In my haste to make her stay, I didn't realize how much anger was radiating from my body. How my hands had tightened around her wrists.

Letting go, I back away, gripping my hair between my fingers. Why do I keep doing this? "Just go," I whisper, turning my back.

My room's never been so quiet, even when I've been alone. The empty space inside of me just grew a little bigger.

I wait until the door clicks before sliding to my knees. I'm lost, completely fucking lost.

Chapter 15

Emery

I USE MY SLEEVES TO WIPE my eyes one last time before opening the door to my room. Kate's probably not here, but if she is, I'm going to have some explaining to do. I drove around for at least an hour, trying to fix my blotchy, red face. It obviously didn't work because I can't stop crying.

When the room is in view, and Kate is nowhere to be seen, I let out a huge breath. It's just me and my misery. We've been quite the pair for a long time now, and the aches and pains in my chest aren't new to me.

With a quick tug, I pull my tear-stained sweatshirt over my head. I don't know if it's just me, but when things happen, things I'd like to forget, I want to get rid of everything that might hold that memory.

I throw my sweatshirt from the night before against the white wall behind my bed, watching it fall in a heap. When my mom left, I clung to some of the dresses she'd bought me. I still have a few of them buried deep inside a box somewhere. Every once in a while I like to take them out and remember the way things were. And sometimes I wonder if she held onto anything of mine. Did she take a piece of me with her, or didn't I matter that much?

Damnit! I hate this. I hate how the sad moments in life bring back memories of every other sad moment I've ever experienced.

I throw on a pair of fresh gray sweatpants and a white tank and fall on my bed, not bothering to wash the make-up from my face. Tears probably washed away most of it anyway.

Curling up, I fold my knees to my chest, and remember the last time I saw my mom. It's the one way I know to make myself cry, and I need to chase more of this sadness from my body.

I walk into the large skating rink with my dad by my side. I've been rubbing my hands raw since he told me to get in his truck. I know what he's up to. He's never been good at surprises.

As we pass the ticket counter and round the corner, the crowd yells, "Surprise!" I look up and HAPPY 13th BIRTHDAY, EMERY hangs on a huge banner on one side of the room. If my dad really knew me, he'd know this isn't my thing. I hate parties. I don't have a ton of friends. Most of these people are probably here for some free cake and a round of skating.

My dad bumps my shoulder with his. "Are you surprised?"

I paint a smile on my face. It's my specialty. "Yes! Thank you, Daddy."

"I love you," he says, tapping his finger on my nose.

"I love you, too," I reply, a genuine smile covering the old, fake one. Deep down, I know his words are true. He tries so hard for me, to make me happy. To make up for all the things he thinks he did wrong with Mom.

He disappears in the crowd. It's an awkward moment for me. Alone. Disconnected. I'm the guest of honor, but I'd rather slip out the side door and sit in the bed of my dad's pickup truck.

I walk around the room for a while, talking to a few kids in my grade, as well as neighbors and family friends. It's not as bad as I thought it would be, but as soon as I've blown out my candles, I make my birthday wish come true and disappear outside without anyone noticing.

I was born in July. One of the hottest, most humid months of the whole year. I shouldn't want to be out here, but it's quiet.

I remember where my dad parked his truck and make my way to the back of the building to find it. My white tennis shoes dig into the gravel, leaving a path of dust. My dad's not going to be happy with me, but then again, he's rarely happy anyway.

Hoisting myself up, I sit with my feet dangling off the bed of his old beat up truck. It's Sunday, and the highway that runs by is quiet, and the air is still.

I sit with my hands pressed to the hot metal and count the minutes until someone will come looking for me. That's when I notice it ... the old blue Chevy driving around the back of the building. I don't recognize it, and that says a lot because I know almost everyone in town and what they drive. My heart races as it comes toward me, slowing as it gets closer. Maybe coming outside alone wasn't such a good idea.

When it's close enough, I can see in the driver's side window, and my heart stops. I recognize the person behind the steering wheel. Even after all these years, I'd know her anywhere.

A soft tap on my door brings me back to reality ... the screen on my old movie going black before it was over. Pulling the covers up higher, I try to ignore the sounds at first, but when I hear them again a few seconds later, I don't feel I have much choice.

I peek out the tiny hole in my door but can't see anything. Against my better judgment, I open it a crack, hoping whoever is messing with me hasn't gone too far.

That's when I see him, sitting against the wall outside my room. Navy lounge pants have replaced his jeans and a gray t-shirt molds to his chest, but what really catches my eye is the agony on his face. His jaw clenched. His brows furrowed. Skin pale. I can't deny how broken he is, and even after everything he's done, there's no denying it ... he's beautiful.

He never takes his eyes off me as he stands, taking slow steps in my direction. "What are you doing here?" I ask quietly.

His head tilts as he watches me carefully. "I couldn't sleep without seeing you again. I think we have unfinished business. Can I come in?"

Without much thought, I open the door the rest of the way, silently inviting him in.

For once, he came to me.

He's fighting back.

I step back into my dark room, not stopping until my legs hit the edge of my bed to put distance between us. I both hate and love when Drake is so close.

I'm not sure what I expected, but he doesn't stop until his toes are practically on top of mine. I watch his hand slowly creep up until it disappears and wraps around the back of my neck, his thumb running against my jawline.

"I'm so sorry," he whispers, lowering his forehead to mine. His voice is like a million pieces of broken glass begging to be put back together.

"Drake—"

His fingertips cover my lips. "Please. Let me touch you. I need to know that you're real. That this is real." He stops, removing his fingers and lightly brushing his lips against mine. "I promise to give you as much of myself as I can, but I need to go slow."

Trust. It happens easily, but it can be broken even easier. Question is, how easy is it to gain it back?

I shake my head. "I don't know."

His lips cover mine again, sweet and slow. "Please. I need this. You need this."

Just as that infamous two-letter word is about to pass through my lips, his hands graze my collarbone, slowly working their way down my chest. All I hear is our mixed breaths as the familiar tingle runs down my spine. My body's betraying me again.

"Be with me," he whispers as his thumbs brush across my nipples. He presses his warm lips to my cheek, repeating it all the way down my neck.

Even if I wanted to, I wouldn't be able to tell him no right now.

Not that I'd ever want to. Even if it's just tonight, it's going to be our night. The way his lips and hands worship my skin, it's going to be a good night.

In a silent answer, I wrap my arms around his neck. He responds by wrapping his muscular arms around my back, ensuring that every inch of the front of my body is touching his.

There's a tiny lingering voice in my head telling me that we shouldn't be doing this. We have too much to work out. Too many unsettled things between us. Deep down, I'm hoping this will open us up to each other.

Our bodies stay pressed together for several seconds before his hands settle on my hips, his fingers working to find the space between my pants and t-shirt. "Lift your arms," he instructs, tugging my shirt over my head. He tosses it onto the bed before settling his hands back on my hips. His eyes fixate on mine as he skims his fingers up my sides and hooks them under my bra straps to pull it down. His hands make quick work of the clasp in the back, allowing the lace garment to fall to my feet. I wonder if he feels how hard my heart is beating. It's thunderous … working hard enough to keep my mind from rethinking this.

With trembling fingers, I touch his stomach, using them to push the soft cotton to reveal one of my favorite parts of him. He has a perfect six-pack. And his chest, it's a sculpted work of art.

"Emery," he growls as my fingers continue their way up his smooth, hot skin.

I pull up on his shirt, and he lifts his arms, allowing me to take it off. We stand, shirtless, eyes locked. My room is dark, but a tiny strip of light comes in from between the curtains. It's enough for me to see the battle isn't over. This time, we're going to win, not the ugly voices in his head.

My shaking hands fumble with the drawstring on his pants, loosening the tight knot and pulling until all that's left is two strings hanging. I glance up at him before moving any further. His mouth opens, but nothing comes out.

My fingers graze his stomach before I slip them inside his waistband. I've never been more nervous or more excited at the same time. He gasps when my hand wraps around his warm cock. Slowly, I begin to move, watching him tilt his head back as his hands tighten their grip on me.

This isn't the first time I've done this, but my experience is limited. When his lips part, it's the reassurance I've been waiting for.

"Stop," he growls, gripping my wrists.

I lower my eyes, not wanting to see any disappointment in his.

"Look at me," he demands, holding my face in his hands. "I stopped you because I didn't want to end the night like that. Don't think for one second that I didn't like it, because, Em, I fucking loved it."

Smiling, I lean in to kiss him. He meets me halfway, much hungrier with this kiss. Hands, his and mine, are everywhere. Adrenaline is high, so high that I have no idea how I ended up on my bed with Drake straddling my thighs. His hot mouth trails down my skin, sucking and lapping each nipple before burning a path down my stomach.

Not a single thought goes through my head with exception of the amazing things Drake Chambers can do to me.

When his fingers slip under my waistband, his eyes search mine. Life's filled with a bunch of forks in the road, and we both know this is a major one. It's a threshold that once we cross we can't get back over. For me, it's a moment that will probably make or break the rest of my college life. I'm not the girl who considers this another college experience. This will become part of my history, good or bad.

Resting my shaky hands on his shoulders, I push lightly. He acknowledges it, pulling my pants down my legs. He stands quickly, letting his own pants fall to the floor before climbing back up the length of my body.

I feel him at my entrance, but he hesitates, studying me carefully. "I'm not a virgin," I whisper, watching as one side of his mouth turns up.

"I never thought you were."

"Everyone assumes," I say, turning my head to the side.

His warm, calloused fingers press against my cheek, forcing me to look up at him again. "I've learned not to make any assumptions about you. You surprise me every day. Every fucking day, Em."

Feeling him enter me, I pinch my eyes shut. Sex is an emotional thing that I've never let myself fully experience. I saw it as an expectation. Another mile on the road to adulthood. But this, with Drake, I want it to be different. I just don't know what that is right now.

He buries his head in my neck, whispering to me as he continues to enter me.

"Relax."

Another slow motion.

"I'm going to take care of you. I promise."

A little deeper. God, it feels so good. My heart swells as he presses all the way in, filling me completely.

"You feel so fucking good wrapped around me."

He moves out, and slowly pushes back in, giving me time to adjust. He repeats this a couple more times before we find our rhythm. I never knew it could be like this, his hands and mouth paying just as much attention to my body as the rest of him. It's never been this way for me.

My fingers tangle in his hair as my legs wrap around his trim torso, bringing us even closer. "Jesus," he says, his lips still pressed to my neck.

"Not quite," I tease, lifting his head to kiss his swollen lips.

He smiles against my skin. "Oh yeah," he says as he speeds up his motions. That familiar pressure I felt in the bathroom with him that night starts again, but this time it's even more intense. With each movement, he's right where I need him, pushing me higher.

I love that feeling. The one that happens right before falling, and this time, I fall hard and fast, my body clenching his tightly.

"Fuck." He pumps into me with one final thrust, curling his fingers in my hair, his face buried in the crook of my neck.

Sweat drenches his hair and our skin. That was the best freaking physical experience I've ever had in my life. It's the first time I've let myself let go. It's the first time I've left the lights turned on, and really let someone see me, let myself see anyone.

"Are you okay?" he asks, kissing my chin. I still feel him inside me, and I want more. This part of me has been locked up for too long.

"More than okay."

"You don't regret it?"

"Not yet. Give me a day or two," I tease, combing my fingers up and down his back.

Grinding his hips against mine, he says, "Then we'll just have to do this again tomorrow, and the next day, so you don't forget how fucking good it was."

"That I won't easily forget."

"Me either." His voice is lower this time.

Chapter 16

DRAKE

AFTER EMERY STORMED OUT of my room earlier, I sat in the same spot for over two hours, staring at the wall. My shoulder wasn't bothering me anymore or maybe it was, but I didn't feel it because my chest hurt more.

I had to check on her to make sure she was okay. I had to see her to make sure I was okay.

I wasn't after she left.

I wasn't until I was in her room, my lips on hers. She forgave me. Now, I have to forgive myself and part of that requires giving her a piece of me. This thing we have is about more than sex, and I need to show that to her. I should have done it after she told me about her mom, but I wasn't ready then. Maybe I'm not ready to let the past out in the open now, but I want Emery to know that she's more than just a game to me. She means something …

Her fingertips blaze a trail on my back, relaxing me as my breathing evens out again. She trusted me. Now, I have to show her that I deserve it.

"My dad died when I was eleven," I say quietly, my lips moving against her neck.

Her fingers stop, and she nudges me, trying to force me to look at her. "Drake."

I need to keep talking, or I may never be able to get it out. I've detached myself … too much.

"He grabbed his coffee one morning, kissed each of us on the top of the head, and climbed into his car. It was the same routine he had every morning, but that morning he was upset with me ..." I stop, trying to swallow down that part of the memory. Now that I look back, he had every right to be angry. I always acted like a punk where my sisters were concerned.

"Drake," Emery whispers, pulling me back.

Her fingers lightly comb through my hair as I take a deep breath and continue. "A few minutes after he left, we heard sirens but didn't think much of it because we lived close to a busy highway. My mom grabbed our lunches from the fridge, and we all climbed in the car to go to school."

The next part is difficult. Emery must sense it because she slides out from under me, laying her cheek against the pillow beside mine. Face to face, nowhere to run but to the truth. To something I've never told anyone. "We drove through our neighborhood like we always did, but when we got to the stoplight along the highway, red and blue lights were flashing everywhere. I guess that's what I was looking at when I heard my mom scream. I'll never forget that scream," I say, lowering my voice. Even now when I close my eyes, I can still hear the gut-wrenching sound that I heard that day. A lump forms in my throat, but I swallow it down again.

"Oh my God," she whispers, pressing her palm to my chest. There's just enough light shining through the window that I can see her eyes watering. I never let any tears fall, not since the first day, but right now, they're threatening.

"His light had turned green so he started across the road, and a drunk driver crashed right into his side of the car. They said he died almost immediately."

She stares into my eyes, cupping my cheek in her hand. "I'm sorry. So so sorry."

Holding my stomach, I attempt to chase away the queasy feeling I have whenever I picture the bent metal that used to be his car. He didn't stand a chance. "I didn't just lose my dad that day. I lost my mom, too. She's never been the same, or even a shadow of who she used to be."

"What was your dad's name?"

"Michael," I answer. I can hear my mom saying it in my mind. I used to know what was going on between them by the way she said his name, whether she was happy, angry, or sad … that's how I knew.

"How old are your sisters?"

"They're fifteen and eleven," I answer, quietly. "I pretty much raised them after he died."

She briefly removes her hand from my cheek, wiping the tears from under her eyes. I don't want her sympathy … I just want her to understand me, why I'm not all warm and fuzzy. Why I have a metal shell around my heart. "What do you mean you raised them? You were only eleven."

I lightly kiss the tip of her nose. "My mom left us, too. Not literally, but she spent days in her room, barely eating. I didn't realize it then, but she'd fallen into a deep depression. A family friend started taking us to and from school, I made our dinner, made sure they took baths, and went to bed on time."

"How long did it take her to come out of it?" She snuggles into my chest, laying her head under my chin.

"She hasn't." I wipe under my eyes, stopping the tears from rolling down my cheeks. This whole day has been too much, especially ending like this.

Her lips press to my chest. "How did you keep up with football? I mean, the practices and stuff."

The vision of my dad in the backyard in his dress pants, button-up shirt, and loosened tie flashes through my mind. Every day, spring through fall, we were out in that backyard perfecting my skills. At first I loved it because of all the attention he was giving me, but there were days it became too much. It still is sometimes.

"Football was his dream. I'm doing everything I can to make it happen," I whisper, wrapping her hair around my fingers.

She straightens, staring into my eyes. "Is it your dream?"

I shake my head. "I don't know anymore."

"Drake," she starts, using her fingertip to straighten the lines that have formed on my forehead. "Have you ever talked about this with anyone? I mean, really talked through it all."

"I can't, not yet anyway. It brings up too many memories that I'd rather forget. Well, until you." I stop, brushing my fingers between her breasts. "Help me forget again, Em. I need to forget."

This whole night has had a pattern: sadness, sex, sadness. I kept my promise and gave her the biggest piece of me, and it actually took some weight off my chest. Now, I want to complete the pattern so I can forget again.

Rolling her onto her back, I seat myself between her legs and get completely lost again.

I didn't spend the whole night with Emery. She mentioned that she didn't know when her roommate would be back, and I took that as my cue.

I don't know what I was expecting to feel when I woke up, but this wasn't it. I crave more of her, even though I've seen it all. There's no regret or guilt. There's this big part of me that just wants to be with her.

My phone buzzes on my nightstand, startling me. I pick it up, immediately seeing the familiar number I usually avoid. Maybe it's my relaxed mood, but I decide to answer. "Hello."

"Drake."

"Yeah, I'm here."

Her usual soft sigh comes over the line. I think knowing I'm here relaxes her. "How's school?"

Covering my forehead with my hand, I rub my temples in a precautionary measure. "It's good. Busy."

"And football?"

"Coach is working us hard, but it's been worth it so far. We're undefeated." Most parents come to at least our home games, but not my mom. I don't even know if she checks the scores.

"I know," she whispers, surprising me a little.

"You should come to a game this year. We have a shot at the Big Ten Championship," I say, holding my breath as soon as the words leave my mouth.

Silence follows, and I bite my lip to keep myself from saying anything else. "I'll see if I can make it. Money's been short, but maybe toward the end of the season." I know what's coming next, and I fucking hate it. It's the real reason she called. "Can I borrow some money? Tessa needs shoes for basketball, and I don't have it."

She doesn't know this, but my sole purpose for having a job is to help cover the things she can't. I work at the field a few nights a week, and every dollar I make goes into an account for moments like this. It doesn't mean I like it, because I don't. I fucking hate this life. "I'll transfer some into your account later today."

"Thank you. I really hate asking you."

"It's no problem," I lie as I scrub my hand over my face.

"I applied for a new job at the insurance office."

"That's good." It's another lie. The whole town knows her, knows what she's like. The chance of her getting a call from there or anywhere is slim.

"Well, I'll let you go. Call me if you need anything."

"I'll talk to you later, Mom."

"Bye."

"Bye."

Tossing my phone onto the end of my bed, I fold my arms over my eyes. This is why I keep pushing Emery away. She's worth more than this fucked up life I live. And I'm so drained from what I give my team and my family … I don't know if I have anything left of me.

Chapter 17

Emery

HE DIDN'T CALL YESTERDAY.

A few times I thought about calling him, even holding my finger over his name. I didn't go through with it, though. I'm tired of being the one who's chasing him. The one who's constantly getting hurt, because I'm putting myself out there, and he doesn't see it.

As I step into the classroom, I grab a seat toward the middle. Not wanting to be front and center or hiding in the back. I just want to blend in. I'm so frustrated with Drake Chambers, I don't know if I want him to see me or not. I guess it would depend on what happens next.

As I wait for the professor to take her spot behind the podium, I start to wonder if Drake will even show. He opened up big time on Saturday night, and it was hard to hear. I wanted to cry for him, but I could tell he was working hard to hold it all in. A few tears escaped, but I didn't let myself completely fall apart. It's his story, not mine.

"Em." Looking up, I see Drake in his low-slung jeans and a fitted black tee. He waits until our eyes meet before he continues. "Is this seat taken?"

"No," I whisper, shaking my head.

He sets his bag on the floor and sits down beside me. I bite the inside of my cheek, waiting impatiently for him to make the next move. Are we back to being friends and enemies, or did what happened the other night mean as much to him as it did me?

It meant everything to me. Drake's the one guy who's been able to break my rules and get away with it.

My eyes stay focused on the front of the room. The uncertainty I feel inside is making this extremely awkward.

His elbow rests on the chair arm between us as he leans in. Knowing what his body can do to mine causes my heart to pound. "I'm sorry I didn't call you yesterday. Things were kind of hectic."

"How's your shoulder?" I ask, avoiding his eyes.

"It's better. I had a friend who gave me some tips." It's that word. The one I was hoping we'd moved past.

"And you followed them?" I still can't look.

"The best I could."

I fidget with the corners of my notebook paper until they're frayed. Out of all days, why is the professor running late today?

A large hand settles on my knee, squeezing it gently. "Can we talk after class?"

I swallow, feeling desire pool in my stomach from that one simple touch. "I have some time before biology."

"Good," he says, squeezing my knee once more before letting go.

I don't know what it is about him, but I'm suddenly having trouble catching my breath. Professor McGill chooses this exact minute to walk in, reining us in with a few loud comments.

This is going to be the longest hour of my life.

I can't repeat one sentence the professor said, but to my relief, class is finally over, and hopefully I can get some answers from Drake.

"Ready?" he asks, picking up his bag off the floor.

"Yeah."

I follow him, hoping we'll discuss what happened the other night and where that leaves us. I don't ask where we're going. It doesn't matter. I'd go anywhere with him.

As soon as we step outside, he turns to me. "Your place or mine?"

"What?" I ask, taken aback.

He glances from side to side before cupping the back of my neck in his hand and drawing my lips to his. "I said, your place or mine?"

This isn't what I had in mind, but is it what I want?

"Kate's probably home. She doesn't have class until later."

He kisses me again, then grabs my hand and pulls me down the long sidewalk. After a few minutes, I realize we're heading to his dorm, not mine. Nervous butterflies pool in my stomach. *Is this what our relationship is going to be about?* Sex. Not talking for days. A few stolen touches here and there that no one else can see.

This isn't what I had in mind. Honestly, I never thought I'd have Drake on my mind, but I don't think there's any way to get him out of it right now.

He opens the door to his building, using his hand to guide me in. Neither of us speaks. I have no idea what we're doing, and he's already proven to be a man of very few words.

The silence continues up the stairs, down the hallway, and as he unlocks his door. After he opens it, he allows me to step inside first, following closely behind.

Two seconds later, my back is pressed against the wall and his hot lips are on my neck. It doesn't take long before my body gets the idea and joins in, my fingers tugging at his hair, my hips grinding into his. I didn't know I needed him like this, but I do.

His hands slide over my covered breasts and brush against my stomach until they find the bottom of my denim button-down. "Are you attached to this shirt?" he asks, his warm breath tickling my neck.

Confused, I shake my head. He immediately pulls both sides of my shirt, and buttons fly across the room. "Drake," I moan, turned on by how aggressive he is.

"You're so sexy, Em. So fucking sexy." His hands touch my shoulders, sliding my sleeves down to my wrists. With one more tug, it's on the floor.

I push his t-shirt up his stomach as his fingers work to unfasten my jeans. His skin is so warm, so smooth. His hard work on the field shows.

After my jeans and panties join my ripped shirt on the floor, I pull his t-shirt over his head. He undoes his jeans just enough to free himself and grips my hips, quickly sinking into me. There's nothing between us now.

"Fuck, Em, I've been thinking about this all morning." He pounds into me over and over. I won't deny that it feels good, but I also wonder if this is what I mean to him, if I'm becoming some sort of physical release for his hurt and frustration.

My fingers tangle in his hair again as his lips explore my neck. At some point, I'm going to have to address this, but right now, it feels too good. "God, Drake," I moan, as he rubs against that spot again. He's driving my body insane with every thrust.

"What are you doing to me?" he asks, as his forehead comes to rest on mine. "I can't get enough. All I want is you, Em."

"I don't want you to leave me again." The words escape me before I have any time to think them over. What I'm saying. What it means.

He freezes, brushing a few strands of hair from my sweat-soaked skin. "Who said I was leaving?"

"You always do. Even Saturday, after everything, you left."

He winces, still buried deep inside me. "Please don't think like that. It's not like that."

I nod, wrapping my arms around his neck. Pressing my forehead back to his, I whisper, "Stop running. I need you. I haven't figured out why yet, but I do."

His eyes close before finding mine again. "Em—"

"Stop. Don't think. Just be with me. Please," I beg, kissing him softly.

His eyes bore into mine for several seconds before he starts thrusting into me again. If I made any headway is yet to be seen, but for right now, I'm stuck in this moment with the most unexpectedly amazing man I've ever met.

My body winds quickly, squeezing him over and over again, and before he finds his own release, he makes me come again, even harder this time. We do it together.

As we both try to regain control of ourselves, we stay in place. I feel him going soft inside of me, but I'm not ready for him to pull away.

He's nitrate, and I'm acid. We're testing the limits, waiting for the explosion, but neither of us can stop.

He lowers me back to the ground, using his fingertips to brush the hair from my sweat-drenched face. "How was that?"

"I can't find the words," I reply, kissing his sculpted chest.

"Hmm, is Emery White speechless?"

I shrug, kissing him again.

"That's a first." His arms envelop me, bringing me to a place I never want to leave. It also makes me realize that we have some talking to do before we continue this. The longer I let myself fall into Drake's arms, the harder it will be to break free again.

I need to know that what we have goes beyond these physical explosions. I never held onto my body like it was a prize to give the guy who showed me he loved me first, but this isn't okay either. Not anymore.

"I think we should talk now."

Kissing my temple, he says, "What is there to talk about? I think we just said pretty much everything there was to say."

I wiggle out of his grasp, picking my clothes up off the floor.

"What are you doing?" he asks, standing in the middle of the room completely naked.

"I'm putting my clothes back on."

"Okay," he says, resting his hands on his hips. "Why are you in such a hurry?"

"We have class."

He shrugs. "Skip it."

"I am not skipping." I pull my jeans back up, before eyeing my torn shirt. "Do you have a shirt I can borrow? Since you ruined mine."

A wicked grin appears on his face. "You look better without it anyway."

"Drake."

"Em."

"Please," I beg, crossing my arms over my bare chest. The room feels a little too cool all of a sudden. I'm not sure if the overexposed feeling comes from that, or the fact that I'm scared that he's going to walk out of here and not talk to me for days again. I can't keep doing this, not like this.

He smiles, his eyes surveying the length of my body before he walks to his dresser and tosses me a long-sleeve gray t-shirt. "Here, this one is small on me."

All I can do is stare as he sweeps his clothes up off the floor and pulls them on, wondering what the hell I'm doing here. He didn't even have to ask, and I was naked in his arms, letting him pound me into the wall. This isn't me. This isn't what I'm about. This isn't what I want our relationship, or any relationship I'm in, to be about.

"You know what, why don't you call me when you want to go on a real date. One that doesn't end with the two of us naked." I leave, slamming the door shut behind me. Maybe I'm overreacting, but the girl I left back in that room wasn't me … I don't know who I am anymore.

Chapter 18

DRAKE

I HAVE NO IDEA WHAT the fuck just happened. One step forward, two steps back, and I'm tired of this dance with Emery.

I have enough going on in my life without adding another drop to my rollercoaster, but something about her won't let me just get off the ride.

I feel something for her. Something new. Something I blocked myself from feeling for so long. I like her, care about her even, or I wouldn't have told her everything I did about my dad. That's something I've guarded and held in close. The fact that I told her says a lot. Right now, I know one thing's for certain—we need to end this stupid game we play, or go our separate ways. This is starting to hurt too fucking much.

I pick up the phone and call the one person who might have something to help me figure her out.

"Hello," he says, his voice scratchy like he hasn't been up for very long.

"Hey, Beau, how you been?"

"Good, good. You?"

My foot bounces on the ground as I sit on the edge of my bed, trying to do something I've never done before ... ask for help. "I've been better. Do you want to grab a beer or something? I need to talk to you."

"You're scaring me," he says, concern evident in his voice.

"I just need some help with a little situation, that's all."

"I have class in ten, but I'm free after that. Why don't you come over? My fridge is still full from the last party I had."

"Thanks. I'll be there."

Angry knuckles pound on the hollow wood door. I don't have to open it to know that it's Dad, and that he's not very happy with me. Anyone who's ever been on my dad's bad side can tell you he's not afraid to show his emotions, good or bad.

"Drake, come out. Now!" Yeah, I'm in a whole lot of trouble.

"Coming," I reply, taking one last look at my hair in the mirror. I've been trying this new thing where I spike it up in the front. It's not quite right yet, but it's getting closer to where I want it to be every morning.

"Drake, if I have to tell you one more time, you're going to be running laps around the block all night in the rain!"

I put one hand on the knob and turn the light off with the other. Here goes nothing.

He stands right outside the door with his hands on his hips, face bright red. Maybe I should have come out the first time he asked.

"What are you doing? Your sisters still need to brush their teeth, and you've been sitting in there for almost half an hour with the door locked."

I shrug, burying my hands deep in my pockets. "I'm sorry. I lost track of time."

"Go eat your breakfast." He sighs, pinching the bridge of his nose.

He's always hard on me, but I rarely hear him yelling at my sisters. It's unfair. Sometimes I just want to throw my favorite shirts and video games in a bag and run away. Anywhere has to be better than this.

"Is that what you're wearing today, Drake?" my mom asks as I step into the kitchen. I look down at my old red t-shirt and jeans with holes in the knees; it's actually one of my favorites.

"It's all that's clean," I lie, pouring some milk into my cereal bowl.

My sisters sit across from me, venom in their eyes. "You got in trouble," Quinn says, sticking out her tongue at me.

I shake my head, watching the light rain fall against the window. I wonder if Coach might cancel practice tonight. We practice seven days a week, almost every month throughout the year. If it's not outside, it's inside. I love football, but living it almost every day is a little overwhelming, especially when my friends are off doing their thing.

"I'm taking off," Dad announces, pulling my mom away from the sink to wrap her in his arms. He's done it every morning since I can remember. It's gross.

He kisses her lips before letting her go to kiss the top of each of my sisters' heads. When he gets to me, he messes up my hair and says, "I love you. Be good."

Usually I say something back. I'd tell him that I love him, but not that morning. I broke the rules that morning, and it nearly broke me.

We all watched him walk out the door, my sisters even waving behind him. I moved my attention back to my full bowl of Frosted Flakes. Dad gets mad at me a lot, but he's usually okay by the next day.

My mom finishes the dishes while we eat the last of our breakfast. I stare out the window in wonder of all the colorful leaves that cover our usually green lawn, and after a few minutes, I hear a series of sirens in the distance.

changing forever

"Mom, what's that?" my sister Quinn asks, running to get closer to the window.

"There's probably another fender bender out on the highway. They've got to fix some of those stop signs." She wipes her hands on a dishtowel and throws it on the counter. "Okay, we need to go. Get your coats and shoes on."

We listen without giving Mom any grief today. Days like this, when we're already on Dad's bad side, we know better than to make it worse.

We're all quiet as we drive out of our sleepy little neighborhood to the main road that goes through our town. I'm completely in a daze with my forehead pressed against the cold window when we come to the stoplight that controls when we get to cross the highway. Lights—red and blue— flash, highlighted even more so by the bleak day.

I'm staring out the window, wondering if we're going to be late for school when I hear her scream. I've never heard my mom like that, even when she's angry with us, and as I watch her run out the door, I see why. The twisted piece of metal in the middle of the road is the same color as my dad's old Ford.

My heart stops ... completely stops in my chest. I'm only eleven, but I'm not stupid.

My mom crumbles to the ground in front of our car. My eyes search frantically for the telltale Southern Iowa Hawks sticker on the bumper of his car. It's older, worn by the sun, and I've never seen another one like it. A painful tightness grips my heart when I spot it. This isn't good. Not one bit.

A tear rolls down my cheek. More want to follow, but I hold them in.

"Drake, what's going on?" Tessa asks from beside me.

Using one hand, I wipe the tear from my face, and with the other, I grab her hand in mine. "It's going to be okay."

I have to be strong. It's what my dad would want me to do.

That day, a drunk driver took my dad's life and destroyed my family, and while I blamed the selfish bastard, I've been harder on myself. In my mind, I thought my actions caused it … by the things I didn't say that morning. I've wondered every day since if he was thinking about me when he was hit. If I hadn't been such a little shit that morning, would he have paid better attention when the light turned? Deep down inside, I think I know it had nothing to do with me, but my guilt makes it feel like it had everything to with me.

That was the only time I didn't say I love you back to my dad, and I've held that regret inside … it's become a permanent part of me. What happened that day has affected every decision I've made since. It's why I keep running, to get away from the monsters that are constantly chasing me. But when you're living in a nightmare, no matter how fast you run, you'll never get away.

I need to find a way to turn this around … football can't be the only thing I have in my life. At some point, I have to start letting him go and live for myself. I need to find forgiveness.

Taking a long, deep breath, I knock on Beau's door. At least five times on the way here, I wanted to turn around and go back home. I hope this doesn't come back to bite me in the ass.

"Hey," Beau says, opening the door to invite me in.

"Thanks for letting me come over, man." I pat his back as I walk past, taking a seat on the edge of the oversized couch. I helped Beau and Cory move their stuff in at the beginning of the semester. It was a bachelor pad back then: white walls, black leather furniture, a few lamps, and a big TV. Their girlfriends have worked wonders with the place, adding some bright red and blue pictures and a big red rug. I think it's crazy they let them do it in the first place.

"You want something to drink?" Beau asks, opening the fridge.

"Beer. Please."

He looks over at the fridge door, his eyebrows pulled in. "Don't you have practice today?"

"Fuck," I groan, rubbing my hand over my face. "I hate football season."

Beau laughs, walking to me with two waters in his hands. "It's only a few months out of the year." Sitting in the chair across from me, he watches me intently. It's time to get this show on the road.

"I need some help."

"Okay, be a little more specific." He twists the cap off his water but never takes his eyes off me.

"Emery." It's one word, but by the way his face relaxes, I think he knows where I'm going with this.

"Go on."

"I like her. Fuck. I mean I like her a lot, and I'm not sure how to show her that in a way that doesn't piss her off. Things will be really good between us for a few hours, or even a day, then I fuck it up."

He glances up at the ceiling, letting out a deep breath. "What the fuck did you do?"

"Nothing. I mean everything. I don't fucking know." Throwing my hands in the air, I accept defeat. Emery 1, Drake 0. This game could go on for eternity, and I think she'd still own it.

He leans in, elbows resting on his knees. Eyes as serious as I've ever seen them. "Just tell me what happened."

"We had that project to do so we were spending time together. You know me. Usually, I don't give a damn if a girl likes me. It's not at the top of my priority list, but Emery, she's different. She's smart, confident, and she doesn't give a fuck that I'm the quarterback of the football team. She just cares about me as a person ... I can't explain it."

I stop, rehearsing the next part in my mind. Beau knows me, but he also knows Emery, and I don't know what he's going to think about the rest of this. "I kissed her one night at a party. She was flirting with Cole, or should I say, he was flirting with her. I pulled her away, and we ended up in the bathroom. We've been doing this stupid back and forth thing ever since. I pull away, she gets pissed at me, then we repeat the whole process all over again a few days later."

Closing his eyes, he asks, "Did you sleep with her?"

"That's really none of your fucking business, Bennett, but yes. We've had sex."

The way his eyes burn into mine when he opens them tells me he thinks I'm a freaking idiot. "Have you established some type of relationship? If all you do when things are good is have sex, you're not going to get very far. I don't know Emery well, but she's not just any girl. She's not the type of girl you fuck just to fuck, Drake. She does everything for a purpose. What's yours?"

His words shatter every thought I had about why Emery and I weren't working up to this point. It's not about what I'm doing, or what we're doing. It's about what I'm *not* doing. "I told her something I hadn't told anyone before. No one here anyway."

"Really? When did you do that?"

"After we had sex for the first time," I admit quietly.

Beau shakes his head as he stands and walks back to the fridge, pulling out a beer this time. "I'm sure she appreciated it, but if you really want something with Emery, you're going to have to do more than pillow talk. Dates? Dinner? Dancing? I don't know, but this is not going to work with her. She's too fucking smart for your shit." He stops, taking a long drink from his beer. "The good news is, she must like you a little bit if she's put up with you this long."

"Okay, I get it. What do I do now?"

He laughs, setting his beer down on the coffee table.

Sitting back, I rest my arms on the top of the couch. This is going to be a long fucking afternoon.

After talking to Beau, I feel better and worse. Better because I know what I have to do, and it's not completely impossible. Worse because he made me see myself through Emery's eyes. It's not a pretty picture. In fact, it's so much fucking worse than ugly.

I texted her on Monday night and told her I had some shit to work out before I could see her again. Shit being myself, but she didn't have to know that. Not yet.

But today, I find myself in class with no option but seeing her. She'd never skip. I wanted to but felt like she'd read too much into it if I did.

I arrive early on purpose, selecting a seat in the middle of the lecture hall. I'm being a coward again; I didn't want to walk into the room and have to decide whether or not it was a good idea to take a seat next to her. I'm not ready to talk about everything.

A few minutes before the lecture starts, I see her out of the corner of my eye. She stops briefly in the aisle right next to my row, but after a short stare down, she continues to the front.

My focus stays on her for most of the class. Her hair is tied up in a bun at the top of her head, and she's wearing these ridiculous dark-rimmed glasses that are actually kind of cute on her.

For sixty minutes, I wait for her to look back at me. I keep thinking that maybe she'll glance back and show the smile that I miss so much. It's rejection. It's fuck you.

When Professor McGill ends her lecture, I stay in my seat, anxious to see what Emery's next move will be. Not surprisingly, she walks straight up the center aisle without even glancing in my direction.

My chest aches, but in the end, watching her was the best thing for me. It gave me the push I needed to do what I should have done a long time ago.

Chapter 19

Emery

DRAKE IS A MISTAKE. A bad choice. I'm part of a game he plays, and he plays it well. He won me over, but if he's winning, someone has to be losing.

And this is why I stick to my game plan, because if I don't, I lose.

And I've most certainly lost this one.

"Are you doing okay?"

I glance over at Kate who's driving us to one of Beau's parties. I made her promise at least ten times that Drake wouldn't be there tonight. "Yeah, I'm actually looking forward to getting out. It's been a long week."

She smiles sympathetically as she turns down Beau's street. "Tonight's going to be a good night. I guarantee it."

I survey the street, noting that it's not quite as packed as it usually is during one of these. "Where is everyone?"

"We're a little early. I told Beau we'd help setup," she says, putting the car in park and straightening the front strands of her hair in the rearview mirror.

"What is there to setup?"

She opens the door, ignoring my question. "Are you coming?"

I climb out of the car and follow her, smoothing out the leather miniskirt she talked me into wearing along the way.

It was on clearance at one of those discount department stores, and I think there was a pretty good reason for that.

The nerves don't start to set in until we're on our way up the stairs. I came to have one last hurrah before I bury myself in my books again, but I don't need to see Drake, or replace him with another Drake.

Kate starts fidgeting with the rings on her fingers as we come to a stop in front of Beau's door. Usually, she'd be the one to knock, but she hasn't done it yet.

"Are you okay?" I ask, trying to read the expression on her face.

She shrugs, clasping her hands in front of her. "Beau and I had a little argument earlier, and I guess I'm just a little nervous."

"Like you have anything to be nervous about," I say, knocking on the old wooden door. Honestly, that guy will love her until the day he dies no matter what she does.

As the door opens, my eyes go wide.

Kate's hand wraps around my arm, pushing me into the apartment. "Don't hate me. This was the only way I could get you here."

The apartment is dark for the most part, lit by a few candles set up on the dining table. There are six white tulips in a vase in the center, and table settings for two. Soft music plays in the background, but it's all too muffled to make out because my heart is beating into my ears.

I turn to Kate who has her bottom lip hidden between her teeth. "What's going on?"

Before she gets a chance to answer, I spot a dark figure coming around the corner. It's hard to make out who it is at first. "This is our first date."

"Drake," I whisper, recognizing the voice. This is ... this is just not okay.

"Em, I want another chance to do this right. I fucked up, and this is my apology."

"What are you sorry for?" I swallow the huge lump in my throat. A part of me wants to back out the door and run home; the other part of me wants to stay.

He takes two steps toward me, the candlelight allowing me to see his face for the first time. "For treating you like you were just another girl."

Two more steps. If he really wanted to, he could touch me.

"Because you're not just another girl."

With a couple more steps, his chest touches mine, and his lips tentatively press to my forehead. He smells so damn good ... like clean citrus. Warmth pools between my legs forcing me to shift on my feet. It shouldn't be this hard to stay away from him.

Why does he have to be my exception?

"Words are just words without meaning. Tell me, Drake, what makes me different?"

I'm expecting him to stumble, to have to think about his words, but he doesn't hesitate. "You're feisty. And you don't put up with my shit. You don't care that I'm the quarterback. You're the girl who wants to know me, not just be seen with me. You're also the girl who'll come to my room to fix my injured shoulder even though I've been a dick."

He cups my face in his hands, rubbing his thumbs along my cheekbones. "You're the only one who can wake me up from my nightmare."

Closing my eyes, I lick my lower lip. For once, I'm going to choose my words carefully. Let my thoughts simmer before I release them. Making hasty decisions hasn't worked out too well for me lately.

"What do you want from me Drake?"

"I just want to be with you, Em. I'm done with this back and forth, this tug-of-war ... I want to erase the doubt you feel every time we're together. I want you to know after I leave that I'm coming back. I want to know that you're there for me even when I try to push you away." He leans in, his warm breath tickling my skin. "What's holding you back? What can I do to fix this?"

Wrapping my hands around the back of his head, I pull his lips to mine. He's my vulnerability, or maybe my strength. Time will tell. All I know right now is it's been five days since his lips were on mine, and that's too damn long.

This kiss is gentle, his lips simply slow dancing with mine. When I press my tongue against the seam of his lips, he denies me, kissing me softly one more time before pulling back. "We're just going to talk tonight."

For once, that word disappoints me, but at the same time, I know we need it. "Okay," I whisper.

He smiles. "I made you dinner."

"You made me dinner?"

Grabbing my hand in his, he leads me to the table. "It's nothing too fancy, but we have roast, potatoes, and carrots. It's my specialty."

"It sounds better than anything I can get in the cafeteria." He lets go of my hand and pulls my chair out, allowing me to sit down.

I watch as he walks to the kitchen. His jeans mold to him perfectly. His blue flannel shirt hugs his chest and arms, showcasing all the hard work on the football field. He could wear just about anything, and it would look good on him. As he comes back my way with a large dish filled with food, I inhale, letting the savory smell overwhelm my nose. "It smells delicious."

"Let's eat. The smell has been playing with my stomach all day. I can't take it any longer. Ladies first." He sits in the chair next to me, adjusting the tongs so I can reach them.

"Thank you," I say, smiling at him.

We're quiet for a couple minutes, each loading our plates with as much as they can possibly hold. It's weird how things don't happen the way you expect them to, but yet they end up happening exactly the way you need. My walls are caving in little by little. It's as if I've stepped into this whole new world of living that makes me wonder if I was ever really alive before.

"You look nice. I like that skirt," Drake says, breaking through the silence.

I feel my face turning a deep red ... I've never been more grateful for a candlelight dinner. "Thank you."

He laughs, reaching across the table for my hand, brushing his fingers across my knuckles. "I'm glad you came."

"Me too," I whisper, feeling the gentle squeeze of his hand.

Everything is quiet again as we enjoy our dinner. It's delicious ... the roast is tender, falling apart in my mouth. The potatoes and carrots are seasoned to perfection. It's really the best thing I've tasted in a really long time.

"I make this for my sisters all the time. It's the one thing besides grilled cheese that they'll both eat."

"Yeah, what are their names by the way?"

He's talked about them here and there, but he's never called them by their names.

"Tessa and Quinn."

"Tell me about them. Are they anything like you?"

He hesitates, eyes focused on his half-eaten plate. If he would just open up ... "Tessa is the younger one. She's eleven now. She likes basketball, but other than that, she's a typical girl. Boys, shoes, and an incredibly large collection of clothes. Quinn is fifteen, and she's a little more complex. I guess you could say she's the female version of me: stubborn and driven."

I entwine my fingers with his. "What about your mom?"

His eyes snap to me. His mouth opens like he wants to say something, but nothing comes out. Not right away, anyway. When he's finally able to speak, his voice is so hushed I can barely hear him. "Em, there are some things that are just really hard for me to talk about. She's one of them."

I run my thumb along the inside of his fingers, feeling the rough, calloused skin I've become accustomed to. "At some point, you need to. You'll get a lot further if you leave the past behind. It's weighing you down."

His jaw works back and forth as he closes his eyes. I wait patiently, hoping that by not pushing him, he'll be able to take this step all by himself. Today might not be the day he opens up to me, but he will someday ... he needs to.

"It's so hard when you rely on someone for everything, and then one day, they're gone. Completely checked out. It's so hard to see her there but not actually feel it." His hand leaves mine, and he rests his elbows on the table, gripping his hair between his fingers. "This might sound bad, but in many ways, losing my mom the way we did was worse than losing Dad. At least with him, we knew he wasn't coming back."

I scoot my chair closer to his, rubbing my hand across his back. His eyes are still pinched shut. It's a way to keep the painful emotions inside. There's so much we release through our eyes without realizing it. "Your sisters are lucky to have you," I whisper, pressing my cheek against his shoulder.

He rests his head on mine. "They might not see it that way when they're ready to date."

"I assumed you weren't going to let them."

He scoffs, nudging me with his shoulder. "We both know that the will of a woman is nothing to fight. They're going to do it whether I let them or not. I might as well just lay down some rules."

"I'm sure they'll be fine."

"Yeah, as long as they stay away from guys like their brother, they'll be great," he says, kissing the top of my head.

I sit up straight, searching for his eyes. I wait until I find them before speaking again. "Really? I don't think he's so bad."

"And you've seen the worst parts of him," he says, running his thumb along my lower lip. I stare at him, letting the silence speak for me while I wait for his mouth to touch mine. Luckily, I don't have to wait long.

When he's done eating, he picks his plate up and reaches for mine. "Are you finished?"

I push my plate forward, a signal for him to take it. While he wanders off to the kitchen to rinse the dishes, I put the leftovers in containers and stick them in the fridge. The normalness of all this puts a smile on my face. Tonight we're acting like a regular couple, doing regular things, and it's by far the best first date I've ever had.

After I'm done, I stretch out on the couch and wait for him. The stupid skirt is cutting into my stomach, and I'm learning that leather is something I should avoid when I plan on eating more than a few leaves of lettuce.

When he's still not back a couple minutes later, I open the movie cabinet by the TV and search for something to watch. I don't know how much time will actually be spent looking at the screen, but I still want to pick something we'll both like.

The first one that catches my eye is *The Fugitive*. I've had this weird obsession with Harrison Ford since I was a kid.

Settling back on the couch, I pull a blanket over me and make myself comfortable.

"*The Fugitive*, huh?"

I lift my head, noticing Drake standing at the end of the couch. "If you don't like it, we can watch something else."

He walks to me, placing one hand behind me on the couch and the other in front, effectively caging me in. "The movie is fine. Do you care if I join you?"

"I've been waiting."

He leans in, tenderly kissing my lips. "Wait no more."

He climbs in behind me, pressing his chest to my back, tangling his legs with mine. It just feels right.

"Em," he whispers, pressing his hand to my stomach. "I need you to know this isn't about sex for me. It never has been. I just ... I don't want you to feel that way."

I flip around to face him, staring into his dark eyes while brushing a few strands of hair from his forehead. "If I ever thought you were just in this for sex, we wouldn't be here now."

Wrapping his hand behind my neck, he draws my lips close to his. "I'm so fucking glad you can see right through me," he says before kissing me.

"You make it pretty easy, Chambers."

"I'm sorry if this night wasn't as exciting as you hoped. I think I suck at this date stuff," he whispers, running the back of his fingers up and down my arm.

"This is one of the best dates I've ever been on."

He laughs, gently brushing his fingers through my hair. "You don't need to feed my ego. It's already big enough."

"True," I say, patting his chest.

"I love when you agree with me."

My eyelids are getting heavier and heavier. I lay my head against his chest, craving the comfort and closeness. "I'm tired, Drake."

"Do you want me to take you home?" he asks, playing with my hair again. "I have dessert, but we can skip it."

"It depends. What do you have?"

As he laughs, his chest vibrates against my side. "Vanilla bean ice cream with berries."

Sitting up, I kiss the cleft of his chin. "How about if we have some ice cream, and then you can take me home."

He kisses me back, on the lips this time. "Deal. Oh, before I forget, I have something for you. Wait here."

I stand and watch as he disappears down the narrow hallway, patiently waiting to see what he has up his sleeve now. Shifting on my feet, I wipe my sweaty palms against my shirt while I come up with ideas of what it could be. In the end, I can't get past the fluttery feeling in my stomach long enough to come up with anything solid.

When he comes back into view, I immediately recognize the gift bag and tissue paper as the same one he'd given me outside of class after our presentation. "You didn't have to get me anything," I say, letting him place the handle on my fingers.

"This is about starting over, Em. Remember that."

I nod, pulling the skinny white handles apart. I throw the tissue paper on the table in front of the couch and reach inside, pulling out the same jersey I'd worn a few weeks ago and another white envelope.

"Will you come to my game tomorrow?" he asks, biting the corner of his lip.

"Of course," I squeal, jumping into his waiting arms. If someone had told me weeks ago that I'd be this excited to go to a football game, I would have told them they were crazy.

Chapter 20
DRAKE

WHEN I DROPPED EMERY OFF, I walked her all the way to her door, holding her hand the entire time. I stayed true to my word, not pushing any of the limits I had set for myself. I wanted it to feel like a first date, with good intentions.

When I kissed her goodnight, I made sure that when she woke up this morning, she'd still remember it. I wanted it to be the type of kiss she'd still think about years from now, and it wasn't that the other ones didn't matter, but this was the first honest kiss.

"Hey, Drake, Coach wants to talk to you in his office."

I groan. It's James, the team manager. I don't have anything against him, but Coach tends to make him do all the crap work, and this can't be good. "Tell him I'll be right there."

I pull my jersey over my pads and lace up my shoes first. I want this game to be over so I can hang out with Emery. We have plans after the game, and I still have a lot to prove.

Knocking on Coach's door, I wait for him to call me in. Common courtesy isn't usually my thing, but it's not a good idea to piss the coach off before a game. He has the power to bench my ass, and if I get benched, I might as well kiss any chance of a pro career goodbye.

"Come in!" he shouts through the door.

I walk right in and sit front of his large wooden desk. The first thing I always do is try to read his expression. If the muscle in his jaw is twitching, it's not going to be good. If his hand is anywhere near his forehead, he's worried about something. The way the top of his head shines under the fluorescent light hints to a lot of time spent doing the later. In fact, his fingers are pressed to his temples right now.

"What's up?"

He sits back in his large, black leather office chair, hands clasped behind his head. "I just wanted to remind you of today's importance. The importance of the rest of the season."

I sigh, rubbing my sweaty palms against my thighs. "You never let me forget it."

He leans forward, sitting as close to me as his desk allows. "And what are you going to do to help us get there?"

"I'm here, aren't I?"

"Are you here, Chambers, because some days I doubt it. Don't let this be one of those days." He pauses, looking down at his expensive gold watch. "Your dad is looking down on you."

My jaw works overtime, trying to hold back a few things I shouldn't say. It's so hard to hold back this much fucking anger, though. I hate when Coach plays that card. For one, he never met my dad, and two, he reminds me that this is my dad's dream.

Not mine.

"Can I go now, Coach? I need to warm up." I brace my arms on the old wooden chair, ready to bolt as soon as I get the chance.

"Go ahead. Do what you have to do to get us the win."

I leave without a goodbye. There's not much point when I know I'm going to see him out on the field again in minutes.

My stomach starts to turn as I walk back into the locker room to pick up my towel. If I didn't already have enough weight on my shoulders, Coach just reminded me how heavy it is.

As I head toward the field, I twist my wristband, over and over again. I survey the green grass, refusing to look up in the stands until I'm in the middle of the field.

As I gaze up into the student section, I feel my feet under me again. A fucking beautiful as hell girl with long dark hair is waving at me. And what makes it even better is she has my number across her chest. God, I'm glad she used the ticket I gave her.

I rub my hand over my chest, a gesture I hope only she picks up on. She smiles, doing the exact same thing.

Yeah, I can do this shit. It's nothing I haven't done before.

It ends up being one of the best games I've played all season. I threw for three touchdowns, ran for one, and didn't throw a single interception. If I can play like that the rest of the season, I won't have any trouble keeping Coach happy.

"You coming to the party tonight, Chambers?" Trip asks. I think he plays for the stupid fucking post-game parties.

"Not tonight."

"Yeah? Is there something going on I don't know about?"

I laugh, using a towel to scrub the excess water from my hair. "Trust me. If there was something better going on, you'd know about it way before I would."

He slams his locker shut and throws his duffle bag over his shoulder. "You're right. I'll see you later, man."

Shaking my head, I watch him disappear out the locker room door. Again, I'm one of the last guys left in the locker room. I pull on my long-sleeve white button-down and throw my blazer over top. It's time to claim my prize.

This time as I step out into the hallway, I don't have to wonder if Emery will be there or not. She's opposite the door, relaxing against the old cement wall.

"Hey," I say, crossing the hallway.

She straightens, a huge smile playing on her lips. "Good game, number twelve."

I cup one side of her face in my hand, brushing my thumb across her lower lip. "Did it earn me a celebratory kiss?"

Her tongue touches the pad of my thumb, teasing me. "I suppose I could swing that."

My eyes lock on hers, mirroring the tender, softness in them. The second my hand moves down to her neck, her arms wrap tightly around me, pulling my lips down to hers. It was my idea to take this slow this time, but moments like this make that so fucking hard. I suck her lower lip between mine, listening to the soft moan that escapes her.

Her hand presses against the back of my head, begging for more. I answer, tangling my tongue with hers. Our lips mold together perfectly. I'm so fucking glad I'm one of the last ones to leave.

I'm not hiding her any longer. If anyone wants to say anything about our relationship, they're going to meet my fist.

I trace the inside of her lips one last time before pulling back. If I don't stop this now, I never will. "Are you ready to go?" I ask, wrapping my hand around hers.

She nods, matching me step for step. The last time we walked out of here together, I fucked up. Not this time. I'm holding onto her as tightly as I can until I don't have any other choice.

"So, where are we going tonight?"

"Kate asked if we wanted to go to a new club downtown with her and Beau? I didn't tell her yes or no yet because I wanted to ask you first." She smiles nervously, looking up at me from the corner of her eye.

I've never had someone care so much about what I think before. It's nice. "I'm up for anything as long as we don't have to play football. Is that what you want to do?"

She shrugs. "I don't know. I don't think clubs are really my scene, but I've never been to one before so I don't know. We could go to that little coffee shop on campus. It's open late."

Club or coffee shop? I'd pick the club every time. This is probably just the beginning of many differences to come. "There's no decision to make there. We're going to the club."

A couple guys are still lingering in the parking lot when we reach my car, and in an effort to erase what happened last time, I envelop her in my arms and kiss her. Her body's tense at first, but then relaxes, leaning into me. When I pull back, I kiss the tip of her nose, noticing how cool her skin feels.

"Was that redemption?" she teases, wrapping her hands around my upper arms.

"You can call it whatever you want, Em. I'm going to stick with fucking amazing."

Her chest vibrates against mine. "At least we agree it was good."

Reaching my arm around her, I open the passenger side door. "Let's get out of here."

She climbs in, appearing relaxed, and stretches her long legs out in front of her. The way she looks up at me with a smile, eyes sparkling, damn near knocks the wind out of me. *What is this girl doing to me?*

I run around the front of the car and jump in, rubbing my cold hands together. I hate the gloves that coach gives me, and I usually refuse to wear them because they mess with my grip on the ball. On days like this, I'm surprised I have any damn feeling left in my hands.

"Do you want me to take you home so you can change before we go out?"

"If we're going to the club tonight, yes." She gets this mischievous look on her face, like a kid with a master plan to rob the cookie jar. I don't think there will be many boring moments with this girl.

"Just make sure you actually wear clothes that cover your whole body," I say, reaching for her hand.

"You don't have to worry about me." She winks, and I know I'm in big trouble.

Fuck.

Chapter 21
Emery

"ARE YOU SURE THIS LOOKS OKAY? I feel like I don't have anything on."

Kate lifts my arms up to the side, surveying the length of my skirt. "You're fine. Beau and I went once before, and that skirt looks long in comparison."

Standing in front of the full-length mirror, I evaluate the outfit Kate helped me pick out. The skirt is red, form fitting and short ... it definitely doesn't pass the straight-arm test. I'm more comfortable with the black off-the-shoulder sweater she picked to go with it, though. The heels, on the other hand, are killer. I stand at least four inches taller than I normally do. *Thank God Drake's six-four.*

"Kate, Drake's not going to like this."

Kate comes up behind me, seeing exactly what I see. "Oh, he'll like it. He just won't like watching other guys like it."

I laugh, pulling some of my curls in front of my shoulders. "That's not likely to happen."

"You'll see," she says, walking back to her closet.

"You don't strike me as the type who enjoys this club stuff," I say honestly. Kate's a lot like me ... we both work hard and generally lay low.

Pulling out a black corset, she holds it in front of her. "I didn't think I was either, but Beau thought I should try it once, and it was fun. It's different than parties, you know? There's a few more rules and a little less, uh, nakedness going on."

"Well, that's reassuring," I say, rolling my eyes.

"You're going to have fun. You'll see." She holds up a green halter-top next. "Which one do you like better?"

"The green, no question."

"I knew you'd say that."

While she finishes getting dressed, I put my money and ID into my black clutch. I check my phone, anxious for ten o'clock to roll around. Things are so new, and I guess I'm afraid that if we're apart too long, he'll change his mind and pull back again.

"How do I look?"

I look up at Kate and smile. She looks like a typical country girl: green halter-top, denim mini skirt, and worn cowboy boots. "You look like you."

She grimaces, sticking her hands in her pockets. "If you don't want to wear that, it's okay. I mean, I want you to be comfortable."

"You know, it would probably be good for me to take a risk every once in a while."

She laughs. "That's not really what I'd call a risk."

A knock at the door interrupts us. Kate runs in front of the mirror, tucking a few strands of hair behind her ear. "It's time."

I'm relieved when she opens the door. I need a few more seconds to prepare myself for what's about to come. Right away, Beau whistles, spinning Kate around in a circle. His smile is as wide as I've ever seen as his bright eyes drink her in.

Behind them is Drake, dressed in jeans and a long-sleeve black button-down, rolled up his forearms. He can make the simplest outfits look good. I stand nervously, one leg crossed over the other as he walks my way.

I expected big eyes or a smile, but instead he wears a scowl on his strong features. "You need to change your skirt," he says, low enough that only I can hear him.

I follow his gaze, getting an eye full of my bare legs. "What's wrong with it?"

He wraps his arms around my waist, pulling me into his body. "If you do anything but stand still in that damn thing, there's not going to be anything left to the imagination." He leans in, pressing his lips to the spot right under my ear. "I'm the only one who doesn't have to use his imagination, Em, and I want to keep it that way."

A shiver runs the length of my body. This whole taking things slow stuff is harder than I thought. "This skirt's so tight it's not going anywhere. Besides, I'm yours no matter what anyone does, says, or sees. You should know that by now."

"Stay by me tonight, got it?"

I nod, looking up at him with wide eyes.

He growls, lifting my chin between his thumb and forefinger. "You're killing me."

"I didn't make the rules."

He kisses me lightly a couple times over. "Fuck the rules."

Beau clears his throat from behind Drake. "Do you guys want us to leave you alone or are you coming?"

"We're coming," Drake answers, pulling away from me. His fingers find mine, guiding me toward the door.

Beau only has room in his truck for two so Drake takes me in his own car. Honestly, I'm relieved to be alone with him. It's when I feel the most comfortable.

"What are you doing for Thanksgiving?" he asks out of the blue. It's only a little over a week away, and I haven't given it any thought.

"I haven't decided yet. I should go home because my dad will be alone, but I don't know if I want to."

"I can't go home that weekend because we have a game on Friday … last one of the season," he says as we pull into downtown.

It's a lot more vibrant than campus with bright lights and sidewalks full of people. I've been in Iowa City for a couple months, but I haven't gotten out much. It's sad when

I think about all the things I could be missing out on while I'm buried in my own little world.

"Do you want company?" I ask, turning my attention back to him.

He pulls into an empty parking spot along the street. "I don't want to hold you back. You should be with your dad."

Without waiting for my response, he opens his door, walking around the front of the car to my side. He helps me out, wrapping my hand in his again.

As soon as we're on the sidewalk, I tug on his arm, halting us in place. "I want to stay here with you. I wouldn't offer if I didn't … you should know that by now."

With one quick motion, my chest is pressed against his, his lips an inch from mine. "I want you here with me."

Brushing some hair from his forehead, I say, "Sounds like we're spending Thanksgiving together."

"I'll get you a ticket to the game. It's the biggest one of the year, you know? Southern Iowa versus Nebraska. If we don't win, I'm going to hear about it for the next twelve months."

"You'll be fine, football stud," I tease, kissing his cool lips.

He releases me, leading us toward a brick building with a red door. It's nothing special on the outside, but two large bouncers standing guard.

Squeezing Drake's hand, I ask, "How old do you have to be to get in here?"

"Eighteen. You're fine," he replies, bumping my shoulder with his.

The bouncers check our IDs and collect the cover before allowing us through the door.

"Do you want something to drink?" Drake asks, pulling us through the crowd that stands inside the entryway.

"Can we find Beau and Kate first? They should be here by now."

He laughs, pointing to the corner near the dance floor. "Found them."

I guess sometimes it pays to be tall, because I'm having trouble seeing what he's seeing. Noticing my struggle, he grips my hips and hoists me up. "See them now?"

Kate's up against the back wall on the dance floor while Beau stands between her parted legs. His hands circle her hips, and his head is buried in her neck. They're definitely here, and they're definitely enjoying each other. "I'll take a water."

He puts me down, pressing his lips to my cheek. "Stay here. I'll be right back."

I wring my hands as I watch him disappear into the crowd. Being alone in the center of a packed club is not my idea of a good time. Guys stare me down as they walk past, while a few girls give me a sideways glance. I do my best to keep my eyes on Drake, silently begging him to hurry up and get back over here.

When I'm about ready to give up and join him at the bar, a Tyga song pumps through the club, setting my body in motion. Growing up, we always listened to country because Dad got to control the radio dial, but inside I've always been a closet hip-hop fan. Country is for when I'm feeling down or just want something mellow in the background while I study. Hip-hop ignites me, giving me energy when I have none.

After a few verses, I'm completely lost in the song. My shoulders, hips, and feet all move to the beat. It's the most relaxing, freeing feeling in the world. As the music speeds up, I close my eyes, burying my fingers in my hair.

I hear low whistles and open my eyes. I'm surrounded by a group of men, but right in front of me is Drake. I stare into his hooded eyes as his tongue sweeps across his lower lip. There's at least 300 people packed into this club, but right now, it feels like we're the only ones in the room.

I've lived nineteen years in a safe little box, but when I feel what I do right now, I wonder why I stayed there so long. I feel so freaking alive.

Without taking my eyes off Drake, I begin to move my hips again. The music's bumping. Smoke is filling the dark room. Lights are flashing in and out. I'm lost in the moment … Drake's lost in me.

I want his hands on me, covering every inch of my skin. I want his warm lips on my neck. He starts toward me, and when I'm close enough to touch, he grips my hips tightly, pulling them to his. His hardness is pressed between my legs; clothes are the only things keeping us from doing what my body is now craving.

He wraps his arm around my lower back, keeping me close while his lips cover every inch of my jawline. "You're so sexy, Em. So sexy."

The music picks up again, his legs mingled with mine. His hot mouth exploring my neck. I've never been more turned on in my whole life. I don't even care that others are watching us.

One of his hands brushes my hair away from my neck, holding it there, while the other finds its way up the back of my shirt. I need to get out of here. Soon. "Drake," I pant, hating myself for interrupting him. I freaking love what he's doing to my body.

"Let's get the fuck out of here, Em. Now." He kisses me on the mouth for the first time since we started dancing and looks deep into my eyes.

I nod, just as anxious to get out of here. His hands move down my ass, tugging my skirt down as far as it will go. He's guarding what's his, and I want to take care of what's mine.

I need him tonight.

He grabs my hand in his, pushing us through the crowd. "Do you think I should go tell Kate we're leaving?" I ask, looking over my shoulder.

He doesn't miss a beat. "Text her."

I'm not going to argue with that.

When the door opens, the cool air hits my skin, and it feels amazing. Drake and that club were just too much.

He's quiet, moving us as fast as he can with my tall heels on. He quickly unlocks the door and opens it for me. I step down from the curb, ready to climb in, but he has other plans for me, wrapping his arm around my waist to pull me to him again. He kisses me like he's been deserted on an island for years and is seeing me for the first time. He's so hungry, and it's making me so damn needy.

"I don't want to stop," he groans, kissing the corner of my mouth.

"I don't want you to."

"I need to be inside you, Emery." He stares at me a little too long.

"Why are we standing here then?"

He practically shoves me in the car and runs to the driver's side. His hand settles on my bare thigh as he drives as fast as legally possible to get us back quickly.

"Are you sure about this?" he asks as we pull into the parking lot.

"Drake, I'm so turned on right now, if you don't take care of it, we're going to have a problem."

"Fuck," he says under his breath.

When the car stops, I hop out before he has a chance to open my door for me.

The anticipation.

The wait.

It's all making me crazy.

Drake walks behind me, his hands on my hips. I use my key to get us through the door and start up the steps.

"Is this as fast as you can go?"

"Heels, Drake."

"Fuck it," he says, lifting me in his big strong arms. He carries me the distance, only putting me down when we reach my door. I quickly unlock it and enter. The door clicks behind me, and seconds later his hand touches my stomach, pulling me back into his hard chest.

I want to savor it. I want him to touch me, to kiss me, but I also need him deep inside me sooner rather than later.

His fingertips trail up my stomach to the space between my breasts before tracing my collarbone. Every nerve in my body tingles.

"Dance with me, Em," he whispers, his warm breath tickling my ear.

Leaning my head back against his shoulder, I circle my hips again, purposefully rubbing against his hard cock. He squeezes my shoulders then slides his hands down to my breasts, his palms brushing against my nipples.

"Drake."

His teeth graze my earlobe, and I moan. I can't take it anymore. I want to face him, but his grip on me is too tight.

He walks us forward until my knees hit the bed. "Do you trust me?" he asks, tracing small circles on my stomach.

I nod. I trust him with everything I have right at this moment.

"How much do you need me, Em?"

"Now, Drake." I'm done talking.

I hear the zipper on his jeans and more moisture instantly pools between my legs. "Put your hands on the bed."

All reason is gone. I don't care what he's going to do as long as he does it soon. His fingers grasp the bottom of my skirt, pulling it up over my ass. My panties are next, being pulled down to my knees. Not even a second later, the tip of his cock is teasing my entrance.

I want him so bad.

"Please," I beg, rolling my hips.

In one motion, he presses all the way into me. The sensation, the way he fills me, is like nothing I've ever felt before. He thrusts into me over and over again. It's carnal. Erotic. If I could talk right now, I'd be begging for more.

His hands cup my breasts, circling underneath them while his thumbs run across the top of my nipples. I love this side of him. I love that he makes it feel okay to do things I never thought I'd do.

"How does that feel?"

I moan, unable to speak.

His fingers find their way between my legs, applying pressure where I need them. "Let go, Em."

His words are enough for me. My muscles clench tightly around him, over and over again. It feels so damn good; I have trouble controlling my screams.

He follows, groaning as he pumps into me, as his fingers dig into my flesh. "Fuck."

His arms wrap around my stomach, his chest pressed to my back. I feel the rapid beat of his heart. It's overpowering, like his heart is mine.

Maybe it is.

"Feel better?" he asks, kissing the center of my back.

"You have no idea," I mumble, pressing my cheek against the comforter. My legs ache; I'm going to be sore tomorrow after the dancing and sex. "Stay with me tonight?"

"Do you want me to?"

"Yes," I whisper. "I want to know you'll still be here in the morning."

His body lifts off mine, and his strong hands pull my upper body from the bed, turning me around. "I'll be here."

I wrap my arms around his neck, kissing his chin. "I know."

Chapter 22

DRAKE

EMERY'S LEGS ARE TANGLED WITH MINE, her head resting in the crook of my arm. It's much like the way we fell asleep last night, which shows just how tired we were. I never pictured life like this, at least not any time soon. I could stare at her long eyelashes and full pink lips all day long.

I run the back of my hand along the smooth skin of her back, remembering everything we did last night. Once wasn't enough ... I can never get enough of her. My fingers continue upward, tangling in her long, soft hair. It always smells like cherries. I hated cherries until I met her.

"Mmm." She wraps her arms tightly around her pillow, looking content.

I brush some hair from her face, giving me a better view of her rosy cheeks. "Hey, sexy, did you sleep well?"

"Yeah." She sighs into her pillow, opening her big brown eyes. "You?"

I lay my head next to hers, placing my palm on her cheek. "Like a baby."

Pressing my lips to hers, I let them linger a little longer than I normally do. A sweet girl like her deserves a sweet morning wake up.

I pull back, gently nuzzling her nose with mine. "What's the plan for today?"

"I have to study for a couple exams and finish a paper. The professors are piling it on me before Thanksgiving break."

"Do you need a study partner?" I wonder if she sees the twinkle in my eye with the bright morning light sneaking through the curtains.

She taps her index finger on my chin, pulling her bottom lip between her teeth. "Wouldn't you consider yourself more of a distraction?"

I laugh, tightly wrapping my arm behind her back. "Call me what you want, but I'm your favorite distraction."

Her eyes brighten. It's like a light bulb went off inside her head. "My favorite quarterback. My favorite study buddy. My favorite distraction. My favorite ..." She pauses, but I know what she was going to say, and a part of me is dying for the word to escape her lips.

"What were you going to say?"

"Nothing. I just got a little carried away with my favorites." Her eyes fixate on my forehead as she uses her fingertips to push a few strands of hair away from my brow.

Grabbing her wrist gently in my hand, I halt her progress. "Please say it."

She swallows, her eyes finding mine again. "My favorite boyfriend." Her voice is only a hair louder than a whisper, hesitant and shaky.

"That's my favorite of your favorites," I whisper, brushing my lips against hers. We've never taken the time to talk about what we are, just that we're investing in each other.

She lets out a breath, and I roll her to her back, seating myself between her bare legs. There are pluses to falling asleep with no clothes on.

I'm going to show Emery my favorite right now.

This place is becoming too familiar. I have my regular spot ... there are actually people here every day who leave it open for me. And the smell of old books … I'm starting to like that, too.

I guess this is the power of a woman on display. Emery could probably get me to go on a historical tour of the city, or sit through one of those stupid ballets or musicals. She could get me to do just about anything.

"What are we studying today?" I ask Emery as I settle into the chair across from her. Her hair is pulled up in a bun, dark glasses perched on her nose, and a pencil tucked behind her ear. She never tries too hard to impress me, and it makes her that much sexier.

Peeking up at me, she smiles. "Anatomy."

I rub my foot against her calf, running the eraser of my pencil across my lower lip. "I can definitely help you with that."

"Drake, is there any topic that doesn't make you think about sex?"

I think about it for a second. Not too much, though, because I already know the answer. "I can't think of many."

She pulls her glasses off, rubbing the skin under her tired eyes. "I can't wait to get a little break. This stuff is so exhausting."

Reaching across the table, I cover her small hand with mine. "Quit being so hard on yourself. Not everything has to be so fucking perfect, Em."

"I'm all I got, Drake. If I don't work hard, I could lose my scholarship. If I lose my undergrad scholarship, there's no freaking chance I'm going to graduate school."

I'm about to tell her that it doesn't matter. That school isn't going to make or break her, but then I remember I'm in the same fucking predicament. Mine just involves tossing a ball around and winning as many games as I can.

I nod, squeezing her hand. "I get it, but maybe we can work on mixing some more fun in with these trips to the library."

"Hey, I think we've been having lots of fun," she says, her eyes growing larger.

"A party." She grimaces, but it doesn't stop me. "I know they're not your favorite, and to be honest, they're not mine either, but my teammates are giving me crap about missing them."

"I have a test in the morning," she says, tilting her head to one side.

"Let's make a deal. You study for the rest of the afternoon while I go to practice, and when I'm done, we'll go, even if it's just for a while."

I can see her wheels turning as she stares at me. "Fine, I'll go, but I'm not staying out late."

Standing up, I walk to her side of the table and kiss the top of her head. "Don't worry, I'll have you home by ten."

"PM," she adds, wrapping her hand around the back of my head.

I lean in, placing my finger under her chin to lift her face and kiss her soft lips. "I'll pick you up at eight. I promise not to be late."

She laughs. "Drake's a poet, and he didn't even know it."

"Oh, he knows it," I say, walking away.

Five hours later, I've completed a grueling practice, thanks to Coach's need to make sure everything is perfect. He played football in college. He should know that no matter how much you prepare, it all comes down to who has it on game day. It's not just about skill.

My phone rings from my back pocket as I walk out onto the parking lot. I pull it out, hoping to see Emery's name across the screen, but I see my sister, Tessa's, instead.

I press the button quickly. She never calls me. "Hello?"

"Hey, Drake, umm, Mom wanted me to call and ask if you're coming home for Thanksgiving."

Of course she'd have my sister call me. I've been avoiding her calls for a few days. "I'm sorry, Tess, I can't."

"But we want you to," she whines. I never feel bad letting Mom down, but my sisters are different. I think my mom knows it, too.

"I have a game on Friday. By the time I get home, I'd have to turn right around and go back to school," I say, rubbing my fingers over my brow.

"Who's going to make the turkey?"

"If I email you the instructions, do you think you and Quinn can handle it this year?" Sadly, I've known how to make a fucking turkey since I was twelve.

She sighs, and the phone remains silent for a few seconds. "I guess."

"Maybe Mom will help. What's she been up to?"

"Working. She got that job at the insurance office, and she's working nights at the steakhouse."

I'm shocked that she got the insurance job, but I recover quickly. "Wow, good for her."

"Yeah, it's been good. I even got a new pair of jeans from the mall," she says excitedly.

"The ones you've been asking me about?" I ask quietly, thinking of all the times she begged me for them. I always had to tell her no.

Looking down at my watch, I notice it's a couple minutes past eight. I'm late picking up Emery. "Hey, Tess, I have somewhere I have to go. I'll call you on Thanksgiving morning to make sure everything is okay?"

"Yeah, sure. Don't forget to email me."

"I won't."

We hang up, and even though I told myself I wouldn't let myself get angry over my mom anymore, I can't help it. For seven years I lived in that house with her, and every day, she walked around like some sort of tame zombie. I supported everyone, and now that I've moved out, she's decided to move on with her life. I guess it's good for my sisters, and I have to just let it go.

I white knuckle it all the way to Emery's dorm, thinking of the times I sold my baseball cards my dad gave me for some extra cash. Or the times in high school I worked way more hours than I should have, burning myself out.

She might be on time to save my sisters, but she's way too fucking late for me.

As I pull into the parking lot, my phone rings again. This time it's Emery. "Hey."

"Hey," she says, sounding worried.

"I'm running a little late, but I'm on my way. Are you ready?"

"I'm ready and waiting."

"Okay, I'm pulling up to your building now if you want to come out. I'll just keep my car running … it's a little chilly out here tonight."

The phone clicks without another word, and I see her running out the front door in her familiar green winter coat. Her dark, tight blue jeans peek out from underneath, and her brown leather boots go up to her knees. But the sexiest thing about her is the white stocking hat with the stupid little ball at the top. I never thought I'd find one of those sexy.

She opens the passenger side door and quickly climbs in, rubbing her bare hands together. "We should get you some gloves. You seem to have everything else."

She scoots across the seat, wrapping her cold hand around the back of my neck. "How does that feel?"

I kiss her. It's been hours … too many fucking hours. "Cold," I mumble against her lips.

"I guess that's what you get for making me go out on a cold night." Her lips touch mine again, much warmer than her ice-cold hand. "It better be worth it."

Pulling back, I run my thumb over her lower lip. "It will be worth it. I promise."

She kisses me again before scooting back to her seat and pulling her seatbelt over her shoulder. As I put my car in reverse, I feel like a little kid right before the bell rings for recess.

When I turn left on the street, she asks, "Aren't the frat houses the other way?"

"Yes."

"Then where are we going?"

"Sit back and enjoy the ride." I grab for her hand, bringing her knuckles to my lips.

"Drake—"

"Seriously, you need to trust me." Everything Emery does is planned out. If I hadn't talked her into going out tonight, we'd be stuck in her room or mine, studying. It's what we've done every night since the club, and I couldn't take another fucking night of it.

"Are you taking me to the movies?"

"No."

"Are we going out for dinner?"

"No, did you eat dinner?"

"Yes. Are you taking me to the mall?"

That earns her a sideways glance. "Do I look like the type of guy who likes to hang out at the mall?"

"No."

"You should just give up. I don't think you'll guess it."

She stares at me, eyes narrowed. "We're not leaving the state, are we?"

I laugh, pulling into a parking space. "Hell no. I'd never get you home by ten then."

She finally notices we've come to a stop and searches the quiet parking lot. "Okay, Drake, you're scaring me a little bit here."

Brushing my fingers against her cheek, I say, "Sit tight."

I open my door and run to her side, eager to unveil the surprise I was able to line up on my way to practice this afternoon. She climbs out of the car, placing her hand in mine. I lead the way to the sidewalk, giving us a view of the city lights again. When we came to the club last weekend, I noticed the sign advertising horse drawn carriage rides from now until Christmas. It's kind of cheesy, but I thought it would be a good way for the two of us to talk without life's distractions getting in the way.

A horse and carriage is stopped along the side of the street with a sign that says Drake & Emery. Squeezing her hand tighter, I walk us toward it, watching out of the corner of my eye for her reaction.

"Did you plan this?" she asks, her eyes wide.

I rub the back of my neck, careful not to let her see too much of my softer side. If I show it to her too much, she'll come to expect it, and I don't know how much of it I have in me. "There was never a party. Not one we were going to go to anyway."

When we're standing next to the carriage, the driver climbs down and holds his hand out to help Emery up. I'm next, but I manage without his help. When we're settled into our seats, he hands us a black and red flannel blanket, which I use to cover our legs. Last, the driver pulls out the two scalding hot cocoas I requested. I thought it would be a nice touch, a way to keep us both warm on a frigid November night.

"You didn't strike me as the type of guy who likes carriage rides," she says, pulling the blanket higher.

"I don't know if I am or not. This is my first time."

She lifts the paper cup to her lips, taking tiny sips. "Mine too."

The streets are relatively quiet as we begin our stroll around downtown Iowa City. The cool air pricks my cheeks, but the rest of my body is warm, pressed against Emery's under the blanket.

The late fall night is as clear as it is cold, giving us a perfect view to the stars. I spend my time glancing between them, the bright, colorful lights that line the street, and people who walk along the sidewalks.

I steal glances at Emery just as often. She looks more relaxed than she has the past few days, and it puts a smile on my face. "What's going through that head of yours?" I ask, entwining my fingers with hers.

"How amazing this is. Thank you," she whispers, pressing her lips to my cheek.

Before she gets too far away, I grab her chin in my fingers. "I think this deserves more than a kiss on the cheek."

She smiles, tucking her lower lip between her teeth. "So you did all this for a kiss?"

I grin, kissing both corners of her mouth. "No, we both know this isn't necessary for that. I did this so we could get away from it all, and just be us. So far, I like us."

"Me too," she whispers.

"Just do me a favor, okay?"

"What's that?"

Moving my lips close to her ear, I whisper, "Don't tell the guys about this. They'll probably make me take a few extra sacks to man me up."

"You're all man. Don't worry about that."

I pull her earlobe between my teeth before kissing the warm skin below her ear. "Will you let me prove it tonight?"

"Every night. You know I will."

The rest of the ride is filled with stolen kisses and stories of playing in the snow as kids. Being with Emery is effortless. I'm not trying to be someone I'm not, or anyone who someone else wants me to be.

Chapter 23
Emery

THANKSGIVING DAY. It's the first one I've spent away from my dad. The fifteenth one I've spent apart from my mom. It's probably dumb to think of it that way, but that's how I've told time since she left.

This is, however, the first Thanksgiving I get to spend with Drake, and I'm already hoping it's not the last. There was a life before Drake, and I'm living in the after … it's by far the best.

The funny part is, we're having Hungry Man frozen dinners on our first holiday together. Not anything Martha Stewart would approve of, but we have to work with what we got.

"I picked up dessert," I say as we finish off the last compartment in our cardboard dinner trays. Not long after we started hanging out, I noticed we both like to eat one food off our plates at a time. I don't know what his excuse is, but I hate when two flavors mix.

"Oreos?" he asks, lifting his brow.

"No, it's a little fancier than that."

"Pie?"

I reach behind me and pull out the container of pumpkin bars with cream cheese frosting. My favorite. "I could probably make them better, but I didn't have access to a kitchen."

He smiles, leaning in to kiss my lips. "They look good, but I can't wait to taste yours."

"Maybe someday."

My phone vibrates on the table, and my dad's name pops up. "I better take this. I don't want him to worry."

Drake nods, turning his attention back to the last of his uneaten food.

"Hello," I say, tracing some of the scratches on the top of the old card table we set up for today.

"Hey, baby, how's Thanksgiving going with your friend?"

"It's good. Just about ready to eat some dessert."

I'd told my daddy I was going home with one of my friends. He wouldn't like it if I told him I stayed here eating frozen dinners with a guy.

"What are y'all having? I just ate some pumpkin pie that I bought at the diner. They treated me pretty good there this year," he says, sounding tired and full.

I look up at Drake who seems lost in a world of cream cheese frosting. "We were just getting ready to have pumpkin pie, too."

I hear him laughing on the other side of the line. "You could never go without your pumpkin. Where did you say you were again?"

I hesitate. I hate lying, and I suck at it. "Carrington with my roommate, Kate."

"Oh yeah, I haven't been to Carrington in forever. Nice place from what I can remember."

I rub my fingertips around my temples, hoping to chase away the building headache. "Yeah, it's great so far."

"Well, baby, I'm going to let you get back at it. Oh, and by the way, Clay says hi. He was at the diner with his parents this morning."

"Okay, Daddy, tell Clay I say hi if you see him again. I'll see you at Christmas."

"Talk to you soon."

"Bye."

Setting my phone back down, I scrub my face with my hands. I'm an adult now so what my daddy knows and thinks shouldn't mean that much to me, but it does. I don't want to disappoint him like my mom did.

When I look up, I notice Drake's not sitting in the chair across from me anymore. He's perched against the wall with his arms folded over his chest. "You told your dad you were in Carrington with Kate?"

My eyes widen. "Yes, I told him I went home with Kate for Thanksgiving. He'd hate the idea of me being here by myself."

He rests the back of his head against the wall, staring up at the ceiling. "Why couldn't you just tell him you're here with me?"

Resting my elbows on the table, I tangle my fingers in my hair. "It's just easier this way. He worries about me too much."

He comes forward, placing his hands on the edge of the table. "Are you afraid your dad won't like me?"

I shake my head, begging him with my eyes to drop it. "No, I just didn't want to explain how long we've been together. Where we met. What your family does for a living. He never stops." I pause, waiting for his eyes to soften. "I'll talk to him when I go home for Christmas break."

"Who is Clay?" he asks, standing up straight again.

I press my fingers to my temples again, working hard just to answer the question—honestly, but carefully enough to not cause any more dents. "My high school boyfriend."

He nods, inhaling a deep breath. When I say that I can see right through Drake, I mean I can read his emotions, but I don't always know what's behind them. Like now, he's pushing away anger, but I can't tell if it's because I didn't tell my dad about him or the mention of Clay's name.

It's hard to explain what Clay and I had exactly. We were great friends. We became lovers, and in the end, we decided we made better friends. There wasn't enough between us for me to stay with him and attempt a long-term relationship, and sadly, I think part of me was holding onto him because my dad liked him so much.

"I should have been honest with him," I whisper, watching his features soften even more.

He walks to me, cupping my face in his calloused hands. "I don't want to fight with you."

"I don't want to fight with you either," I say, leaning into his touch.

"I just never feel like I'm good enough. Not for my family. Not for football, and definitely not for you."

I kiss the palm of his hand. "You're good to me, Drake. That's all that matters."

Tilting my head back, he presses his lips to mine. He treads carefully, nibbling my lower lip first before pulling my upper lip between his. When I'm fully expecting him to deepen it, he breaks contact, pressing his forehead to mine. "I'm going to work on me. I'm going to try and see what you see."

I'd never really admit it out loud, but I like the raw feeling I have inside after an argument. I've spent most of my nineteen years going through the motions, locking things deep within. Letting them out makes me lighter, like it's some magical overnight diet for a struggling soul.

And I want to feel less of that struggle. I want him to know how much he means to me … how much I trust him.

There's something I've never talked to anyone about. Something that's been eating me up, and I think Drake might be the only person who understands. "Remember when I said I saw my mom one time after she left?"

He nods, moving back enough to look into my eyes.

"It was my thirteenth birthday. I'd gone outside to get some fresh air, and a car slowly drove past me. I was scared at first, thinking it was a creeper, but when I saw it was her … it hurt me so much. It was every painful moment I've ever been through wrapped up in one."

"What did she say?" He takes my hands in his as he kneels in front of me.

Tilting my head up, I try to keep my tears at bay. "She drove off without saying a single word." It's all I can say. Anything more and I won't be able to control my emotions. There's so much pain I've kept locked inside for years. It sucks holding it all in, but letting it go scares me even more.

Drake shakes his head, squeezing my hands in his. "Why would she do that?"

Closing my eyes, I think back to when I asked Dad about it a while back … after so much time spent holding it all in. "My dad knew she was in town, and when she asked if she could see me, he told her only if she planned on staying." I pause, trying to gain enough strength to continue. It hurts … so much. "She didn't plan on sticking around so he told her it would be better if she kept her distance. He saw first-hand what it did to me when she left the first time, and didn't want to watch it again. Anyway, I don't think she meant for me to see her that day, but I did … and I haven't seen her since."

Before I even realize what's happening, I'm off the chair, lifted up in strong arms. It's the comfort I never had when I really needed it, and as I wrap my arms tightly around his neck, resting my cheek against his chest, the tears start to flow.

How can there be this much hurt after all this time?

"Let it out, Em. I promise you'll feel better after you do," Drake whispers, brushing his lips against my forehead.

For the first time in fifteen years, I let everything I felt the day mom left come to the surface. I let myself drown for far too long, and now it's even harder to catch my breath.

I have a lot of work to do.

"What she did … it had nothing to do with you. There's nothing you could have done to change her. You're a beautiful person, inside and out; she's missing out, not you."

I grip the front of his t-shirt, fighting to believe his words. God, I want to, but when you're left like that as a little girl, it's hard to tell yourself that it's not because of you.

"Why did she drive by without saying anything? I mean … Dad asked her not to but after she saw me …"

His arms tighten around me. "Maybe she wasn't sure it was you."

Pinching my eyes closed, I say, "My dad had that same truck when I was four. He couldn't afford anything else."

"Fuck, Em, I'm so sorry. When my mom fell into her depression, I never questioned why. I only questioned why she didn't come back. Maybe when we're older, it will make sense." He runs his fingers along my spine before gently combing them through my hair.

"And what if it never does?"

His fingers still. "Then we move on with what we know. We live our own lives, aiming to be something we never had."

I need something to help me forget. I need something to help ease the bleeding in my soul. Sometimes this life is too much. Sometimes it's just enough, but right now, I need it to be just right, and I know exactly how to get there.

Wrapping my hands around the back of Drake's neck, I let my fingers curl into the hair at the base of it. One more look in my needy, pained eyes, and he knows what I'm asking. His tongue slides along my collarbone while he wraps my hair around his hands. As his lips move higher on my neck, his hard length presses between my legs, causing a wonderful friction.

"You taste so fucking good," he says, placing tiny kisses along my jawline.

"Drake," I moan right before his lips capture mine. It's hot. Unrelenting. He kisses me like this might be the last time. Like it's the first. Like it's the sum of every kiss we've ever shared.

He breaks his lips away from mine just long enough to give me some instructions. "Arms up."

I comply, letting him pull my sweater over my head. I lay my back against his bed, but his fingers manage to snake under my back and unfasten my bra, leaving me bare from the waist up.

His fingertips trace the line of my shoulders before dragging down between my breasts. They continue down, stopping to unbutton my jeans.

He splays his hand across my stomach, using his lips to sear the skin his fingertips just touched.

"Hips," he groans, lifting them off the bed. He grips the waistband on my jeans, pulling them down to my ankles. I wiggle and stretch my legs to help him free me completely.

Stretching my arms over my head on the pillow, I watch as he stands and performs his own little strip show. He makes his way back to me, working his mouth up my calves to the inside of my thighs. There's nothing short of an ocean between my legs. He does this to me.

His hot mouth settles between my thighs. "Drake." He uses his tongue to lap my sensitive skin. Closing my eyes, I tug his hair between my fingers. He blows warm air against my aroused skin, sending me closer to the edge.

This is the best feeling in the world. When my body is climbing, all thoughts are gone except for those of the pleasure I'm about to feel, and the way his fingers and tongue dance carefully over my skin.

"Oh my God," I pant, feeling the first orgasm tear through my body. Drake doesn't stop until it's over, continuing to tease me the whole way through.

As he moves back up my body, he nips at my skin, tugging it between his teeth. It's sexy. It's sensual. It's pure bliss. And when his lips touch my throat, he enters me in one fluid motion.

"You fit me so perfectly, Em," he whispers, slowly moving in and out of me. He's right … the way it feels when our bodies are fitted together is impossible to describe.

"You're mine, beautiful. I always want to be your favorite," he breathes against my ear. He pushes into me over and over again, whispering sweet things to me the entire way through. As I build up to my second orgasm, he builds to his, quickening his pace.

"Emery," he growls, pumping into me. I wrap my arms tightly around him, needing to have him as close as possible. Even after sex, he feels so right inside of me. I wish life would leave us uninterrupted so we could live in moments like this.

After a couple minutes, he looks into my eyes through the darkness and gently kisses my lips. "I'm sorry about earlier, Em. I'm stressed out, and I guess I just lost my shit." He kisses me again before laying his flushed cheek against my chest.

"I should be the one saying sorry. I should have been honest with my dad," I whisper, running my fingers up and down his bare back. "Why are you stressed? Is there something I can do?"

"Big game tomorrow. Do or die, you know?" His voice is more full of emotion than I usually hear. Drake appears tough, but he's fragile. I think I'm the only person he lets see it.

"I'll be there."

He lifts his head, kissing the skin between my breasts. "Knowing you're close always helps."

"I'm glad," I whisper tracing the lines on his forehead. "You'll do great. You always do."

Without another word, his eyes begin to drift closed, and he falls asleep with his cheek pressed to my chest. Even with frozen dinners, and our little argument, it's the best Thanksgiving I've ever had.

And I never did get any of those pumpkin bars.

Chapter 24

DRAKE

THIS IS THE ONLY FRIDAY we play football all year. The big post Thanksgiving game between Southern Iowa and Nebraska. These are the days that most guys on my team live for. The days the fans come from miles around for. Since my dad's been gone, the joy behind these days is gone. It's not about me anymore. It's my job. I do it for my team. I do it for my family. I can't say I hate it, because it's the one part of my dad I still have, but my relationship with it has definitely changed over the years. I'm just going through the motions.

"How's the shoulder feeling?" Looking behind me, I see Cole pulling on his pads.

"Nothing to be concerned about," I say, throwing my gloves in my locker.

"If you need us to run shorter routes or anything today, let me know."

I slam my locker door shut, the loud sound of metal quieting the entire locker room. "It's fine. Drop it."

These guys have known me long enough that it shouldn't be new to them that I don't like to be coddled. My dad instilled in me that mental toughness is the most important aspect of the game. I can hear his words in my head right now, *"If you get knocked down, you have to get right back up, kid. Not even Joe Montana could win a game lying down."*

Lisa De Jong

When I walk out of the tunnel, the first thing I notice is the packed stadium. This is one of the biggest games of the year. Each team is undefeated, and the winner gets their ticket to the conference championship stamped. This is one of the goals I've been pressuring myself to reach for years. What my coach has drilled into my head week after week in those meetings I try to avoid.

There's sixty more minutes.

Four more quarters.

One more game until we know we're in it, or it's done.

If we don't make it, there's no way we can play in the National Championship game. There are too many good teams week in, week out that are vying for one of those two spots. They're only awarded to greatness.

"Ready, Chambers?" Coach asks, placing his heavy hand on my shoulder.

I nod, tossing the football around in my hands. "It's no different than any other game. We just have to execute. No mistakes."

"Good, good. James has a few gloves for you to try. It's cold and wet out here."

My stomach turns through the first couple plays. After working with me for almost two years, my offensive coordinator knows how I work and calls two easy run plays. By the time I go under center for the third time, my feet are firmly planted under me, my nerves just a trace of what they were before.

On the third play, with six yards to go for a first down, I drop back, scanning my eyes over the field looking for an open receiver. This is where being calm helps. On my first pass over the field, no one is open, but I keep my shit together and quickly start a second pass. My tight end has freed himself on my right side, raising his hand to give me the signal.

He catches it, gaining even more yardage after the catch. The home crowd roars, and the rest of the tension leaves my body. We score two touchdowns before Nebraska scores their first, and going into halftime, we have a one score lead.

"Good job out there, Chambers," Coach says, patting me on the shoulder. "If the defense can hold up, and you do that again in the second half, the game is ours."

I nod, feeling some of the pressure falling back on my shoulders. I'm good at just doing things, and as soon as someone starts reminding me, I feel like they have no confidence in my abilities. Maybe it's just me. Maybe I read too much into this stupid shit.

When we step back out on the field, the rain is coming down faster, small puddles forming across the field. I've played in these conditions before, and if one thing is for certain, we'll be running the ball a lot more in this half.

You ready to go?" I ask Trevon, our first string running back.

He rolls his neck and bends his knees a couple times. "I'm always ready."

"I'm going to need you a lot this half."

"I'll do what I've got to do for the team," he says, stretching his shoulders out.

Nebraska has the ball first in the second half, but we hold them to a three and out. When the ball is back in my hands, I pass it to Trevon, over and over again, moving the chains several times. I place it in his hands again in the red zone, and he runs hard on third down but is brought down before getting a first down. I start walking away, expecting Coach to bring out the field goal unit. I don't realize that Trevon isn't getting up until I see the training staff run past me.

I squint my eyes, trying to see across the field. It doesn't look good. His arms and legs aren't moving, and after a couple minutes of coaching from the training staff, the cart goes out to the field. I'm trying not to let it get to me because we have a game to finish, but the guy's the heart of our team. We need him.

We make the field goal, but Nebraska scores a touchdown on the next two drives, putting us down by four points. My back-up running back fumbled the ball on his first drive in, and since then, I've been trying to come up with new ways to get down the field.

It's the fourth quarter now. It's go time.

With only a few minutes left to score a touchdown, I take matters into my own hands when I see an opening in the line. I'm not as fast as Trevon, but I'm not the worst running quarterback either. I slice right on through, gaining a first down. The next play, I take a chance and throw it down the field, but it slips through the receiver's hands, landing on the wet ground. If I'm going to do this, it's got to be now.

In the huddle, I call a quarterback run, something so rare it earns me a few dirty looks. I ignore them, getting everyone lined up. After the ball is hiked to me, I tuck it under my arm and take off down the center of the field again. A few tacklers slip, missing me and I speed up.

I didn't see him coming.

The front of my body came down hard on the ground, knocking all the air out of me.

A second later, something hard and heavy hits the center of my back, sending a shooting pain down my spine.

Then everything goes black.

Chapter 25
Emery

I HATE HOSPITALS. The sterile smell makes my stomach roll.

I've never had to stay in one overnight or visit anyone for any other reason than they have a new baby. It's white walls, white tiles, and just a few patches of blue carpet in the small seating area.

"I'm here to see Drake Chambers," I announce to the lady at the reception desk.

Her fingers work on the small keyboard before she looks up at me. "Name?"

"Emery. Emery White," I reply nervously, tapping my fingertips along the top of her desk.

"You're not on my list. Are you family?"

"Not exactly. He's my boyfriend. I don't think his family is coming, at least not tonight anyway." I tuck some hair behind my ear and watch her nervously. If she doesn't let me see him, I'm going to have to find another way.

I can't leave him.

Her eyes skim my features before she picks up the receiver. "Have a seat. I'll make a call and see what I can do."

I step back before she has time to change her mind. "Thanks,"

I mumble, running my hand up and down my purse strap.

I stare up at the old tube TV and wait nervously while that last play flashes through my mind over and over again.

I watched for many agonizing minutes as the medics worked on him. I've never felt more helpless. All I could do was pray that things weren't as bad as they looked.

They couldn't get him up after working on him for a few minutes. The only thing that gave me a sliver of hope was a simple nod of his head. But as I watched the cart come out to the field, my chest tightened. Never a good sign.

The wait seems long, but it probably isn't more than a few minutes before the receptionist calls me back to the desk. "You can go in for about an hour. Visiting hours end at nine."

I nod, grateful that I get the chance to see him. "Thank you."

"Don't thank me. Thank the nurse. She said he could use a little company," she pauses, a slight smile forming on her face, "He's in room 214."

Bolting down the small hallway, I find the elevator and push the up arrow. I find myself waiting again. I hate that it's taking me so long to get to him.

The elevator dings, and two people step out before I'm able to get in. I press the two button and wait one more time. As soon as it opens, I rush to find his door, reading the numbers twice to make sure I'm in the right place.

I press against the wood and step inside, staring at his motionless form. I guess I had this vision that I'd walk in and he'd walk right over to me, telling me everything is going to be okay. That's not how it's going to play out.

As I walk closer, I have to cover my mouth to hold back the tears begging to fall. Drake looks so helpless lying there, but when I look at his face, it looks like every other time I've watched him sleep.

A voice from behind startles me. "He's going to be out of it for a while. He was in quite a bit of pain when they brought him in."

A nurse dressed in light blue scrubs comes up beside me, wrapping one hand around his wrist while counting the seconds on her watch. "Is he going to be okay?"

She smiles sympathetically. "The doctor should be in shortly to talk to him. He'll be able to answer any questions you have."

"Thank you."

She squeezes my shoulder, leaving the room without saying another word.

The last couple hours have been so crazy, I didn't realize how late it was getting, or how tired and achy my body was from pushing my way through the crowd to get out of the stadium.

I spot the wooden chair in the corner of the room and slide it close to Drake's bed. Just as I sit down, his eyes flutter open. He stares at me, appearing confused. "Hey," I say, wrapping my hand around his.

He just watches me, eyes filled with pain. I'd do anything to take it all away, to make it my own.

"Just rest, okay." I gently squeeze his hand, running mine across the top of it.

His eyes drift shut again, and I'm content to rest my cheek against the white sheets that cover his bed and watch him.

I'm not sure how long I slept, but when I open my eyes, Drake is watching me. I've missed those blue eyes of his.

"How are you feeling?" I ask, entwining our fingers.

He opens his mouth to speak, but the door clicks open, interrupting him. "Good morning. I'm Dr. Gates, and I'll be the one observing you while you're here."

My focus stays on Drake, watching as he wrinkles his brow. For the first time I notice the dark circles under his eyes and wonder how much he slept last night.

Lisa De Jong

A heavy hand covers my shoulder. "Can I have a moment with our patient? I need to examine him."

I'm nervous about leaving him, but he gently squeezes my fingers to let me know he'll be okay. "I'll wait outside," I say, leaning in to press my lips to his cheek.

I step out in the hallway and rest my back against the wall. There's no way they're going to get me any farther away from him than this. A few nurses pass me. Maybe I should feel self-conscious over my wrinkled clothes and tousled hair, but that's one of the last things on my mind. I fell asleep watching Drake, and nobody woke me up to let me know that visiting hours were over.

Maybe they wanted to, and realized it was pointless to even try. My dad always tells me I have stubborn written all over me. I'm going to do what I want to do, not matter what.

It feels like hours pass before Drake's door opens. I glance up at the doctor, noticing how much his expression darkened from what it had been before I left the room.

Standing, I ask, "Can I go back in?"

Dr. Gates opens his mouth to say something but quickly closes it again. He looks down at the floor then back at me. "You can go back in." I walk around him, pressing my palm to the cool wood. Taking a long, deep breath, I push against the door and hesitantly step in.

At first, the mood doesn't feel that much different than when I left, but as I move closer to Drake's bed, his body language tells me something is wrong. The pain's evident on his brow, the tension showing on his jaw. Whatever the doctor had to say ... he didn't like it. Which tells me I'm probably going to hate it.

"Drake," I whisper, covering his forearm with my hand. I can feel the tension even in that.

He swallows hard, but his eyes stay locked on the tiled ceiling. "You need to go." His voice is so devoid of any emotion. My heart always aches when I hear tears in someone's voice, but something about this cuts a little deeper.

"What?" I ask, my fingers digging into his skin.

He shakes his head. "We can't do this anymore, Emery."

He hasn't said my full name in forever. It feels so impersonal, like miles worth of space is coming between us.

"Do what, Drake?"

"Us," he says, grinding his teeth together.

I touch the base of my neck, searching for the familiar silver locket. I've worn it every day since I was four. It's a constant, a source of comfort. I'm searching for words, but he beats me to it.

"Why do you bother with that thing? She's gone, Emery, and she's not coming back. She made her choice."

My chin quivers as I rub the warm metal between my fingers. "Why are you talking like this?"

For the first time, his eyes make contact with mine. "Because it's true. You can't hold onto the past forever … it's fucking with your head. If you really want to be someone, you need to grow up. Move on."

My eyes widen and fill with unshed tears. This is not how I pictured tonight, or ever. He can't really mean any of this. My voice shakes uncontrollably when I speak again. "Drake, I think you need to go back to sleep. We can talk after your drugs wear off."

"The drugs have nothing to do with this. Don't you get it? I'm saying everything I should have said weeks ago. We're too different. Too fucked up. This wasn't ever going to work."

"But last night—"

"We both got carried away. We're both passionate people, Emery. Shit happens." His voice gives me nothing. No sympathy. No I'm sorry. It's as cold as a Midwest winter.

"So what was I to you? Nothing?" I pause, using my sleeve to wipe the tears from my cheek. It feels like my mom all over again. I feel like I'm never enough. "If you tell me I meant absolutely nothing to you, I'll walk out that door, Drake, but know that when I'm gone, *we are done*!

There are no more second chances. We've done this too many times."

My chest is absolutely flaming, a deep searing pain, as I wait for him to say something. When he still can't look at me, the agony builds. This isn't going to end the way I want.

He swallows hard. "You were just another curve in the road. Another thing holding me back from what I should be concentrating on. You're the reason I'm here, Emery. You."

Hurt and agony are joined by anger. If he weren't already laid up in a hospital bed, I'd find a way for him to get there. For the first time in my life, I feel used. Before Drake, I was smart enough not to give anyone the opportunity to break me like this.

The anger boils inside of me. I'm pissed at him for what he's doing to me and pissed at myself for letting us get to the point where he could have this effect on me.

"Fuck you, Drake! Fuck you!"

Closing his eyes, he shoots the final bullet into my heart. "I was trying so hard to impress you, so hard to be the type of guy you'd want, and this is where it got me. Stuck in a fucking hospital bed."

Realizing my hand is still on his arm, I quickly remove it, noticing the marks I left behind. He deserves it and so much more. I walk backward, intent on getting as far away from this place as I can. Intent on never seeing him again.

"Have a nice life, and when you go back to having meaningless flings and you're lonely ... remember that you're the one who pushed me away." He grimaces at my words, and all I can think is that he deserves it. I swing the door open, wishing there was a way to make the stupid thing slam. Never in my life has something hurt this much. What did I do to deserve this?

The hospital staff move around, business as usual, nurses pacing up and down the hallways, phones ringing, machines buzzing. I feel like I don't belong here, or anywhere anymore.

Chapter 26

DRAKE

I CAN'T WATCH HER LEAVE. It hurts too fucking much.

There are two parts of my life I was sure of yesterday: football and Emery.

Now they're both gone ... and I don't have a fucking clue what's left of me. I spent years living in this dream, whether it was mine or his, and now there's nothing left of it. All because of one play. One decision that ended my dream, and any chance I had at a normal life.

They always say you should fight for your dreams. Well, I fought hard, and now all I have is the memory of a dream that will never be.

That's all I got ... a bunch of broken, scattered dreams.

When the door finally clicks shut, I wince and open my eyes. My heart aches something brutal, because everything I just said is wrong. It's a lie. But it's necessary. There's nothing left of me. I can't offer anything to anyone.

When my dad died, I didn't have any control over it. I had control over what happened between Emery and me, and it hurts so much more because of that.

This pain is self-inflicted.

And honestly, right now, I'd rather be dead. A part of me is dead.

I didn't mean a word I said to Emery, but it's what's best for her. She has so much life left in front of her, and she doesn't need me holding her back. I just couldn't be honest with her. I couldn't tell her the real reason I was letting her go, because she would have stayed. I know that girl too well.

I wish I didn't know what I know. I wish I hadn't heard what I heard.

"How did your night go?" I heard as I drifted in and out of sleep. I look to my side to see Emery's head lying next to me on the bed—her hair covering most of her face.

"It wasn't too bad. We took in a couple of new patients, this one included, but both have been sleeping most of the night," the other female says. There's only a tiny bit of light shining through the window in the door, but I can see the two nurses standing near the small whiteboard.

"What's the story with this one?"

The one sighs audibly before answering. "He plays for the Hawks. Drake Chambers, quarterback. He took a knee to the back, and the preliminary tests show some damage that may be irreparable."

"What kind of damage?"

When the taller nurse replies again, she lowers her voice, but I can still hear her. "Spine injury. He may never walk again, but I'm waiting for Dr. Gates to come in and examine him."

My ears ring painfully loud. I don't hear another word as I stare at the sleeping beauty next to me. Someone just tore through my dreams like it was a cheap sheet of paper. Not only that, my life's been taken from me.

And when the doctor came in, I asked him the prognosis, and he gave it to me straight. There was a chance I'd never walk again. It was all I needed to hear.

My whole identity, everything I worked so hard for is gone. I can no longer be Drake, the star quarterback. I can no longer provide for my family in the way they need. Most importantly, I have nothing left to offer anyone ... including Emery.

For the next two hours, I watched her sleep, weighing my options. It all brought me to one conclusion. I had to let her go. I had to step back because with me in her life, she'd have to give up on some of her dreams. She doesn't need anyone holding her back ... she's worked for years to make sure that no one does.

My resolve almost slipped as I watched her react to my words. It was harsh; I know that, but it was the only way. I had to make her hate me, but when you take goodness, add fire and gasoline, it fucking burns. I can only pray I didn't leave too many scars on that beautiful girl. I will never forgive myself for that.

The door opens again, letting in the light from the hallway. I'm half expecting Emery to come through it with her fighting gloves on, but it's the nurse from this morning. The one who unintentionally sealed my fate with a few words. She's older, probably my mom's age, with short blonde hair and small wire glasses.

"Hey, Mr. Chambers, how are you feeling this morning?" she asks, wrapping the blood pressure cuff around my bicep.

"Never been better," I answer with a little more bite than I intended.

"I hear that a lot around here," she says with a warm smile. Usually, I'd feel bad, but I'm so numb inside that it doesn't matter. Nothing's going to matter without Emery in my life.

After taking my blood pressure, she takes my temperature and asks how I'm doing pain-wise. I'm sure something is physically hurting right now, but it's nothing compared to the piercing pain in my heart.

"Okay, I'm going to grab one of my aides, and we'll get you down to radiology for tests." I turn my attention to the window, watching rain slide down the panes. It brings back the memories of last night when I woke up in the emergency room with medical professionals surrounding me. What I thought was just a concussion or a back sprain turned into this.

Lisa De Jong

The room remains quiet for a few minutes before the nurse and her aide come in to wheel me down the hall to an open elevator. I close my eyes and let myself drift off. This has been the worst fucking day, and I don't need to hear any more of the bad news they want to give me.

Chapter 27
Emery

IT'S BEEN FIVE WEEKS SINCE I walked out of that hospital room. The rest of that Saturday was a daze. I remember Kate coming home and asking why I wasn't at the hospital. I remember her crawling into bed with me while I cried until there were no tears left to shed. She tried to get me to eat but wasn't successful for a couple days. I even skipped class on Monday and Tuesday, something I had never contemplated before.

After that, I put my focus back where it should have been the last few months: my studies. I buried myself in them. I never went anywhere except class and the library, but even that was hard. The classes I had with Drake were now without him. The library he'd frequented with me wasn't as fun anymore.

Drake never returned. I heard he was transferred to a rehab facility, which works with athletes who have severe injuries.

There were so many times I wanted to call him to see how he was doing, but then his words would play in my head, and the anger would build up again.

You were just another curve in the road. Another thing holding me back from what I should be concentrating on. You're the reason I'm here, Emery. You.

Lisa De Jong

I came home for Christmas break a little over a week ago. I went through the motions of holiday parties with my dad's extended family, and then cooked a small ham for the two of us on Christmas day. It was starting to feel like my old life ... a sad, miserable life. *How did I ever let myself live like this for so long?*

A couple weeks ago, I started feeling really tired, even after a full night's sleep. I thought it was the stress of everything—Drake, finals, making plans to go home for break—but then a few days ago, I woke up feeling nauseous. It's the same feeling I've had every morning since.

And now, here I am.

Never in my wildest dreams did I think that at nineteen, I'd be sitting on the edge of the old claw foot tub waiting to see if one or two blue lines appear on a white, plastic stick.

It wasn't part of my dream, but lately my best-laid plans have been ripped to shreds. This is one consequence that lasts forever. It's one I never pictured myself facing alone, but I don't have much of a choice if this test comes out positive.

There's a part of me that wants to throw it back in the box and pretend like everything is okay. If it's not confirmed, it can't be true, right? But deep down, I know I have to face this. This is not something that's just going to go away. Maybe this is my punishment for letting myself get off track with Drake. The guy's practically a walking warning sign, and I fell right into his trap. With every minute, every word, every touch I became his.

He's the one person who's been able to throw me off my path, and the weird part is, I was my happiest when I wasn't living by my plan.

My cell phone buzzes, signaling the five-minute wait is up, but I hesitate. I close my eyes tightly and say a silent prayer to God, asking him to forgive me for whatever I did that brought me here. I ask him to give me one more chance to live the type of life I should, to make everything okay so I can move on ... past Drake.

Feeling sick to my stomach, I wrap my trembling fingers around the little white handle and lift it up to get a closer look.

My dreams have changed.

This life isn't just about me anymore.

I decided to make an appointment with my doctor before I say anything to my dad, or anyone for that matter. I need to know I'm not rearranging my whole life for nothing. I'm supposed to go back to school in a week, and I have some big decisions to make.

"Emery White," the nurse calls as she holds open the door.

I've been sitting in the waiting room surrounded by screaming babies and pregnant women for almost thirty minutes. As much as I've dreaded this appointment, I'm relieved to make my way to the exam room.

I follow the nurse back down a narrow hall, stopping in front of the scale to get my weight. "One twenty-two," she announces, making a note on her clipboard.

It's a few pounds lighter than I was, but my sickness has only increased since I took the test a couple weeks ago.

"Do you think you can use the restroom? I need a urine sample."

"Yeah, I drank some water before I came," I reply, trying not to think too hard about what I'm about to do.

"Okay, there is a cup on the sink. Fill it the best you can, and then set it inside the small metal door next to the toilet. We're going to go back to room three, so I'll wait for you there."

I close and lock the door, picking up the small plastic container that reads my name across the side. Being here is making this so real, and when the doctor comes in to tell me the results, I won't be able to stay in denial any longer.

I quickly fill it, using my shaky hands to place it inside the metal door. I pull my jeans back up and stand in front of the sink to wash my hands, getting a glimpse of myself in the mirror. Either the lighting in here is terrible, or the crap I've gone through these past couple months is wearing on me physically as much as it is mentally.

Dark circles surround my eyes.

My hair looks like a nest, mostly because I've been too sick and tired in the morning to do anything with it.

My cheeks are sunken. My skin is ashen.

Yet, I think I look the worst on the inside. Everything feels broken in there.

As I walk to room three, I rub my hands together in an attempt to lessen my nerves. It's not working … I'm on the verge of a panic attack. I can tell by the tingle in my hands and jaw. I wish this could all be over.

The nurse is there waiting, a knowing look on her face. I'm sure I'm not the only teenage girl she's seen in here. "Take a seat on the exam table. I'm going to get your vitals and ask a few questions, and then I'll send the doctor in.

I nod, unable to do much more.

She asks me to open my mouth and sticks a thermometer under my tongue. Her only comment is "perfect." Next, she takes my blood pressure and jots that down on her paper. After going through my whole family medical history, she finally gets to the real reason I'm here.

"It says here that you took a pregnancy test at home, and it came back positive. How long ago was that?"

"A couple weeks ago."

"And when was your last period?"

I inhale a deep breath. I hate talking about this stuff. "I don't remember the exact day because things were busy at school, but it was around the middle of November. Sometime between the tenth and fifteenth maybe."

She nods, making another note. "It says in your records that Dr. Brandt had been giving you birth control shots the last few years. Had you gotten them anywhere else but here?"

I shake my head as I try to calculate the last time I'd had one. My quick conclusion is it's been too long. Something else to add to the series of mistakes I've made lately.

"Okay, Emery, I'm going to get the doctor."

As I wait, my feet dangle off the side of the exam table, the rubber soles of my shoes hitting the metal drawers over and over again. I wish I didn't have to do this alone.

A soft knock at the door startles me, and Dr. Brandt walks in dressed in his white lab coat. I've seen him since I was a little girl, which made my yearly exams awkward after I became sexually active. Asking for birth control wasn't easy at all, but I told myself that if I was old enough to have sex, I was old enough to talk to my doctor about it.

He sits in his round leather chair and wheels himself close to where I sit, his expression more sympathetic than usual. "Well, I have your test results, and it confirmed the test you took at home. You're pregnant."

The whole room spins as the words, "You're pregnant," ring over and over in my ears. It's one thing to see it, but it's a whole other game when the words come out of your doctor's mouth.

"Are you okay?" he asks softly.

I nod, but tears form in my eyes. Dr. Brandt just took a paintbrush, and crossed a black X over the portrait of my future. Actually, no, I did that by not keeping track of my shots, and not once did Drake use protection with me. I never asked him to.

Taking a few deep breaths, I try my hardest to pull my shit together. "How far along am I?"

He looks down at the clipboard that I recognize as the one the nurse carried around with her. "From your last period, I would say eight weeks or so. The baby would have been conceived around Thanksgiving. We'll do an ultrasound to confirm at your next appointment."

My mind flashes back to Thanksgiving. It was the second to last day I had with Drake … the last time we slept together.

"Now, Emery, this might not be the time for this, but I have to ask. Were you using any protection? Looking at your chart, it seems you were about a month behind on your shot, but this still could have been avoided if—"

"No, I didn't," I say, pinching my eyes closed tightly.

"If it's okay, I'd like to take some blood work to run a couple tests. Just as a precaution."

"It was just one guy," I whisper, wondering what's going on in his head. Drake's only the second guy I've been with, and I'm not one of those girls.

"It's just a precaution."

I nod, too tired to argue.

After the doctor writes me a prescription for prenatal vitamins, the nurse comes back in to draw my blood and give me a few guidelines on what not to do and what not to eat. I take as much of it in as possible, but my mind is elsewhere.

How am I going to do this?

The minute I get home, I crawl under my old, warm comforter and let the tears roll down my cheeks. I wonder what Drake would think of this? If I was just a curve in the road, what would our baby be?

You always think you know someone until they prove you wrong. I have no idea how he'd react to this. The Drake I thought I knew would have helped me through; the one I saw in the hospital … I don't even want to think about that.

I pick my cell phone up off the bed and call the one person I feel won't judge me right now.

"Thank God. You finally decided to call me back."

"I'm sorry. I've been busy." I can't hold back the sniffle that follows.

"Are you crying?" Kate asks, her voice louder than usual.

"No, I mean, I was. I feel a little better now."

"What is going on? Did you talk to Drake?"

I cover my eyes with my forearm, wishing night would just come so I can go to sleep. "No, I haven't seen or spoken to him at all."

"What is it then? Come on, Emery, you can tell me."

Silence falls between us as I try to form the words. I realize I've never said it out loud. This will be the first.

"I'm pregnant," I whisper, the tears welling in my eyes again.

"Wait. What?"

"I'm pregnant, Kate. I'm pregnant with Drake Fucking Chambers's baby, and he wants absolutely nothing to do with me." Days' worth of frustration comes out. I can't help it.

"Oh my God," she whispers.

"Eight weeks. Eight weeks pregnant."

"Jesus, what are you going to do? Have you told your dad?" She sounds more frantic now, mirroring what I feel.

I sigh. "I haven't thought about it much yet. I mean … I'm going to have the baby. There's no choice to make there." I pause, turning my body to look at the picture of my daddy and I that I keep on my bedside table. "I haven't told my dad yet. I don't know what he'll say."

Kate's voice is soft when she responds. "You'll be okay. You have friends and family who love you. I'll help you in any way I can."

"I hope so, because I can't do this one my own."

"Are you going to tell Drake?"

Just thinking about telling him makes me sick. I can't imagine that conversation going well. He'd probably just say I did it on purpose … to keep him. I'm not going down that road.

"No. I can't."

"He deserves to know. I grew up never really knowing who my dad was, and it sucked Emery. Don't let your baby go through that, too."

"I don't even know if I'll keep it," I say honestly. What can I give a baby? I don't have a college degree or a job.

"You need to think about this. Really, really think about it."

"I think I just need some time to let it all sink in. I feel like I'm on the outside looking in … like this isn't really happening to me," I cry, using my sleeve to wipe the tears from my cheeks.

"Emery, you are one of the smartest, strongest girls I've ever met. If anyone can deal with this, it's you."

"I hope you're right." I hear the front door slam shut and look out my window, spotting Dad's old truck in front of the house. "I should probably get going. My dad's home."

"Okay, I'll call you in a few days to see how you're doing. Get some rest, and talk to your dad."

"I'll tell him soon. I need some time to think about this before I get everyone else's opinion."

"So, I'll talk to you later?"

"Yes. And thank you for listening to me."

"I will always be here if you need me."

"Bye, Kate."

"Bye, Em."

Em. That's what he always called me, I think as I nestle my head into my pillow. He could get me to do just about anything with that voice.

The waterworks are coming again. I hope this is only a temporary rise in hormones because this sucks. I'm not this girl.

Deciding to take some of Kate's advice, I pick up my phone from the end table and press my finger over Drake's name.

My knees bounce nervously as I wait. One ring. Two ring. Three. I take a deep breath, preparing myself to leave a voicemail, but it's answered before the fourth.

"Hello." It sounds like a young girl.

"Oh, I must've dialed the wrong number," I say, brushing my hand over my forehead. All this stress, and I have to start all over.

"If you're calling for Drake Chambers, you have the right number. I'm just answering because he's sleeping. Do you want me to give him a message?" It must be his sister. At least I hope it is.

"Yeah, can you tell him to call Emery? It's kind of important," I reply, tightly closing my eyes.

"Don't worry. I'll let him know."

"Thanks," I say, ending the call.

This might be a big mistake because he could let me down all over again, but I'm hanging on to the possibility that it will all be okay.

A short time later, I hear my dad's footsteps coming down the hallway. He's going to check on me before he goes to bed. He always does. I roll over so my back is facing the door and take advantage of the darkness, pretending to sleep. Like clockwork, he opens the door and walks a few feet inside. I wait until the old door creaks again, then, for the first time since I found out I was going to be a mom, I place my hand over my stomach.

The tears fall hard and fast late into the night.

I really don't want to face this alone.

Chapter 28

DRAKE

"DRAKE, WHAT DO YOU WANT FOR DINNER?"

"I don't care. Surprise me."

"Do you care about anything anymore?" Tessa asks, putting her hands on her hips.

I've been sitting in the same spot on the couch all day, only getting up a couple times to use the bathroom. This is my whole fucking existence right now with a few weekly trips to therapy mixed in.

"Tess, it's food. I really don't care."

"Jesus, Drake, you don't have to be such an asshole all the time!" she yells, stomping off to the kitchen.

"Watch your mouth!" I shout after her. If I could move a little faster in this stupid wheelchair, I'd be in her face right now.

After my injury, I was in the hospital for over a week, then transferred to a rehab facility where I stayed for almost two months. I've been here ever since ... it's been two months of fucking misery.

Quinn comes in, sitting in the old, worn recliner. "Can you see if there are any movies on? I'm sick of watching these stupid reality shows about cars."

"Well, Quinn, you get out of the house. This just happens to be the only entertainment I have."

Her head snaps toward me, venom pouring out of her eyes. "You know what? I think if you really wanted to, you

219

could walk. You just don't want to. For some dumb reason, you're happy hanging out in this stupid pity party you've been throwing for yourself."

I bite my tongue to hold back things I should never say to my sister. Besides, she's right.

When my tests came back at the hospital, they discovered my injuries might not be as permanent as they first seemed. I completely fucking shut down at that point.

I have to stay like this. If I don't, everything I said to Emery will be for nothing. I could never live with myself if I let her go for no reason.

My life is in the motherfucking spin cycle right now, and I don't know when or where it will stop.

But I do know I don't deserve her.

"Drake, can I come in?" my mom asks softly, peering through my half-open door.

"Not like I can stop you." I've been sitting in my dark room for hours, staring at the light from outside that reflects on my wall.

For the most part, my mom has kept her distance. I've gone off on her the same way I have my sisters. No one is immune.

She tries.

In fact, since I moved back home, she's been in way better shape than I have. She mentioned the doctor had given her new drugs to treat her depression. I haven't seen her out of her room this much since before my dad died. Sometimes, she even cooks when she doesn't have to work at night.

"Tess said you were in a bad mood so I thought I'd come check on you before I go to bed."

"Tess just knows all the right buttons to push. I'm fine," I reply, grabbing the small rubber football from my nightstand. Tossing it up in the air gives me something to do. Something to focus my energy on to keep my temper in check. "You can sit on my bed, you know. I don't bite."

She laughs nervously, barely sitting on the corner of my bed. "You know, Drake, I sucked at this mom stuff after your daddy died. I failed you and your sisters. You especially, but Drake, I can't let you do this to yourself. I won't let you turn into me."

I shake my head as I continue to stare at the ball as it goes up into the air then falls perfectly into my hands.

"Now, you listen to me," she says, raising her voice. "You deserve better than this. You *are* better than this. Don't let this be the end for you ... it's just a setback."

I don't know where this woman came from all the sudden. Where was she when I needed her? "He said there was a fifty percent chance I'd never walk again."

"Yeah, and what about the fifty percent chance that you can?" She scoots farther onto my bed.

"I don't want to fail," I say honestly.

"What are you doing right now, Drake?" she whispers, squeezing my foot. A few weeks ago, I wouldn't have been able to feel it, but now I can. It should be hope. It should make me feel something positive, but it's ruining me.

"I did something I can never take back. Whether I walk again or not doesn't matter."

I want to tell her about Emery, but I can't.

Not yet.

"The injury wasn't your fault, and if you never play football again, your life will still go on. You're a smart, good-looking guy, Drake. Concentrate on what you have." She stops, covering her mouth with her shaky hand. Her voice isn't as steady when she starts speaking again. "I should have focused on you kids when your daddy died, but I didn't. I lost so much time. I cost you so much."

"Just give me some time to figure all this out. I don't even know what I want anymore."

She pats my arm, slowly moving off my bed. "Let me know if you need help figuring it out. I'm here."

I watch her walk out of my room, and when she's gone, I stay still for over an hour, working my tense jaw back and forth while playing my mom's words over in my head.

Maybe I am being stupid.

Maybe there is something left in this world for me.

But what?

I push myself up on my bed like I always do when I'm going to get into my wheelchair, but this time I grab my crutches. Just learning to stand on my feet again is so fucking difficult. I fall back four times before I successfully get myself up with my calves resting against my bedframe. My therapist makes me try this all the time, but I never succeed because I've never given it my all.

I slide my right foot against the hardwood floors, trying to take the tiniest of steps, but I end up falling back again. If I'm ever going to do this, it's going to take a lot of damn work.

I attempt it over and over again with the exact same result.

"Shit," I mutter under my breath, deciding it's time to settle in for the night.

Maybe by tomorrow I'll decide it's not worth it again.

Today is my first physical therapy session since my mom gave me her version of a pep talk. I've been thinking about everything she said, and I do owe this to myself. Life may never be my idea of perfect again, but it doesn't have to be this bad ... it should be worth living at least.

As I wheel myself into the fitness room, my therapist smiles tightly. I've been anything but easy to work with, but that's all about to change.

"Hey, Drake, how are you doing?" Keith, my therapist, asks, crossing his arms over his chest.

Up until now, I've always given him the same answer. *How do you think I'm doing? I'm stuck in a fucking wheelchair.* Today may shock him. "I was able to get up on crutches."

His eyes widen, and he can't hide his grin. "That's good. Do you want to try holding onto the bars and walking between them? It might help you gain back some leg strength."

I've been dreading this moment, and the potential for failure, but I'm not going to let it hold me back. "Let's do it."

He helps me up and waits for me to gain my balance using mainly my arms. When he finally lets go, I slowly shuffle my feet, determined to get from one end to the other. When I struggle, I picture Emery standing at the other end waiting for me. It's a dream I wish could be a reality, one that hurts even more because I lived it once. I would still be inside of it if I had just let her be there for me. Maybe this is where I belong ... back in a nightmare.

My loneliness. My misery. My struggles ... they're all on me, and the cure is gone from my life forever.

It takes me almost the whole session, but I make it to the other end, letting memories of Emery guide me there.

Chapter 29
Emery

MY WHOLE WORLD HAS TURNED upside down since the last time I saw Drake Chambers.

I waited around the house for days after I called Drake, and he never called back. After two days full of ice cream, sad movies, and a few boxes of Kleenex, I decided I had to move on ... resigned to raise this baby on my own. Drake doesn't want me, and maybe he never did, and there are consequences I now have to face.

There is a piece of both of us growing inside me, and while the idea scared the crap out of me at first, I'm getting used to it now.

The first time I felt our baby move in my stomach, something changed. This is real. My love for this child is real. I had to stop running so I can give this baby the home it deserves.

During my last appointment, my doctor had asked if I wanted to know the sex, and I said no. There aren't many surprises in life, and when I'm in labor, feeling like I want to give up, the desire to know if I'm having a son or daughter will help me through.

I waited until a few days after my doctor's appointment to tell my dad about the baby. It went exactly how I expected.

"You want me to make you some breakfast?" he asks, disappearing behind the fridge door.

Just thinking about eating anything makes my stomach roll, especially eggs. "No, I'm not hungry."

He looks up over the door, brows pulled in. "Are you okay? You haven't been eating much lately."

I hesitate, trying to form the perfect lie in my head, but in the end, I know it's inevitable. "I'm pregnant," I whisper, holding the tears at bay.

The fridge door quickly slams shut. "What?" he asks, looking at me wide-eyed.

"I'm pregnant, Daddy."

"What do you mean you're pregnant? How?"

If it were anyone but me, I'd laugh at him right now, but this isn't funny at all. All I can do is tap my fingernails on the table and wait.

"I'm going to kill that son of a bitch!" he yells, standing over the sink.

"You don't even know him, Daddy."

He spins around so fast, it almost doesn't seem possible. "What do you mean I don't know him? Isn't it Clay's?"

I shake my head, wishing I hadn't picked this exact moment to tell him.

"Then whose is it, Emery?"

"You don't know him. I met him at school."

"Well, where is he right now?"

I shrug. I honestly don't know, but the last time I heard, he was in a rehab facility for his legs.

"Does he plan on helping you?"

I shake my head, letting a tear slip down my cheek. "He doesn't know. I tried to tell him but he never called me back."

Dad runs his fingers through his hair. "Jesus, Emery."

"I'm so sorry, Daddy."

He looks out over the sink again toward the endless meadow. I was his pride and joy. He bragged about how smart a girl I was every chance he got.

I don't feel too smart anymore.

"What about school? You worked so hard for that scholarship." He won't look at me.

"I'm going to take some classes at the community college this semester, and then I'll see what happens after the baby comes. I'm not giving up." Just saying that kills me.

He nods, bracing his hands against the edge of the sink. He stays like that forever, without a look in my direction or a word spoken. It's some of the worst minutes of quiet I've ever endured.

"I'm going out in the field. Call my cell if you need me," he says, slamming the door behind him.

I spend most of the day crying. I've never felt more alone.

"Emery, I'm going out in the field. Are you going to be okay?"

My dad's been treating me like I'm a little girl again, cooking me dinner and making sure I have everything I need before he leaves, even if it's only for a short time. It feels good.

"I'm fine. Besides, Clay's coming over, and we're going into town to catch a movie."

My dad's eyes narrow. He does that a lot when he wants to say something but doesn't necessarily think it's his place. "Clay?"

"Yeah, you know Clay. And before you get any ideas, we're friends," I say in an attempt to put an end to this conversation. My dad's always liked Clay, and I think it's because they're similar in so many ways. Clay decided to leave school behind to work on the family farm just like my dad. Clay's kind, predictable, and when he commits to something, he sees it through … just like my dad. There's nothing wrong with that, but I realized a long time ago, Clay wasn't the guy for me.

"I see," my dad says with a smile. I should squash his dream like a pesky little bug right now, but he won't listen. He never does.

But with Kate so far away, Dad and Clay are all I have left.

"Do you want me to bring lunch out to the tractor today?" I ask, peeling the skin from my orange. I used to hate most fruits, but these days, I can't get enough.

Walking over to kiss my forehead, he says, "I already packed a sandwich. Have fun today."

I nod, watching him walk out the door. He does this every day for hours in the spring and fall. I used to think he was miserable just because I didn't see how anyone could be happy with this life. But these last few months, I've realized he is content. I just wish he had someone to share his life with.

As soon as my dad disappears into the machine shed, I head upstairs to get ready for my trip into town. It might sound crazy, but this is a lot of excitement for most people who live in the country. I've been stuck in this old house for almost a week now, watching old movies and catching up on my reading list.

The excitement lessens as I open my closet and scan my clothing options. Being seven months pregnant doesn't suit my once-stylish wardrobe. At least most of the weight gain has stayed on my stomach and breasts.

I pull out a royal blue maxi dress with thick straps to give me the support I need. Next, I pin my hair up in a high ponytail and apply a thin layer of mascara and lip-gloss.

I finish just as the doorbell rings, and hurry down the stairs as fast as I can, opening it before Clay gets another chance to push the button.

"Hey," he says, looking me up and down. His smile widens along the way creating some of the uneasiness I feel when we're alone.

"Hey, are you ready to go?"

"More than ready. I have a little surprise for you."

"Clay, I hate surprises." I remember the last surprise I got … the carriage ride with Drake. The heavy weight I've been trying to escape drops in my chest again.

I hate surprises. Absolutely hate them.

"Come on. This is every pregnant woman's dream," he says, tilting his head to the side with the cocky smile I've known for years. He's nothing like Drake. He's only a few inches taller than me with dark hair and soft green eyes.

He's cute; I can't argue that. He's also been there for me since the day I told him about the baby.

"Okay." I grab my purse off the hook and follow him to his truck. It's so hot I can feel my hair curling against my neck. "Does this surprise include ice cream because if it doesn't, I can't consider it a dream?"

He laughs, opening the door for me. "Of course it does."

"Good, let's get out of here then."

Chapter 30

DRAKE

EVERY SUMMER, I TAKE MY FAMILY to the state fair. It's a tradition, and as sad as it sounds, it's become our annual family vacation ... our getaway doesn't involve a single night spent away from home, but my sisters look forward to it.

I still haven't figured out what I'm going to do with my life, but at least I know I can have one now. It took a few weeks, but after I set my mind to it, I was able to walk without my crutches. Progress was slow, but other than some weakness after long distances, I'm almost back to normal. I may never run again, and football is out of the cards, but for now, I'm dealing with life the best I can.

The part of this entire situation that stings the worst was my own doing. I chose to let Emery go, but I didn't do it for myself. I did it for her, and every day I question whether I made the right decision. Is she happier now? Has she moved on? Does she still think of me?

I've grabbed my keys, ready to go after her more times than I can count, but I always talk myself out of it. She deserves more than the life I'd be able to give her. I think I've always known that, and my injury put me back in my place.

"Drake, can we get funnel cake?" Tessa asks as I pull into the parking lot next to the fairgrounds.

"Yeah, you can get a funnel cake, but you have to share it with Quinn?" I glance up in the rearview mirror, watching as she shakes her head.

After I park the car, I turn to my two sisters who are waiting patiently in the back seat. "I want you guys to stay close to me, got it?"

Quinn rolls her eyes. "I'm fifteen. You don't have to treat me like I'm four anymore, Drake."

Girls are not easy to deal with. Quinn solidifies this every day.

"There are thousands of people in there. I'm not going to spend hours looking for you when it's time to go."

"You should just let me get a cell phone," she says, crossing her arms over her chest.

Taking a deep breath, I calm myself down before answering … controlling my temper has always been an issue—more so since my injury. "We're not talking about this again today. Now, let's go." I climb out of the car before she has time to respond. I can't even afford two funnel cakes, so how the fuck would I buy her a cellphone?

"If Daddy were still here, he'd buy me one."

I hate when she plays that card with me. It digs up painful memories that I've been working hard to forget and fills me with guilt. Every day I wonder if my dad would be proud of me. Would he think I'm doing a good job with my sisters? What would he say about the way I've handled my mom?

I'll never know.

"I'm serious. Let it go, or you can sit in the car." I watch her closely as she steps out, and to my surprise, she doesn't say another word.

As we walk toward the entrance gate, I pull the cash and loose change from my pocket, making sure we have enough. I pay the lady behind the counter and carefully tuck the rest back in my pocket.

"What do you want to do first?" I ask, stepping off to the side.

"Rides!" Tessa yells.

"Concert tent," Quinn adds.

"Okay, here's the deal. We'll all go to the concert tent, and when that's over, we'll do rides before we hit the food stands. Good?"

No words greet me, but silence is just as good with these two.

As we weave our way through the crowds, I keep Tessa at my side, and Quinn in front of me. I know they both think I'm an overbearing asshole, but it's my job to protect them. It has been since Dad died.

When we step into the concert tent, a local country band is playing. They're pretty good, which makes it hard to find a seat. After scanning the crowded space a couple times, I spot two empty chairs toward the back and escort the girls to them.

"Sit here. I'm going to stand in the back."

I walk to the corner of the tent and prop myself against a large wooden pillar. I'd never admit it to anyone out loud, but walking around for more than a few minutes still kills makes me weak. When the doctor said I'd never be able to play football again, I didn't think he meant I'd have this lingering pain long after the accident. The worst fucking part is that I'm getting used to it.

As I let myself relax to the sound of the guitar, the band sings typical country song about a guy who'd do anything to be with the woman he loves. The singer's voice trails off. *"I should have never let her go, because then I wouldn't be here."* And that's when I see her seated on the other side of the tent with her back to me. I'd recognize her from any angle, because when we were together, I never took my eyes off her.

I'd convinced myself that I was doing okay without her. I convinced myself that she was better without me.

But now I don't know who I was fucking kidding. I've been lonely, miserable, and almost impossible to be around. All because I'm missing her.

Something like a magnetic force or a strong current has always pulled me to her. I'm feeling it right now. As I take one step toward her, she stands suddenly. That's when I notice it for the first time.

The swell of her belly. The curve of her breasts. When I look up, I notice the glow on her cheeks. The weight on my chest holds me in place. So many thoughts are racing through my head. Is that mine? Why didn't she tell me? Actually, I know why she wouldn't tell me; I told her I didn't want anything to do with her the last time I saw her. What do I expect?

My feet slowly start moving forward again as I try to talk myself into facing her. I've never been more scared in my life. Imagine that ... Drake Chambers scared of speaking to a girl. A few more steps, and I notice him. He comes up beside her and places his hand on her lower back. I have no idea who he is, but I fucking hate him. My eyes shift again, spotting his other hand on her stomach.

I watch her as she smiles up at him, and a sick feeling comes over me. It's his. The baby that brought the glow to Emery's beautiful face is his, and any chance I may have had to get her back is gone. For a second, I imagine walking up to her. I imagine her telling me about the baby, and things being different between us. Maybe I want it to be mine.

It doesn't matter. Maybe I didn't matter to her because it doesn't look like it took her that long to move on. I can't even look at another girl without feeling like I'm cheating on Emery, and we haven't been together for almost seven months.

Pain pierces my heart. I thought what Emery and I had meant something, and seeing her here with him, carrying his baby ... it hurts. So fucking much, it hurts.

This is what I wanted for her when I let her go ... or so I thought.

Emery's always been about dreams and stability. I certainly can't make her dreams come true, and I have no idea what stability feels like.

After watching them disappear from the tent, I gather Tessa and Quinn so we can hit the rides and get out of here. The last thing I want to do is run into the happy couple, but

I'm going to take a wild guess and assume they won't be enjoying the rides with Emery's current condition.

"I wasn't ready to leave yet," Tessa whines, not keeping pace with Quinn and me.

"I read there's a chance of rain, so we better keep moving or we might not get to everything," I say, slowing my steps so she can catch up.

"Are we still going to have time to get a funnel cake? You promised."

"We'll grab a funnel cake on our way out if you quit whining." I'm being a complete asshole, but I couldn't control it right now if I tried. Anger, disappointment, and sadness are running through my veins, and there's nothing I can do about it while we're here. The only thing that's going to fix this is a twelve-pack and a few rounds with my punching bag.

"You're mean," Tessa scoffs, walking in front of me.

With nothing to say to that, I follow after her. After buying them each enough tickets for a few rides, I stand back and watch as they bounce from ride to ride. It gives me time to try and get ahold of the monster feelings I'm grappling with internally. It doesn't work, and by the time they've used all their tickets, I'm ready to get out of here.

Out of the corner of my eye, I see the familiar long blue dress. I take a chance and turn my head, watching Emery on the other side of the midway as she stands beside the guy she was with in the tent. He's playing a game, one where you toss three balls into the impossible hoop. I should walk away before she sees me, but my curiosity holds me in place. She's even more beautiful with her swollen belly. Even with the turmoil and confusion inside of me, I can admit that much.

I watch as she stares at a large stuffed green frog that hangs next to her, smiling as she squeezes one of its legs. I've seen that look before—it's one of want and excitement. If I were that guy, I'd do whatever it takes to get it for her.

After a few more tries with the ball, he turns to her and throws his arms up in defeat. She shrugs, following him to the next game, but I don't miss when she glances back at the frog again and how close she is to seeing me.

I'm ready to get out of here. I need to get out of here. I find my sisters watching the bumper cars and head in their direction.

"Let's grab your funnel cake and leave before it starts to sprinkle," I mumble, walking to a concession stand in the middle of the midway.

Quinn places her hand over her eyes and looks up to the sky. "There's not a cloud in the sky, Drake."

"They're coming," I say, not really referring to the weather. It's life, or at least it's my life. There's always a cloud forming over the horizon.

I order two funnel cakes in an effort to smooth over our hurried trip and grab enough napkins for a kindergarten classroom before heading to my car.

I wish it wasn't an hour-long drive, but with any luck, they'll fall asleep, and I can think. The girls are behind me, but I hear their shoes hitting the gravel parking lot so I don't bother slowing my pace. I'm lost in my own world when I hear a familiar voice say my name. My whole world freezes as I glance to my left and see her standing next to a new white Ford truck with the unnamed asshole by her side.

I turn, causing Tessa and Quinn to run into me because they aren't paying attention to anything but their funnel cakes. "Go wait in the car. I'll be there in a minute." I hand Quinn my keys and watch to make sure they follow my directions for once. As it turns out, it's easier to get them to do something when they have food.

When my eyes find Emery again, she's in a heated debate. I walk over to where they stand in case she needs my help.

"Clay, just give me a few minutes. I need to do this by myself," I hear her say in a hushed tone. *Clay,* her high school boyfriend. I don't know if that makes this better or worse.

He looks at me then back down at her, carefully brushing a few strands of hair off her cheek. I'm supposed to be the one doing that. "I'm going to sit in the truck. Don't go far, okay?"

"I'm staying right here."

Clay nods, throwing me a look of disgust before going around to the driver's side. I don't know what he's so bent up about.

Emery and I each take a few steps until we find ourselves face to face. It's strange being this close to her but not being able to touch her like I once did.

"You're walking again," she whispers just loud enough that I can hear her. Is that all she has to say?

"I've been going to physical therapy."

"Oh, I thought they said you would never walk again." She crosses her arms over her chest, but it's anything but cold out today.

"That's what they said," I say, glancing to my right to see two heads of long blonde hair through my rearview window. Looking back at Emery, I say, "It looks like you've moved on. Is this the part where I'm supposed to offer you my congratulations?"

Her eyes gloss over almost immediately. I should feel guilty for talking to her like this, but anger is the only thing inside me right now. "What?" Her voice is shaky, full of emotion.

I want to hurt her. I want her to feel even a little of what I'm feeling right now. "The baby, Emery. Was Clay your backup plan? How many days did you wait before you hopped into his bed? One? Two?" The pain etched in her eyes and the quiver of her lower lip should be enough to stop me, but it just fuels my anger. "I guess it doesn't matter because you were just another girl."

A tear rolls down her cheek, but I still can't stop. "Has he put a ring on your finger yet? Did you get yourselves a little house and a dog?" I stop, gripping my hair in my fingers. "God, I don't know why I even care. Goodbye, Emery. Have a nice—whatever."

I'm too much of a coward to look at the damage I've done before I walk away. I thought the things I said would help me feel better on some level, but they don't. Now I just feel like a sad, angry asshole all over again.

"Drake!" I hear her footsteps as she walks up behind me, but I don't bother turning around.

"If you think what we had meant so little to me that I went and screwed someone right after you told me to fuck off, you're wrong. Even if you didn't love me, I loved you. You meant so much to me that I was willing to change my whole idea of forever to be with you. You're an idiot, Drake Chambers."

Looking up to the darkening sky, I say, "I never pretended to be anything more."

"Yeah, well I guess I was wrong about you, too," she cries, raising her voice.

I quickly walk to my car. I need to get the fuck out of here and away from her. When my hand grips the warm metal handle, I hear her voice again. "The baby isn't Clay's. The baby is yours, Drake. Yours and mine."

My whole body freezes in place as her words play over and over in my head. The baby growing inside of her is ours. She could be lying to me, but I know Emery White better than that. She's not that type of girl, and that's one of the reasons I was so drawn to her in the first place. She's the most real thing I've ever known.

When I finally get the courage to face her, she's climbing into Clay's truck. She's not going to wait to see my reaction, and after everything I just said to her, she probably doesn't care.

It's not until I'm in my car, pulling my seatbelt on, that it hits me. Not only did Emery tell me she's carrying our baby, but she also admitted for the first time that she loves me. I didn't say it back, but the overwhelming burn in my chest tells me I love her, too. If I didn't, this wouldn't hurt so much.

And if today taught me anything, it's that she really does deserve someone better than me.

Chapter 31
Emery

"WAS THAT HIM?" Clay asks as soon as he puts his truck in drive.

Tears blur my eyes, but not enough to miss the tension in his jaw. He doesn't need to explain the *him* to me. "Yes," I whisper.

"What happened out there, Emery? What the fuck did he want after all this time?"

Pinching my eyes closed, I shake my head. The tears fall fast, and I don't have the energy to hold them back. "Just take me home, Clay. I need to go home."

Out of the corner of my eye, I see him fuming. He only knows one side of the story, though. Actually, he doesn't even know that ... he thinks I came home because I got pregnant. He doesn't know what Drake said to me. He doesn't know that, until today, Drake wasn't aware that we were having a baby.

And now that he found out, I wish I had done it differently. I wish I would've told him sooner so we could have avoided today. It doesn't matter that I tried ... I should have tried even harder. I should've made him listen to me.

When the truck comes to a stop on the highway, I feel his hand lightly squeeze my knee. I've been so lost in my own world, replaying the last couple hours in my head, I'd almost forgotten I wasn't the only one here. "Emery," he says quietly, never taking his hand off me. "For what it's worth, I'm here for you. Always have been and always will be."

Resting my forehead against the passenger side window, I completely lose it. I've been dying to hear those words for months, but Clay isn't the person I wanted to hear saying them.

Without warning, Clay pulls to the side of the road and puts the truck in park. "Emery?"

I catch a glimpse of his concerned eyes and crumble, instantly feeling his arms pulling me close. It feels wrong taking comfort from the guy who wants me while I'm crying over the one who doesn't. I guess life hasn't been fair to either of us.

"It's going to be okay," he whispers, running his hand up and down my spine. "We'll get through this."

His words make me tense up. There is no *we* ... not in the way Clay wants. Pulling back, I wipe my tears away and take a deep breath. "I'll be okay. It's just not how I wanted him to find out."

"He didn't know?" Clay asks, sitting back in his seat.

Tears slip from my eyes again. "No, I mean, I left a message once, but he never called back. He doesn't want anything to do with me, and I wasn't going to force him with a baby."

"He's an idiot not to want you," he says softly, squeezing my hand before putting his truck back in drive.

The rest of the drive is quiet, which is good because I'm sure anything Clay wants to say will cut me deeper. I know what it's like to love someone but not be able to be with them. He's a sweet guy, but he's not the one for me. He's a safe walk across the sidewalk when what I really want is a walk across a tight rope. I'm slowly learning, though, that while one is more fun, the other is less likely to shatter me.

By the time we pull into my gravel drive, the sky is completely dark, and the only light that remains on in my house is the one above the sink in the kitchen, which means my dad has gone to sleep.

"Sit tight," Clay says, climbing out of the truck. Sitting back against my seat, I anticipate my door opening any second now.

When he pulls it open, he steps into the open space, making it impossible for me to get out. The way he stares at me makes my hands sweat. "Do you want me to stay with you tonight?"

Without hesitating, I say, "No, I think I need to be alone. Besides, Clay, I can't go back to being the us you want us to be. I need to figure out who Emery is right now."

He reaches up, using his thumbs to brush the tears from my eyes. "I know who you are. You're a smart, determined, stubborn woman. You're not typical, but that's what makes you so special."

Shaking my head, I try to free my face from his hands. It's not the right time for this. "Emery, please, just listen to me."

"I'm tired, Clay."

"Just do me one favor … whatever you do, wherever you end up, make sure you're happy. You've worked too hard to settle for anything less." He lets go of me, stepping back.

Our eyes remain locked. I haven't felt this open and raw in a long time. Not even when my mom left, or the day I saw her again driving past my dad's truck. I either didn't let myself fall this far, or those events didn't push me this hard. I'm older. I've seen more. I feel more.

And one thing I know for certain … the guy standing in front of me with sad eyes and a defeated stance is the most unselfish person I've ever met.

"I'm sorry about today," I whisper, breaking the silence.

He grabs my hands in his, gently pulling me forward until my feet are firmly planted on the ground. When his lips press to my forehead, I close my eyes, letting his touch soothe me.

"The first part was fun," he says, smiling sadly. "Come on, I'll walk you to the front door."

I nod, following his lead. All I want to do right now is let my head fall against the pillow. With any luck, I'll get some sleep.

We stop in front of my door. It reminds me so much of our first date. Neither of us knows exactly what to say or do. "Thank you for everything, Clay."

His lips touch my forehead one more time. "You take care of yourself."

Nodding, I open the door and disappear inside.

Chapter 32

DRAKE

AFTER I DROP MY SISTERS OFF AT HOME, I drive through the darkness, no destination in sight. I'm too numb to fully process the consequences of what happened today, or how my actions in that hospital room months ago affected the rest of my life. I want to go somewhere and forget all my problems by drowning myself in alcohol, but I know when I wake up in the morning, I'm going to feel exactly like I do now. Nothing can be worse than this, and I never deserve better.

This is my forever … the one I was destined to have anyway.

There's something about country roads. They never get you to where you want to go too quickly, but when you do get there, you've gotten the best form of free therapy. It's crazy what a little time to think can do for you.

After a couple hours, I find myself pulling into the parking lot of B&B's. It's one of the two bars in town, but it's my personal favorite because it's more low-key. Not the place a guy goes for a hook-up or a fight. Just a place to sulk and forget.

As I walk in the door, I spot the regulars sitting up at the bar, nursing their drinks. That's not where I'm heading tonight, not if I'm driving.

"Hey, Chambers, what can I get you tonight?" Bill, the owner shouts from over the bar.

"I'll take a Coke." He stares at me curiously for a few seconds before throwing some ice in a glass and grabbing a can from the cooler. I drink often when I come here, but tonight I don't have a ride home, and one thing I'll never do is drive drunk … not after what happened to my dad.

While I wait for my drink, I switch on the dartboard and pull the darts from the center. This is what I do when I need to focus on something other than what's swirling in my head.

"Where do you want it?" Bill asks.

I don't even bother looking at him. "Just set it on the table next to the jukebox."

As I throw my first set of darts, I hear the glass clink against the table. "What's eating you, kid?"

"I'm not a kid."

His voice is lighter when he speaks again. "To me, you'll always be a kid."

Without responding, I pull my darts from the board and stand back to throw my second round. I didn't come here to talk.

"How's your momma doing?"

Fuck. "I didn't come here to talk, Bill." I throw another set of darts, hoping he takes the hint and finds his way back to the bar.

"Your mom and dad used to be the king and queen of this town. I've been praying for her since the day he died."

"I'm not in the mood for this, Bill," I mumble, hoping he'll just walk away.

He lets out a short laugh. "Every woman in town was jealous of her because your dad was quite a catch. Handsome, and he'd gone to college. Hell, all the guys envied him because he could get a woman to look at him like your mom did. He was a lucky bastard." The last word fades away as I finally look over at him. My dad may have been lucky in life, but it ended too soon. Way too soon, and we're all paying for it.

"Some luck," I say, swallowing the lump in my throat. My dad was my best friend, and I still haven't dealt with his death the way I should've, because I've been too busy taking care of everyone else.

"Look, I'm sorry. I didn't mean it like that."

I nod, my silent way of letting him know that I'm okay. Or at least that's what I want him to believe.

"Anyway, if you ever need anything, I'm here. I know you don't know me that well, but your dad and I were good friends. He loved you, and I know he'd hate to see you like this."

I stop, rubbing my fingers over my brow. I try so hard to keep everything to myself, to hide it so deep that no one can see, but this guy I barely know is reading me like a children's book. "It's been a long day. I think I'm just going to head home."

"Avoidance isn't going to solve any problem," he says as he places his hand on my shoulder.

He walks away before I have a chance to say anything, not that there's much to say. He's right. I've been running for as long as I can remember. When my dad was killed, I took care of everyone else so I wouldn't have time to deal with my own grief. I practiced football for hours each day so when I wasn't in school, I wouldn't have to think. School. Football. Sleep. That's all I did. When I was old enough to work, I got a job at the local grocery store, working every weekend and all through the summer.

I monopolized my time. I avoided serious relationships. I didn't have many friendships. And where has it gotten me?

A life of fucking misery. Even if I could play football and made it to the NFL, I'd still be this guy. I can't believe it took me this long to realize it.

I grab my keys from the table and head out the door. It's time to stop running. I'm too fucking tired ... I have been for a long time.

This time, as I drive home, I let my mind go free, thinking about what it is that I want. What would make me happy? I've made such a mess of things that it's hard to sort through it.

As soon as I pull in my driveway, I shut off my headlights, careful not to wake my family. I want to get inside and throw myself on top of my bed.

After an attempt to open the front door quietly, I make my way toward the stairs, careful not to step on the creaky boards.

"Drake, is that you?" From the sound of my mom's voice, I know she's been sleeping.

"Yeah, Mom. Go back to sleep," I say, running my fingers through my hair.

I spot her dark form sitting up on the couch. "I must have fallen asleep watching *Pretty Woman* with your sisters. They never get sick of that one."

I can't help but laugh a little. I've watched that movie more than any man should.

"Where have you been? You weren't drinking, were you?"

"No, I went to B&B's to throw some darts," I say, rotating my neck to release some of the tension.

She stands, walking in my direction, her eyes taking in my features. "Are you okay? Tess said you were acting strange at the fair, and she saw you arguing with a girl. You can talk to me, Drake."

Looking up to the ceiling, I inhale a deep breath. "I met a girl at school, and we dated for a while. Anyway, I ran into her at the fair today, and let's just say things didn't go well."

"There's only one reason seeing her would bother you like this. She must have really meant something to you."

I could have really used my mom all these years. "I know," I reply, quickly skipping up the stairs.

I don't want to talk anymore.

I know what I want, but I just don't know how I'm going to get it.

Or if I even can.

Chapter 33
Emery

THERE ARE ONLY SIX WEEKS LEFT until my baby will be in my arms. Time's gone by so fast, and it really hasn't even sunk in yet. I wonder if it's like this for everyone. I've spent months preparing, making sure I have everything, but does anyone really feel emotionally ready?

Tonight I'm finally getting some time to myself. My dad's suffocating me. Clay's smothering me. I know they only want what's best for me, but I'm starting to lose my sense of self. And also my mind.

Daddy rarely lets me out of his sight, and Clay likes to pop by once a day to make sure I'm okay. Usually we watch some TV, or if it's not too hot, we sit on the front porch and talk. And he's given me more space, making our friendship stronger. I don't feel the pressure to be anything more than his friend.

I throw a bag of popcorn in the microwave and pour myself a big glass of lemonade. The nights are getting hotter, and it's getting more and more difficult to chase the humidity out of the house. As soon as the sun went down tonight, I opened the windows and cranked up the ceiling fans.

The microwave beeps, and the smell of fresh kettle corn hits my nose, making my stomach growl.

Right as I'm about to take my usual seat on the couch, the doorbell rings. Glancing up at the clock, I notice that it's almost ten, and my heart rate picks up. Dad is out of town on an overnight camping and fishing trip, and last I heard, Clay went with him.

I hesitate for a few seconds, looking down at my short cotton shorts and oversized white t-shirt. I could just hide out, but all the lights are on and my car is parked outside the garage. It's a little too obvious.

I tighten my ponytail, deciding to chance a peek through the side window. As I'm taking small steps against the wall to stay out of view, the bell rings again. Then again.

You know that feeling you get when you are watching a horror movie, and you know something really bad is about to happen? That's how I feel as I peel the curtain back. I've watched way too many episodes of those true crime shows … it always starts like this.

At first, I can't make out my visitor's face in the darkness, but as I look in the distance, I spot a familiar car parked in front of my house. I swear my heart rate just doubled as I brace my hands against the wall to stabilize my weak knees.

I last saw that car almost three weeks ago in the parking lot at the fairgrounds, which means the dark figure on the other side of my door is someone I don't want to see right now. Or maybe ever.

But yet I want to know why he's here. Drake Chambers doesn't do anything unless he wants to. Why would he want to be here?

Taking a deep, cleansing breath, I try to get my emotions in check. He's hurt me so much. Done things I'll never forget. And I've asked myself over and over if I'd ever be able to forgive him.

I honestly don't know.

Slowly, I grip the doorknob, closing my eyes as I pull it open. When I think it's safe, I open them again and let them take in the familiar features of the guy I let myself fall hard and fast for months ago. The guy who turned me upside down and spun me around before standing me back up and walking away, leaving me staggering.

"Hi." His voice is quiet and screams of fear. I've never seen Drake Chambers quite like this. He's played on much bigger fields.

His eyes stay on mine, but then they roam down, taking in my breasts and my ever-growing belly. They linger there, and when his eyes finally come back up to my face, his head stays down. There's more remorse written there than could ever be expressed in words.

I stand frozen, still shocked he's even here ... on my front porch. I notice things about him that I didn't a few weeks ago. His hair is a little longer than it was when we were still in college, and he's lost weight. I can tell by the way his khaki shorts hang lower on his waist, and the way his t-shirt hugs his thinner abs.

"Em, are you okay?" he asks, taking a step closer.

I flinch, not wanting him in my space. "What are you doing here? How did you find out where I live?"

Now it's his turn to flinch. He grips the top of the doorjamb and stares at me with those blue eyes where I used to get so lost. He used to be able to talk me into anything.

I wonder if he looks at me long enough, like he is right now, if he still could.

"I need to talk to you, and it's not hard to find anyone in this state. There aren't that many of us."

"What could you possibly have to say that you haven't already?" I ask, crossing my arms over my chest. They're my armor ... my heart's protection.

If only that were possible.

"Just give me a few minutes, Em. That's all I want."

The way he says my name ... my resolve to push him away is slipping.

Falling.

Deeper and deeper.

I have to know why he's here at least. Otherwise, I'll sit and wonder. Just like I have with my mom. I don't want to go through that again.

"Wait out here," I say, pointing to the old patio furniture that adorns one end of our front porch. "I'm going to grab a different shirt."

He looks past me, rubbing the back of his neck. "Is anyone home?"

I shake my head, gripping the side of the door. "Just wait out here," I say, pushing the screen door closed.

When I'm back in my house alone, I lean over the sink and take a few seconds to catch my breath. Seeing him is doing all sorts of things to me, and none are reactions I expected to have. I thought I'd scream at him until I had no voice left, but all I need right now is closure. We each need to say what we need to say and go our own way.

And what if he wants to be part of our baby's life?

After grabbing my gray t-shirt from the laundry room, I walk back to the front door, opening it slowly. Drake's seated on one of the old wooden rocking chairs, giving me a choice between the old porch swing and the other chair.

"I don't bite," he jokes, resting his elbows on his knees.

"That's debatable."

"I get that you're pissed at me, but will you please just sit down and let me say what I need to say? I think we both need this."

I rub my fingers over my temples. The headaches I've been getting these last few weeks are starting to get to me. "Five minutes," I say, finally sitting in the chair next to him.

He does nothing but watch me for a while. It's dark, and the only sound that fills the country air is the crickets … the same sound that puts me to sleep every night.

"First, I have to ask you something. What you said a few weeks ago about the baby being mine—"

"It's yours," I say, cutting him off. If he came to question me about Clay and the baby, this conversation isn't even going to last five minutes. It's going to be done now.

He stands, pacing back and forth on the porch. "Why didn't you tell me?"

"I tried. I called one day and left a message," I reply, resting my elbows on my knees. Since I ran into Drake at the fair, I've felt guilty about not trying harder. Even after everything he did, he deserved more from me.

"I never got a message," he says, stopping in front of me with his hands on his hips.

I sigh, feeling the frustration of this. Of all of it. "I left it with a girl. She said she would give it to you."

"Damn it!" he shouts, taking his seat again. "Tess must've answered it. I've told her a hundred times to leave my phone alone."

"Maybe I should have tried again, but I thought you wanted nothing to do with me. I just couldn't do it, Drake."

He leans forward in his chair, burying his head in his hands. "I'm sorry." His fingers grip his hair, pulling it away from his scalp almost painfully so. "I'm so sorry."

"For what?" I ask, throwing my hands in the air. "Are you sorry for pushing me away in the hospital? Are you sorry for telling me your injury was my fault? Or are you sorry because you thought I slept with someone else right after you broke my heart? What exactly are you sorry for, Drake?"

He lifts his head, but it's hard to see his expression under the pale moonlight. "All the above. I'm also sorry I wasn't there with you when you found out. I'm sorry I didn't get to go to your first doctor's appointment. I'm sorry that what we did together sent you back here."

He pauses, glaring up at the stars. "I'm sorry I didn't tell you I loved you, too, because I do, Em. I love you so much that everything I did to you hurts like hell. Deep down in my chest, Em, I feel it."

Leaning forward, I mimic his position from before, pressing my forehead to my palms. I don't want to look at him. I'm slipping. Falling. Deeper. "The things you said in the hospital … I will never forget them. Why would you say those things if you loved me? Please, help me understand."

Before I realize what's going on, he's kneeling in front of me, lifting my chin with his fingers. "Look at me. Please."

I comply, tears pooling. His voice has never been more sincere, gentler. It's wrapping itself around my heart, and all I can do is listen.

"That morning, in the hospital, I heard the nurses talking about me. About how I may never walk again, and I couldn't put you through that. I knew you'd stay with me, but I also knew your dreams. If you were with me, you would have had to choose, so I chose for you."

"Drake," I say, biting the inside of my cheeks to keep my emotions locked up. I've shed too many tears over this. So many nights spent laying in my room listening to the saddest fucking slow songs I could find while staring into space. "Look where I am right now!" I yell, throwing my arms in the air again.

His face moves closer to mine, his breath hitting my lips. "I said I'm sorry."

"You made me feel hated. You made me feel stupid. No one has ever made me feel that way ... not even my mom."

He grabs my face in his hands. "I knew the only way you'd leave is if I made you hate me. I thought it was the only way. Don't you get it?"

"No," I cry, shaking my head. "I don't get it. I could never hurt someone like that, especially if I loved them."

Gripping my face tighter, the dim light hits his face at just the right angle. Unshed tears glisten in his eyes, and the path of a fallen one shows on his cheek. "It's a fucked up form of love, but it's the one I know. I've spent years protecting my mom and my sisters ... I thought I was loving you by giving you what you wanted. I didn't want to stand in your way."

"Did you ever stop and think that maybe it was you I wanted?"

He shakes his head slowly. "I couldn't see a reason for you to love me enough to give everything up. Football has always defined me, and I don't have that anymore."

"So what's different now?" I whisper, entranced in every word he says.

"I've had time to think about what's important to me. Football was important to my dad. It was his dream, and you know what? After they told me I probably wouldn't be able to play again, I was torn up, but it didn't have anything to do with the game. It was always you. I've missed you so much."

I want to wrap my hands around every word he says, but there's this wall that won't come down. I can't quite reach over.

"Why are you here now? After all these months?" I ask, gripping his wrists. I try to pull his hands away from my face, but either his hold is too strong, or I don't really want him to let go.

"I finally feel like I deserve you," he whispers.

Those words clamp my heart. Tight. Squeezing. I hope that I didn't do anything to make him feel undeserving before. He was good enough to make me forget about all my dreams for a while. If he only knew it takes a special person to do that.

"I broke all my rules for you. That should tell you something."

He sweeps his thumb across my cheek. "I see that now," he says, looking down at my round stomach.

"So what do you want exactly?"

He lets go of me, sitting back on his heels to grab something from his back pocket. When he kneels in front of me again, a small dark box sits in the center of his hand.

Pinching my eyes closed, I take a deep breath. This is too much. I can't handle such a swing of emotions in one evening. Ten minutes ago I was pissed and annoyed. Five minutes ago, I was confused and hurt. Now, well, now I have no idea what to think.

He opens the box, and though the contents are hard to see, the sparkle in the center stands out. The pissed and annoyed phase is creeping back … this isn't how I thought this moment in my life would happen, and I'm not going to accept it.

"Don't," I say, grabbing the box from his hand and snapping it shut. I place it back in his hand and stand, forcing him back. "I can't do this right now. Not like this."

"Emery! Please."

Walking toward the door, I try to pretend he's not even here. He won't let me. I feel him right behind me as I spin around, intent on making my point known. "If we were meant to be, things wouldn't be this difficult."

I turn back around, but he grabs onto my hand. "I'm not giving up, on you or our baby. I'm going to be here."

Looking over my shoulder, I say, "I won't keep you from our baby, if that's what you're worried about."

He lets go of my hand, running his long fingers through his hair. "Is that all you think I'm worried about?"

"It's all that matters anymore." I take a few quick steps and disappear through the old screen door without a second glance.

I shut and lock the inside door in case he gets any ideas about following me. When I'm only steps away, there's more knocking. Without giving it much thought, I turn back around and open the door. I need him to leave, everything that needed to be said has been. "Drake, please."

"I forgot to give you something," he says softly, looking down at me with sad eyes.

I open my mouth, thinking he's going to bring up the ring, but he pulls an oversized stuffed frog from behind his back. I've always had a thing about the small green creatures, but I've never told him that.

"I saw you eyeing one like this at the fair. I want to prove to you that I can give you what you want so I searched until I found one like it." He swallows, hesitantly reaching his finger up to brush against my jaw. "I want to give you everything … especially the things that make you smile."

"Drake, I—"

His finger presses to my lips. "Don't say anything. Just think about it … I'll wait for you."

Before I disappear inside again, he places the frog in my arms, smiling sadly. Maybe I shouldn't take it, but I don't want to let it go. "Goodbye, Drake," I whisper, shutting the door behind me.

I grab my uneaten bowl of popcorn from the coffee table and dump the whole thing into the garbage. After quickly turning off all the lights, I head upstairs and try to get comfortable in my bed with my new gift tucked under my arm. I don't want to like it, but I do. It's soft and smells just like him.

Closing my eyes, I try to fall to sleep. I'm doing what I do best … blocking everything out and pretending like it never even happened. It's impossible, though, because all I can think about is Drake.

I barely slept a wink last night. All I could think about was what he said, the proposal he had planned …

It was too little too late.

I think …

I don't want to look back at my decision to shut him out and regret it. There's so much anger inside me overriding the things he said, but there is a faint beat in my heart that's pushing me to take him back. Especially when he shows up on my doorstep with sad eyes and a stuffed animal. He sees me in a way that no one else ever will.

He gets me.

"Emery!" I jump at the sound of my name. It's my dad. He must have come home early.

"Yeah, Dad?" I yell back, pulling my robe on.

"Can you come down here a minute?"

After tightly securing my robe, I open the door and head down the hall. As I turn the corner to walk downstairs, I see rain pouring down the small window above the landing. That's why Dad's home early.

As I move down the last flight of stairs, I see him standing at the bottom of the stairs with his arm resting on the railing, eyes trained out the front window.

"Hey, baby, I came home a little early and found a young man sitting against our front door. Said he wasn't leaving until he talked to you."

I open my mouth to speak, but nothing comes out right away. How much has Drake told him, or how much has he figured out on his own?

"He's still here?" I ask, my voice barely above a whisper.

"What do you mean 'still here'?"

I rub my hand over my brow, trying to see Drake through the window. "He came last night. He probably never left."

"I'm going to tell him to leave. The idiot doesn't belong here anyway." He makes his way toward the door.

"No, don't. I'll take care of it."

He stops, turning to me again. "Is he the son of a bitch who did this?"

My head snaps up, my eyes blur. I've thought so many times about what it will mean for me to be a mother. I haven't given much thought to Drake. I nod, rubbing my temples with my fingertips. "Yes. Can you just give me a minute alone with him? I have a few things I need to say."

He watches me, more than likely gauging my ability to handle this on my own. I wonder if he'll ever see me as anything but his little girl. "I'll be in the kitchen if you need me," he finally replies, walking away before he has any time to second-guess himself.

I hesitate for a minute, rehearsing what I want to say in my head. I think there's a small chance that maybe someday we'll be able to give us another chance. This just isn't the time, but I want him to be as involved as he wants in the rest of this pregnancy and the baby's life.

I unlock the door and pull it open, scanning the front porch for Drake. Like a skydiver without a parachute, I fall.

He's gone.

I'm too late.

Stepping back inside, I bolt the door shut again, letting myself rest against it.

Slowly, I slide down to the floor as tears spill from my eyes. I had a second chance, and I took it for granted. At some point last night, I started to forgive Drake because what he was saying made sense.

And now my own stubborn nature ruined it.

Using my long cotton sleeves, I wipe the fresh tears from my face, knowing they'll be replaced with new ones soon. I always thought life would get easier as I got older. I'd have more control over the decisions that affected me, but I was wrong. First, Drake got the best of me, now my emotions.

This is a life lesson for me. One I'll never forget. One I may never get over.

A sound comes from outside on the porch, startling me. I stand, bracing my hands against the wall to peer out the small side window. My breath hitches when I see Drake fumbling with a small bag and two paper cups. He came back, or should I say, he never really left.

Closing my eyes, I say a silent prayer while I squeeze the metal knob in my hand. When I finally open the door, Drake stands right in front of it with the bag tucked under his chin. I reach forward and grab it as he eyes me carefully. He's probably wondering what's going through my head ... most of the time, I'm wondering what's going through it.

"I brought you breakfast," he finally says, pointing his finger toward the bag in my hand.

I nod, unable to speak in fear of completely falling apart.

"I have coffee, too. I mean, I know you like it so I got decaf for you and the baby," he says, handing me a cup. I take it from him, unable to hold back the water works anymore. It's one of the sweetest things anyone's ever done for me, and the fact that he's already thinking about our baby does something inside of me.

"Thank you," I mouth, wiping the tears from my cheeks.

He slowly closes the space between us, running the back of his hand along my tear-stained cheek. "Give me another chance, Em. I want to show you how much you mean to me. How much I love you, and how much I want this baby with you … please, let me, Em."

Chapter 34

DRAKE

I HATE WAITING FOR ANSWERS, and I never stick myself out there like this. When I handed her the frog last night, I felt a bit of hope with the way her eyes lit up. It turned into a false hope, but I don't regret it. I want her to be with me, but it's even more important that she's happy.

Now, I'm waiting again, staring down at a glint of hope. This could be one of the best days of my life ... or it could be one of the worst. Whatever it ends up being, it's going to change my life, one way or another.

"I know I don't deserve it, but will you give me another chance? I need you, Emery, and more importantly, I want you. You're the only one I want."

Her face contorts as a single tear rolls down her cheek. Slowly, I'm breaking her ... but in a good way this time. In a way that I'm hoping will make both of us happy.

"I'm not perfect, and I never will be, but I want to be everything you need."

I watch her crumble, her hands covering her face. My arms are begging to hold her, to give her the comfort I should have given her the last few months.

I just wish I knew what she wanted from me.

"Emery," I whisper, running my fingertips along her bare forearm.

She lowers her hands enough that I can see her beautiful brown eyes. I hold my breath and wait for a sign from her. She shakes her head, lowering her finger at me. "If you hurt me like that again—"

"I won't," I say, brushing the back of my fingers across her cheek. "I love you."

"I love you, too." Her lower lip quivers as her mouth forms a small smile. It's the first one I've seen on her face in a long time.

It's progress.

I smile back, folding her in my arms. She's my everything. She defines a better me, and I'm going to make sure I do the same for her.

"Are you okay?" I whisper next to her ear.

She nods, pressing her forehead to my shoulder. "I didn't think we'd ever get back to this point."

"I give you permission to hit me next time. Yell at me. Whatever you have to do; just don't ever let me spend another day away from you."

She laughs, looking up at me through her long eyelashes. "Can I start now?"

"I haven't done anything yet."

"Shouldn't I be allowed to let out all the frustration from the last time so we can start with a clean slate?" she teases, showing an even wider smile.

I slide my hands to her rounded stomach, rubbing small circles with my palms. "Can I put my old football pads on first? That one might hurt."

"Well, I'm pregnant so that works in your favor. I'm not supposed to do anything too strenuous."

That painful ping returns to my chest. I hate thinking about her facing this alone. I hate that I put her in a place where she couldn't even call and talk to me about it. A lot of good days are going to have to come before I feel okay about it.

The past is something I can't change.

"You know I'm going to spend years making these last several months up to you. Consider me wrapped around your finger."

Her eyes are glued to my lips, but she looks nervous. I've wanted to kiss her since I saw her last night.

Cupping her face in my hands, I rub my thumbs along her jawline. "I want to kiss you, Em."

She pulls her bottom lip between her teeth, the nervous look on her face replaced with mischief. "How much? If you ask nicely, I might let you."

I lean in until I'm so close she shuts her eyes. "Did you think I was going to kiss you?"

Her eyes find mine again. "You're not being very nice right now."

"Let's try that again then." Tilting her face, I bring her lips up to mine. For the longest time, I don't move. I like being able to just feel her warm skin against mine. I never thought I'd be able to do this again. They're just like I remembered—soft and full—and as I deepen it, pressing my tongue between the seam, I remember how good she tastes.

There's nothing about this girl that isn't perfect for me, and the fact that she's standing here is a miracle. I'm never going to let myself forget that.

As I pull back, I kiss the tip of her nose, her cheeks, and the sensitive spot below each ear.

Looking into her eyes, I say, "We need to talk some more."

She nods, nervously biting her lower lip. "Would you be uncomfortable around my dad?"

After what I did to his daughter, he scares the shit out of me. I have to get over it, though, if we're going to have a future of any kind. "No, I have enough donuts for everyone."

Laughing, she wraps her hand around mine. "Let's go see how far those will get you with him."

My jaw tingles as I follow Emery through the front door. I think everyone is scared to meet the parents, but this is on a whole new level.

"Don't worry," she whispers, looking back over her shoulder. "He'll like you just fine."

changing forever

All I can think about is how I'd feel if some guy impregnated my daughter the first semester of college then left her to deal with it herself. Emery's probably not right about her father … deep down inside, I know he wants to kick my ass.

As we make our way through the small living room, I see him leaning against the counter with a coffee cup in his hand. I convince myself that it won't be nearly as bad as I think it's going to be, but then his eyes meet mine.

I'm screwed, so screwed, but for Emery, I'll take it.

"Dad," Emery says, pulling me forward. "I want you to meet Drake."

After setting his coffee cup down, he rubs his palms across his jeans. The look on his face terrifies me as he reaches his hand up. "John," he says.

"Drake." He grips my hand so tightly; I might as well have put it in a clamp. Maybe I should just stick my head in an alligator's mouth to get it over with. "I just want to say, I'm sorry about these last several months. I was immature and selfish … it will never happen again."

The scowl on his face doesn't change at all. He's scaring me more than any defensive back ever did. "I love your daughter. I'm going to take care of her and our baby. That I can promise you."

"She's all I got," he remarks, loosening the hold he has on my hand.

I nod, glancing over at the girl who changed me forever. "She means everything to me."

"How are you planning on taking care of her?"

"I'm going to find us an apartment in Iowa City so we can finish school. I know how important it is to her, and I want her to have it. Things will be tight for a while, but I'll work as hard as I need to in order for her and the baby to have everything they need. And someday, when she's ready, I'm going to marry her. I know that for certain, and I'll wait for as long as it takes."

He looks over to Emery who smiles anxiously. This can't be easy on her either. I swear I'm seeing some sort of secret language pass between them; I miss having my dad around because he used to do the same exact thing.

When John's eyes shift to me again, I swallow nervously. It feels like I'm on the edge of a cliff with hands pressed to my back, waiting to see if I'm going to be pushed over, and the silence is just making the feeling worse.

"Do you want coffee?" he asks.

I glance over at Emery whose smile widens. "No, sir, I'm not much of a coffee drinker," I reply, grinning big.

"The stuff's not that good for you anyway," he says, reaching for his cup. Emery gently squeezes my hand, and I know everything is going to be all right. For the first time in a long time, things are where they are supposed to be. Life's changed for the better.

Chapter 35

Emery

WITH TWO WEEKS LEFT until my due date, we're finally settled into our apartment. It's not much, but it's close to campus and has two bedrooms to accommodate our growing family.

"Are you ready for your date with Kate?" Drake asks, wrapping his arms around me from behind. He's been unpacking everything himself the last two days, and I love him for it.

"Yep, I just need to find shoes that still fit on my feet. Does this dress fit okay?"

I spin around and follow his eyes as they take in the long, navy dress I borrowed from Kate. It's not maternity, but it's flowy and fits perfectly. "Let's put it this way ... if you don't leave soon, that dress will be on the floor, and you'll be under me in bed."

I smile, taking that as a yes. My cell buzzes. It's Kate, texting me to let me know she's here. "I need to go. My ride awaits."

He cups my face in his hands and kisses me slowly, his lips lingering on mine. He kisses each corner of my lips before pulling away. "Have fun, but hurry back. I already miss you."

"I'll miss you, too," I say, brushing some hair from his forehead.

He grabs my hand, bringing it down to his lips to kiss my palm. "Love you, Em."

"Love you, too."

He smiles as I walk past him toward the door. Things have been going really well the last several weeks. After he left my house, we each took a couple weeks to tie up loose ends so we could put our lives back together. After lots of searching, we found this apartment. It wasn't easy because we could only afford so much, and Drake was picky about the neighborhood. He wanted it to be safe for the baby and me when he wasn't home. I think we did okay.

I sold my car to get enough money to help with the deposit and first month's rent. We're going to have to make do with one car, but Drake and I were raised to make it through with what we have. We're professional survivors.

When I walk outside, I spot Kate's little red car sitting in front of the building. She waves and hops out to open my door for me. Everyone's been treating me like I'm going to break if they don't baby me. I only have a couple weeks left, though, so I guess I'll allow it.

"Are you ready?" she asks, climbing back into her seat.

I laugh, feeling the baby against my ribs. "As long as there's food, you can take me anywhere."

"So like vegetables and fruit?" she jokes, pulling out onto the street.

"You better be kidding. I need cheese and salsa. Oh, I hope we're going for Mexican?" I ask, placing my arm over my bulging stomach.

"It's a surprise … how many of those do you get in life?"

Looking down, I say, "Well, over this last year, I'd say I've had my fair share."

"You're lucky, though."

"I know, but it's weird saying that because I'm pregnant at twenty, living in a small apartment, and I have to work all over again to earn my scholarship. I guess it doesn't matter what I have or what I've accomplished. Happiness was all I needed."

"I could have told you that," she says, pulling into the parking lot in front of a salon and spa.

"What are we doing here?"

"Well, since you didn't have a baby shower, I wanted to do something special for you. I have an appointment for each of us to get a pedicure, and then we're doing lunch."

"Seriously, Kate, you didn't have to do this."

"I wanted to. You deserve it." She turns the car off and reaches behind the seat, pulling out a soft green gift bag. "Here."

"This is too much," I say, pulling the bag onto my lap. I've never had a friend who's been as good to me as Kate.

"Open it," she instructs, biting her lower lip.

Reaching inside, I pull out the white tissue paper followed by a soft fleece blanket. It's a light yellow with green polka dots and has the little ties around the edges. I roll the material between my fingertips, imagining the little baby growing inside of me lying on top, cooing and kicking. It brings an instant smile to my face but also makes me tear up.

"I made it," she says quietly. "I know it's not much."

"I love it. Really." I drop the blanket back into the bag and pull my best friend into a hug. "Thank you."

"You're welcome," she whispers, squeezing me back. When she pulls away, she reaches in the back and pulls out another small yellow bag. "Rachel wanted to be here, but she couldn't because of what happened with Cory. She told me to give you this."

My life hasn't been perfect, but I couldn't imagine what it would be like to be in Rachel's shoes right now. I went to the Cory's funeral, but I haven't seen her since. Pulling the small bag open, I find a Target gift card with a cute little note in Rachel's handwriting. "Buy what you need. Love, Rachel."

"Did you talk to her?" I ask, tucking it back into the bag.

"I did the other day when she called to make sure I got this. She's a mess. It doesn't sound like she's coming back this semester."

"I wish there was something we could do." I run my fingers along the top of the gift bag, trying to imagine what Rachel's going through. In all honesty, I think it would be very hard to move on ... impossible really.

"She just needs time. I told her to call if she wants to come visit, but I think it's going to be a while before she's ready."

"That's totally understandable. It just sucks."

She grabs her purse from the backseat and places her hand over the doorknob. "Are you ready to be pampered?"

Smiling, I say, "I don't know. This is a first for me."

"Well, let's show you what you've been missing, and when we're done, I'll get you some chips and enchiladas."

"Have I ever told you you're my best friend?"

"Every day, but I don't mind hearing it."

By the time I step back into my apartment, I'm exhausted. After we finished our pedicures, we each had a plate full of enchiladas, and then went to Target to buy a few necessities with the gift card Rachel gave me. It was fun to relax and hang out, but I'm ready to lie in bed with my feet up.

I notice that the only light on is the small lamp next to the couch, and Drake is nowhere in sight. Usually, he'd be at the door waiting for me. He's not in the kitchen either, so I look down the small hallway that leads to the bedrooms, and notice a light peeking out from underneath the nursery door. We haven't done much with it yet, but we plan to start tomorrow.

I slip my sandals off and follow the light. "Drake," I yell as I push the door open.

I cover my mouth with my hands, taking in everything. When I left earlier, the room was a blank slate, white walls and tan carpet. Now, there are little characters on the walls from my favorite Dr. Seuss books, as well as a crib, changing table, and rocker. The giant frog Drake had given me a while back rests against the corner of the crib. A perfect touch, a symbol of the start of our new life.

Tears well in my eyes, and I feel Drake's arms wrapping around me. "Do you like it? I did what I could since we don't know if the baby's a boy or girl."

I nod, still too in shock to put anything into words. I recognize the crib as the same one from all my baby pictures. The changing table looks new, but the wooden rocker was also mine. The curtains and bedding are a light green, yellow, brown and orange with hints of cream. It's beautiful ... more than I could have ever imagined.

"Em," Drake whispers against my ear. "When I said I wanted you and the baby to have everything, I meant it. I love you."

His hands move in circles along my stomach as the trail of tears start to fall. "It's perfect. I couldn't have done it better."

"I was afraid you'd be mad because I did it without you, but I wanted to surprise you. I called your dad, and he helped me pull it all together." He kisses the top of my head, squeezing me tightly again.

"I have pictures of my mom and me in that rocker. I didn't realize that Dad still had it."

"It looks like he kept everything up in your attic. He even brought you baptism outfit in case it's a girl, as well as some of your old toys. I think he had fun helping."

"Is he still here?"

"No, he left an hour ago. He wanted this moment to be ours." Over these last several months, I've realized how much my dad loves me. He did the best he could with me when I was growing up, and I think he'll make a fantastic grandpa.

Lisa De Jong

Turning in Drake's arms, I wrap my arms around his neck, pressing my lips to his collarbone. He holds me so tight, I swear he's never going to let me go. "I love you, Chambers."

"And every day I'm grateful for that because I love you so damn much, Em."

After kissing a trail up his neck, I look up into his blue eyes, remembering the first day I ran into him. It's weird how life gets us from one point to another. "Do you remember when you said you were going to marry me someday when I'm ready?"

He nods, watching my curiously.

"I'm ready. I don't ever want to think about not being with you."

His eyes widen, and he leans in to kiss my forehead. "I'll be right back," he says, running out of the room.

While I wait for him, I look around the room some more. He put a bookshelf in the corner beside the rocking chair, and it's full of all of my favorite childhood books. Reading is important to me, and Drake knows it. I look forward to reading to our baby every night before bed. It was one of my favorite things to do with my mom.

When I turn back around, Drakes is in front of me on one knee. For the second time today, my hands cover my face. I've seen him like this before, but this time I'm ready.

"Emery," he says, emotion pouring from his voice. "There are two versions of forever: the one I dreamed of every day as a kid, and the one I made my own after the old dreams faded away. The old dreams weren't meant to be, but this one is. You're my forever. I just had to take a few wrong turns to find you, and now that I have, I never want to live without you. Will you marry me?"

His hand shakes as he holds up a small black box with a small round solitaire inside. It's simple, but perfect. The same way I like my life.

I nod, kneeling down to get closer. "You changed my idea of perfect, and this version makes me happy. I can't

267

imagine ever going to bed without you by my side, or waking up and not seeing your face."

His trembling fingers pull the ring from the box. He uses one hand to hold mine, and the other to place the ring on my finger. "I love you," he says, pulling me into his arms.

"I love you, too," I say, wrapping my arms around him.

Epilogue

FIVE YEARS LATER

Emery

WHEN I LOOK BACK AT EVERYTHING that has changed over the last five years, it's like I was thrown into a dream. Not everything has been perfect, but I've learned the more you struggle, the more you appreciate what you have when everything falls into place.

Drake is the total package for me, but when I look at him on paper, he's everything I always thought I'd avoid. I didn't want to meet anyone in college. I was never going to let anyone step in my path, especially an arrogant, stubborn guy from Iowa. He's not a big city guy. He'll never be a doctor or a lawyer, but he loves me in a way that makes me a better person. He's shown me that every day is worth something, no matter what I do for a career or what zip code I'm in.

He changed my forever. He showed me a rose garden can grow anywhere if it has the right conditions.

And little Michael completes our perfect picture. Time has gone so fast, and it's hard to believe he starts kindergarten in a few short months. With his dad's athletic talent and his mom's brains, he makes us both incredibly proud. We've been working really hard to not push him too hard because we want him to build his own dreams.

"Em, are you about done in there? I need to get ready for work."

Looking down at the timer on my phone, I yell back, "Give me two more minutes."

"You better hurry, or I'm going to make sure we're both late for work," he teases through the door. We both work in the same school in one of the smaller towns outside Des Moines—me as a school counselor and Drake as a physical education teacher. Not quite what we set out to do, but we're happy.

The little beeper on my phone goes off, and I pick up the familiar white plastic stick ... much like the one that changed my life almost six years ago. Drake and I have been talking about having another baby for months now, but we wanted nature to take its course.

"Em, come on."

I unlock the door, aware that if I don't, he'll find another way in. Drake usually gets what he wants.

As soon as it opens, he steps in, walking toward me like a crazed cat on the prowl. He looks sexy with his bare, muscular chest and lounge pants hanging low on his waist. He may not play football anymore, but he still stays in shape. When my back hits the counter, I know I'm in trouble. There's this little game he likes to play.

"Where's Michael?"

"He's still sleeping," he says, pushing my hair behind my back. His lips press to my neck as I grip his shoulders.

"Drake."

"Hmmm," he moans, sliding my shirt down to expose my shoulder, giving his lips better access.

"Aren't we going to be late for work?"

He raises his head, his eyes searing into mine as his hands squeeze my thighs and slowly work my nightgown up my legs. "I just need a few minutes," he whispers, kissing the corners of my lips.

I wrap my arms around his neck as he unties his pajama pants and lets them fall down his legs. His fingers slide between my thighs, massaging the sensitive skin between them.

"No panties again, huh?" he whispers, entering me with two fingers.

"I like to make things easy for you, Mr. Chambers."

"So thoughtful," he says, replacing his fingers with his cock. "Always ready for me, aren't you, Mrs. Chambers."

I moan in his ear, feeling the pressure building quickly. His hands know every inch of my body, where I like to be touched and teased, and how to drive me over the top.

He pauses, lifting the nightgown over my head. He thrusts into me again as his hands press to my back, allowing me to lean against them. His mouth teases my nipples, his tongue lapping the sensitive skin.

"Drake."

"Yeah?" he asks, bringing his head back up.

"Harder, I'm so close."

He complies, pounding into me until my body goes into overdrive. He fills me perfectly, creating the right amount of friction.

"Come for me, Em. Let go for me, baby."

The feeling of complete euphoria sweeps over me almost immediately. Amazing. Soon after, Drake pumps into me one last time, finding his release.

I love that, after all these years, we still share these little moments on a regular basis. Maybe we'll be one of those lucky couples, and every day will feel like a honeymoon.

"You're not still mad at me for hogging the bathroom, are you?" I ask, burying my face in his neck.

"No, I think that anger has been erased now."

He runs his fingers up and down my bare back.

"Good, because I have to tell you something."

"Did you buy something online again?"

"No, it's bigger than that." Reaching behind my back, I pull up the white stick and wave it between our bodies.

His eyebrows draw in as he studies it. "You're pregnant?"

I nod, my eyes welling with tears. This is how I always imagined announcing a pregnancy. Being married to the man I love, having a home and a steady job ... last time wasn't ideal.

"Oh my God, Em," he says, wrapping me up in his muscular arms. "Are you okay? I didn't hurt you just now did I?"

Smiling, I comb my fingers through his hair. "No, you didn't hurt me. In fact, I remember being really freaking horny the first few months of my last pregnancy."

He pulls back, cupping my cheeks in his hands. "You know how sorry I am that I missed that." He kisses the tip of my nose, brushing his thumbs along my cheekbones.

"I'll make sure you make it up to me."

"That will be my pleasure."

"Mommy!"

"Shit," Drake mutters under his breath. "I hope I locked the door."

Grabbing my nightgown from the counter, I pull it over my head while Drake pulls out of me and quickly slides his pants back on.

"Coming, Michael."

"Not anymore you're not," Drake whispers, a crazy ass grin forming on his face. I hop off the counter and smack his shoulder, turning his smile into a grimace.

"Hurry, Mommy, I need to go potty." I hate to say it, but we live in the same one-bathroom type house I grew up in. It's okay, though, because I love the people who share it with me. I like the closeness.

Drake unlocks the door, and our little monkey comes running in. "Why do you guys always lock the bathroom? What if I really need to go?"

I rub the back of my neck, waiting for Drake to come in and save us both with the answer. "Daddy just likes to spend time with Mommy before she goes to work."

"Yeah, me too," Michael answers. "I can't wait until I go to her school."

"I'm excited too, baby," I answer, scrubbing my fingers through his sandy blond hair. He looks a lot like his daddy right now, but his hair is getting darker with every passing year. I love this little boy something fierce, but I'd like a little girl, too.

As soon as he's done, he runs right out of the room. I'd bet money that cartoons will be on in less than sixty seconds, followed by demands for fruity cereal.

Drake leans in to kiss my cheek, resting his hand across my stomach. "I'll take care of him while you finish getting ready for work, Mommy."

"I promise not to take too long." He winks before leaving me to finish. Looking in the mirror, I finger the locket that still hangs around my neck every day. Although, now one side has my mom and me, while the other has a picture of Drake, Michael, and me. It's truly my past, present, and future.

While there are things I wish hadn't happened in my life, there are plenty of things I'm glad did. My dad has been excellent, taking Michael for a weekend here and there to give Drake and me a break. Kate and Rachel are still in my life, and even though we live in different parts of the state, we get together a few times a year.

Drake and Michael are the reasons I wake up in the morning. They're my forever, and that's never going to change.

They say you should dream like you'll live forever, and live like you'll die tomorrow. This is my life and my dream … it just took a while for me to see that in order to have them both, I had to change my idea of forever.

Coming late Summer 2014:
Rachel's Story ... *Living With Regret*

Also coming this fall:
Always Imperfect, the first book in the Imperfect Series

Acknowledgments

FIRST, AND FOREMOST, I have to thank my husband and kids for being so patient with me when I need my time with my imaginary friends. Your continued support is what allows me to do what I do.

I'd also like to thank my family and friends who have been more than understanding and supportive. I couldn't have done it without you.

To my beta readers, Autumn, Melissa, Amy, Jennifer and Megan. You feedback helped immensely on this one, and *Thank You* doesn't seem like enough.

Jessica, you are a rock star. You've helped me so much with my writing and became a great friend in the process. Your turn is coming.

To my editor, Madison, thank you for putting up with me, even when I want to use clichés and such. I promise to cause those elusive butterflies with my next project.

To my agent, Jill, without your guidance, Drake and Emery would not exist. Thank you for pushing me to do more.

And last, but not least, to the readers and bloggers who have supported my work, THANK YOU! I never thought I'd be where I am today, and I owe it to you.